THE PLAGUE

2/04

THE PLAGUE STONE

STONE

Gillian White

G.K. Hall & Co. • **Chivers Press**
Thorndike, Maine USA   Bath, Avon, England

This Large Print edition is published by G.K. Hall & Co., USA and by Chivers Press, England.

Published in 1996 in the U.S. by arrangement with The Orion Publishing Group Ltd.

Published in 1996 in the U.K. by arrangement with the author.

U.S. Softcover 0-7838-1679-0 (Paperback Collection Edition)
U.K. Hardcover 0-7451-4808-5 (Chivers Large Print)
U.K. Softcover 0-7451-4809-3 (Camden Large Print)

G.K. Hall Large Print Paperback Collection.

The text of this Large Print edition is unabridged.
Other aspects of the book may vary from the original edition.

Set in 16 pt. News Plantin by Minnie B. Raven.

Printed in the United States on permanent paper.

British Library Cataloguing in Publication Data available

Library of Congress Cataloging in Publication Data

White, Gill.
    The plague stone / Gillian White.
       p.   cm.
    ISBN 0-7838-1679-0 (lg. print : lsc)
    1. Large type books. I. Title.
  [PR6073.H4925P58   1996]
  823'.914—dc20   96-4335

To Ron, Lucy, Nat, Dan and Beck.
With Love.

CHAPTER ONE

Now I am not a superstitious man. I can't afford to be. I work all day with icons and masks, totems and artefacts . . . relics musty with magic from bygone times when superstition gripped the world. If I believed in any of it I would go crazy.

But superstitious or not, by the time my investigations ended, I understood why the villagers of Meadcombe unanimously demanded the removal of the Plague Stone from their midst, from their memories and from the centre of their village square.

They imagined they could ask and it would be done . . . just like that! No forms, no official investigations, nothing! Bulldozers in, men with tin hats, excavate the megalith, into the lorry and away with it . . . dumped somewhere, anywhere, so long as it was away from Meadcombe and out of their sight.

It doesn't work like that. There are forms to be filled in, enquiries to be made, you can't just move something that has been a feature of an area for millions of years. The Plague Stone was well-documented. It was listed, an ancient monument. It belonged to the nation. History had woven itself around the place where it stood.

Tourists flocked to see it. Scarred like an old

whale, barnacled and beached by time, it was the sort of thing you travel to see and then wonder why you bothered. It was the kind of object you need to touch rather than look at. You feel it like a thousand fingers have felt it before you, and try to absorb the reality of its great age. You can't. The brain can't tolerate that sort of timelessness. It's grotesque. Humiliating for humanity, hopeless as standing on the moors and opening out your arms so that time can come in. It wasn't so much its bulk, and that was impressive enough, it was the aura of the thing.

Before the petition arrived at the Ministry's door I had never even heard of Meadcombe. By the time my investigations were finished, I knew it well — I knew some of the survivors personally. The police made their own enquiries of course, and most of those I have read. My reports were professional, short and to the point. I used the facts. But there are other considerations besides facts, considerations nearer to the truth but in which the authorities take no interest. Human nature . . . the peculiar oppression of English village life, the behaviour of women, social roles and expectations and downright evil . . . the fuel that fired the magic pot hundreds of years ago.

Atmosphere. There has to be atmosphere. The bleak streets of a modern new town could not have nurtured the phenomenon, could they?

So imagine . . . there is no sign at all of the gathering storm. No wind, nothing. In olden days, on nights like these, while paling autumns gave way to winters, old women told tales at chimney corners as they sat by their cottage fires.

Night — and the village of Meadcombe is buried by the mauve candlewick of the surrounding hills. White, it peeps from its covers like a slumbering unicorn curved round a church spire horn. White-washed walls, gloss gates, and, by day, Persil-white washing flapping on its garden lines.

The Plague Stone has always looked uncomfortable slumped in the centre of the square like that. In such an ordinary village. Out of place. Sinister, even. It glares down through pitted, stony eyes at its spindly sibling, the war memorial, as if that structured edifice is vulgar, as if a puff of wind might easily bear it and its wretched lists of irrelevancies away. For the Plague Stone is much, much older, and is not here on a petty whim of man. The Plague Stone, wrought from the birthing of the earth, spewed from a bubbling, white-hot womb, was ground into its present position millions of years later by a creeping, glacial tide. And no one can say for how many millions of years it will stay.

After nightfall on the nineteenth of September, three dark wishes hit the Plague Stone simultaneously. One comes from across the road, from a cottage bedroom which overlooks the village square. From a cottage where tatty rose heads fall back lifelessly from the trellis, petals veined and tinder dry, like the cheeks of the old woman in the brass bed upstairs.

The second wish comes from the girl who sits beside the Stone itself, irreligiously stubbing out a cigarette end on its wide, granite base, and the third comes out on the smell of frying onions, through the cosy red mullioned windows of the village pub.

Each wish in its own way is evil, but the wishers do not think so. Each wish is directed at God, in the form of a prayer, but the Plague Stone intercepts the straight line between the wishes and the church spire, deflecting them.

The first wish comes from Marian Law. And it is that her mother-in-law will die tonight . . . or if not tonight, certainly some time soon.

The second comes from Melanie Tandy, and it is for freedom from this sodding village, her sodding family and sodding school.

The third wish comes from Sonia Hanaford, and it is that Paul and she will somehow stave off the mortification of bankruptcy.

I talked to friends of Marian Law.

Marian's wish, most naturally, comes in the form of a prayer. Not that she believes, not that she has ever believed, but the habit dates right back to childhood ritual, semi-buried, that she learnt at her desk in the one-roomed village school. She is searching through the window, weary-eyed, for the church, and the Plague Stone gets in the way.

'God, I can't bear it,' she says not quite stand-ing, holding her back, after putting away the orthopaedic slippers and slipping Constance's fat white feet between the sheets. 'My burden is too heavy. Let her die, dear God. It would be a release — oh God, it would be a mercy! Help me, help me, please somebody help me.'

Where, she wonders, is breaking point. And she treads heavily on the stairs that take her down into that roaring cavern of silence where she is always alone.

At least you've got the children, people said, seven months and three days ago, when Roger died. Yes, she has the children. But they are never home.

I talked, at the hospital, to Janey Tandy. It was uphill work. I talked to her acquaintances . . . or those who would agree to talk to me.

Janey Tandy would have been the first to uphold her daughter Melanie's wish for freedom. The Tandys' little, respectable home, in a row of six farmworkers' cottages next door but one to the Laws', crackles with tension every time the girl comes home. And even when she isn't there her petulant, aggressive face dominates the sitting room as obviously as the gilt-framed mirror over the fireplace, clanking a little on its chains, ghostly, when the fire gets too hot.

'Jesus Christ let me get out of this place,' mutters the changeling child, the dark-haired daughter, the small, neat, olive-skinned one with the fringe cut straight as a Russian doll's across the top of her eyes. The years she has spent in

11

the village have all been dishonest, she knows, although, as a child, she never had a choice. She was never one of these people, for, although born in the village, she was not of it in the way that her father was. Just as the Stone had no choice . . . part and yet never really part. For a second a flaring match throws her shadow across the Stone, it leaps up thinly, cobweb-frail, and shrinks as the brilliance fades and dies.

I found the villagers were always keen to talk about the Hanafords.

Nobody but husband Paul, and perhaps the twins, would have underwritten Sonia Hanaford's wish for a monetary miracle, for everyone, especially her friends, would cruelly enjoy to watch the downfall of the snobby inhabitants of The Manor . . . they would be glad to know of the looming drama, secretly feeling that Sonia has not suffered enough, not suffered as they have done. She never looks as if she has suffered. She never talks as if she has suffered. And it's hard having a friend like that. No, Sonia has never really been one of them. Sonia has led a superficial, easy existence compared, they think, to their own firsthand dealings with grief and penury. And Sonia and Paul Hanaford, although he is a local lad, are nouveau riche, Yuppies, and don't know how to possess money graciously like, for instance, the ancient Bloggs family who have farmed the local estates for generations.

'Stan, we're basically only asking for a loan.'

Sonia Hanaford is begging as she wishes, wringing her hands and begging over a plateful of Chicken Kiev. 'Wanker,' she thinks, as she pleads, the habitual disdain wiped right off her face.

Stanley Hanaford's empurpled, manic face glares at her over a dish of braised celery. Her use of the word 'basically,' has got up his nose. Father-in-law, secondhand dealer, rich Stanley Hanaford with his heavy gold watch on his hairy white arm, who could help them if he wanted to, would also be happy to see his son go under, mainly because of his deplorably snooty wife. Sonia, naturally, regrets that she hasn't been nicer to this brute of a man, wishes she had welcomed him and his sparse-haired peroxide wife into their gracious home, wishes she had treated him with courtesy over the years instead of a kind of patronising, aloof disgust.

But even now, with all the worries and pressures that sit like a yoke upon her paisley-scarfed shoulders, she feels embarrassment at being seen with him here in the Weary Ploughman. A huge-headed man of sixty who has always longed to be a cowboy, look at him in his pink shirt, denim jacket and high-heeled cowboy boots . . . God, please, don't let Paul go bankrupt. Don't let me be beholden to people like Stan for ever!

'A hundred thousand, Stan,' she says, and the secondhand dealer's piggy little eyes turn redder under Sonia's frosty glances.

She fears she is wasting her time, and that Paul's last plan has gone the way of all the others.

13

Meadcombe. I wandered round it. I probed its history. It would have become a town but the railway missed it. Its hills were too high.

In prehistoric times, the Stone was of such a height and size that, to the hunter passing by, it soon became a landmark. Presently, two woodland paths converged here. One, two huts were built where the paths met, and a primitive village was born.

Centuries passed. In those days a squirrel could leap from tree to tree the length and breadth of the land. The Jacobite rebellion, and Lord Henry Grey's Jacobite friends tucked secret messages in the Stone's crevices . . . to be collected. These were fetched away early in the mornings by a small boy called Nog who wore laurel leaves in his hair for luck. One morning he was seen and pursued by the King's men. The leaves were washed off in fast-flowing river water and they caught him. Nog was boiled alive in a cauldron . . . so the story goes . . .

'It's funny,' thinks Marian Law, settling down into her chair beside the woodburner thirty yards from the Plague Stone with stout stone walls between. She puts her stockinged feet on the handmade rug, woven with autumn colours and speckled with cinders that take the effect of fallen leaves. She has half an hour of peace and quiet before the children come home from their evening out. She's never sure whether she looks forward to their return or not. 'It's funny how life erupts every now and then, like a volcano, changing landscapes with rivers of lava, covering the world with dust. Then it settles for a while, you just get used to how it is, and then there's another explosion.'

Having children was an explosion. Carving out new routes . . . routes to schools, to doctors' surgeries, to nursery groups and other children's parties. The dust — fish fingers, plimsolls, nappies, Lego, pantomimes, firework nights . . .

Roger's death was just such an explosion . . . dusty, yes, and it certainly hasn't settled yet, the new routes are still being scorched into the weeping earth of her soul. Great, searing ruts. Long routes, lonely routes, going to Tesco alone and up the stairs to bed. But this time one great gob of a molten spume has solidified into the form of Roger's mother. Constance, who has cunningly waited until after his death to go so viciously senile . . .

'It's funny,' she thinks, angrily, pooled in the light of a standard lamp which she prefers to the harsher light of the paper bamboo ball in the room's centre. 'It's funny, and it's so unfair.' She aches with the missing of him. She aches because she cannot complain to him about his mother, because big, fat incontinent Constance with the Eton crop and the dew-dropped moustache seems to be the only lasting legacy he has left her. And she can't remember what Roger looked like any more. All she can see when she tries to conjure him back is the way his overlarge Adam's apple jerked when he laughed . . . something she never liked very much. And there's not a lot to laugh at now, Roger, is there? CAN YOU HEAR ME, I SAID, IS THERE?

She aches. She aches.

Melanie Tandy thinks she will go home now. Not that she ought to go home because her mother will be worried. That sort of thinking doesn't enter Melanie Tandy's range of imagination . . . deliberately. She will go home because she is getting cold and she fancies a cup of coffee and a bacon butty. As usual there is nothing doing in this Godforsaken dead-end hold of a place. Angrily she shoves another cigarette end into the scarlet post box in the ivy-covered wall.

Meadcombe is quiet at night. In the distance a farm dog barks. Far away a train shushes through the darkness. But nearer there is nothing. Not even from the Weary Ploughman, the Mecca of Meadcombe, the jovial, cosy heart of the place.

Yes, the Weary Ploughman says it all, thinks Melanie, with its firedogs, its cobwebby corners and its two-faced, simplistic suggestions of real ale and mung bean stews. Just so that the overfed can pretend to be peasants.

Melanie would love to squat in the square, raise her head and howl at the obscenity of all of it. People are starving, dammit, and yet the people of Meadcombe file into church with their sizzling new clothes and their roasts neat in the oven.

16

People are homeless, yet the residents of Mead-combe clean cars and browse through brochures. The world is ending, but the householders of Meadcombe spray their bogs with pine, tearing away at the very edges of the atmosphere.

They all pretend to like each other. In reality they only like themselves. And a good drama, oh yes, they love a drama. She doesn't want to be like them. The sallow colour of her skin pro-claims her different, she thinks. She wishes she was black. She doesn't want to grow up and have hanging breasts and pubic hair that sprouts from the gusset of her swimming costume like her mother's does. The irony, bloody smell that comes from her every month is bad enough. Her body is letting her down, her mother is letting her down, her father is letting her down, everyone is letting her down, and it's worse because she lives in a horse's arsehole like Meadcombe.

Good thinking, deep thinking Melanie Tandy. The dark child of fourteen years who can see through it all and wants to change and punish. It's her age.

'Oh, give me land lots of land . . . don't fence me in . . .' Stan's juke box choice plays incredibly quietly, almost tastefully. It's hardly worth put-ting the money in. Doubtless *My Way* will be next. It's one of his favourites.

Now she knows there isn't a hope in hell of getting a penny out of him, Sonia can relax and act as bored as she likes. She wastes precious energy by despising Stan, but she doesn't care. And she drinks too heavily tonight. It's just the thought of telling the children they'll have to leave the school they love and go, with the other village kids, by bus, to the comprehensive. No good explaining the horrors of this to Stan, he just wouldn't understand.

A police photo-fit, that's what he looks like, with his vast, square face divided clearly into four sections and a drooping Mexican moustache of the sort you get in Mr Potato Head packs. Little eyes and great big fat lips. And cowboy silver hair.

He will not grow old, she thinks, as we that are left grow old, because he bloody well doesn't give a damn about anything or anyone.

'Coffee?'

'Yes, I'll have some coffee.'

Her own hair is thick and brown and curly, and she still has some of her Greek suntan left . . . they didn't take the children. They left them with friends. The suntan goes well with the gold coin bracelet at her wrist, and the green eyeshadow over her dark brown eyes. Stanley Hanaford also wears a bracelet . . . a large, be-ringed bracelet that puts her in mind of bulls' noses. She stares at it as she says, 'So you don't think . . .' She toys with the pudding, spoon loose in long fingers.

'Don't believe in it, never have,' says Stan in his drawling, country accent. 'All my children have had to stand on their own two feet, make their own way in the world . . .'

'And would Beryl feel the same way?'

'This has nothing to do with Beryl. She's always left those sorts of decisions to me. No, Paul has made his own bed and he must lie in it.' But he makes it sound as if it is her fault. How he is enjoying this conversation! How he is enjoying watching Sonia crawl!

Sonia feels her hatred harden. She knows it shows in her face. She watches his words come out, fascinated by the scum at the corners of his mouth.

'It will mean we have to sell the Manor.' She's saying these things, she's saying the very worst thing of all, and yet for some reason she doesn't care any more. Sonia is very tired. They didn't really believe Stan would help them, but Paul thought it was worth a try. 'It's pointless talking about it any more. I don't want to start raking it all over tonight.'

Sonia Hanaford rubs a little piece of window squeakily and puts her eye to it. She sees the girl Melanie Tandy, dressed all in black, moving across the square away from the Stone. Her own childhood seems so far away. The days when she could truthfully run about shouting with happiness, swinging her little tartan bag up over her head as she went. Her life seems to have gradually grown darker and darker. She's always waiting for somebody else to switch the light on. She sees the lights go out in the Laws' house. They put her in mind of tired eyes closing. It is late.

She's done her best. It's time to go home and break the bad news to Paul — unless . . . She still has one trick up her sleeve and Sonia Hanaford is a most determined woman.

Cholera. 1783. And the villagers of Meadcombe would have starved if the farmers hadn't helped them, bringing produce to the Plague Stone in the dead of the night. The desperate, grateful villagers left their money in pools of vinegar, in the pocked side of the Stone, in the holes that look like a fat man's eyes.

It was after this that they gave it mystery, called it magic and proclaimed it powerful. It was unlucky to ride round the stone 'widdershins', contrary to the course of the sun. It was lucky to walk round it three times backwards on the night of a full moon. Women, young girls, came out of their cottages bearing dreams in their arms like bunches of flowers.

There was talk of witchcraft. When the witch came in the night to claim your child you only had to stand with your back to the Plague Stone, call your baby's name, and all would be well. Only a decade ago a little tragedy had been acted out, according to reports. A young mother, one of the Telfords, gone from the village now, had stood in the square in the darkness, desperate enough to test the theory. Pushing back against the stone, maddened by grief, she had called out the name of her son, 'Sasha, Sasha' . . . It hadn't prevented him from dying of leukaemia. Chilling!

People who'd heard her said it had made their hackles rise.

Little rhymes sprouted up thicker than moss.

If snow on Christmas Day there be
Beat the Stone with laurels three.
If sunshine touches stony head
In January bring out your dead . . .

and so forth.

Strange things started happening around the Stone — rituals, chants, magic-making. The Meadcombe trials began. The widow Garner was drowned in Dolan's pond . . . Mother Kiery was another. The church procession avoided the Stone during the beating of the bounds, looping round it in their purple robes, their noses in the air and their eyes rolling darkly, inadvertently making it the centre point of the ceremonial route. Graven image! They considered the Stone satanic, attaching fearful importance to its reputation. If it had been a person, it would have started believing these stories about itself — it might even have been able to make them come true.

But it isn't a person. It is a megalith. It is only a stone.

And yet by dawn on 20 September, Constance Law is dead, Melanie Tandy is missing from home and Sonia Hanaford holds a cheque for a quarter of a million pounds in between the fingers of a well-groomed hand.

21

CHAPTER TWO

To understand what happened in Meadcombe that fateful winter you have first to understand about Melanie Tandy . . . the child who stalks the square at night with anger in her heart. Not so strange. There are thousands like her. There she is, a figure in black, wanting so much to be a little girl again, but knowing she can never be. She has been happy. She forgets that. She has been loved. She forgets that, too.

And growing up, when you don't want to grow up, is a frightening thing.

Her breath went with the piston puffs of a toy steam engine. The first frost of autumn began to grip the gravel. Precisely twenty-three strides to get Melanie Tandy home, and at every one she grew a little angrier, moved a little more jerkily.

SOMEONE NEEDED PUNISHING, AND THAT SOME-ONE WOULD HAVE TO BE HER MOTHER.

When Melanie opened the door, Janey was at the sink. She didn't speak. She didn't have to. The accusation was plain in her lowered eyes, in the way she balanced the clean dishes on the draining board, and in the way the pinny stretched in tight wrinkles round her waist, forehead wrinkles round her waist. Still clearing up at twenty past ten and blaming somebody for it. Forever humble and subservient, but bitter with it. Other mothers didn't wear pinnies . . . and if they did they certainly didn't call them pinnies like Janey did.

Melanie brought frost into the fluorescent kitchen. She went straight to the kettle and pushed the button home. She crossed the room, picked up a newly-washed mug, still wet, and threw a teaspoon of instant coffee into the bottom. It went a hard, dark brown. Three heaped spoonfuls of sugar. She knew she was annoying Janey. She forgot about the bacon butty. The eyes of this mother and daughter rarely met any more. Each was afraid of the other. Each excited for a confrontation, yet fearing one, lest they said things that would take them into a void from whence there might be no return . . . ever. And neither was sure they could deal with that.

Finally, sounding thoroughly fed up with it all, 'You're back then.'

Melanie wasn't going to answer such a feeble silence-breaker. She stirred her coffee, violently, so that some of it slopped over on to the clean surface. Time stopped as four eyes watched the spattered mess. Janey's soft with cow-brown acceptance, Melanie's tiny nuggets of coke.

The television noise from the other room remained subdued. A man's cough made a perfect match with a reverent snooker commentary. But it seemed to parry with the action in the kitchen, loosening the knot and allowing the thread of movement to flow smoothly again. Melanie lowered an arm and wiped the spillage with the sleeve of her jumper. 'Well?' It was a challenge. Sometimes Melanie frightened herself.

'You should be more careful.'

'My fault! My fault! Mea culpa . . . mea culpa.' Her head started to throb, threatening to split like a zit, as it often did these days when she was with her mother.

'Don't be silly, Melanie. And now I shall have to wash that jersey.'

'It's OK. There's nothing wrong with it.'

'Melanie, you can't go to school tomorrow with coffee all over your sleeve.'

'It's not such a big thing, Mum. Leave it out, will you. You have to over-react.'

'Dad might like a cup of tea, as the kettle's boiled.' There was a wheedle in her voice.

'Let him come and get one then.'

'He's watching something on telly.'

'Well, I'm busy drinking my coffee.' Melanie shrugged as Janey's face tightened. Her mother looked trapped, ratlike. Her nose was thin and red, like a cartoon rat's, her tangled hair rat-brown sprinkled with grey. Melanie wasn't bothered. She was bored to death with her mother's self-imposed misery. She wasn't going to bow and scrape to him in there like she did. Depressed, my arse. Lazy slob.

Melanie sat at the kitchen table and huddled over her coffee, rocking herself for comfort. Being unkind to Janey, though necessary, made her feel solid and sticky inside, as if she was building something up there that needed passing. But she couldn't help it. She had to do it.

And Janey desperately searched the immaculate kitchen for something else to do. Anything to avoid having to sit across the table from her sullen-faced daughter, anything rather than go into the lounge and sit in the semi-darkness, pretending to watch the snooker next to her silent man. Oh yes, Janey Tandy understood why Melanie liked to go outside and sit by herself in the square.

There were times when Janey still loved Melanie. Now love caught in her chest as she noticed her daughter's narrow, childlike shoulders. So brittle, so vulnerable. Still such a child. She felt inexpressibly sad. When Melanie was born somebody wrote under *'How lovely . . . a daughter!'* that she would never now lack a best friend. She couldn't remember who it was sent the card, but she could recall the writing . . . it was spidery and sprawling, the writing of an old person, a great aunt or an ancient family friend. And Janey thought to herself that that might well have been the case in the olden days. Not now.

Janey tried to be normal once more. She longed for a slackening of tension. 'Daniel was sent home from school again today. He must have a bug. He seems all right in the mornings but then he says he starts feeling hot at break-time . . .'

Her lost daughter was ignoring her, was flicking through a magazine, licking the rim of her mug as if to compound the insult.

Then, surprisingly, because Janey hadn't expected her to bother, 'He's having you on, Mum.'

'Oh, I don't think . . .'

And Melanie started to hum. Her mother, once the most solid thing in her life, she now found distasteful. She wondered how she'd ever loved her as she had. Her stupidity corrupted her, made her betray herself as a woman. Made her betray her daughter . . . or try to . . . making her servile . . . making her carry cups of tea and wash up, clean her room and help with the ironing. The great betrayal. While the man in the lounge sat studiously watching snooker, hankering all the while for the cup of tea he pointedly refused to make. And the boys were never expected to help in the house, as if somehow, by being male they had inherited their father's sickness, as if he had passed it on, debilitating them, too. No. Melanie would not sympathise with Janey, not now, she could no longer climb on her lap and hide her head in her pinny, or peel the flaky pastry from her fingers.

She kept her eyes carefully hostile. She pulled her sleeves down under the arms of the jacket she refused to take off. She pulled them over her hands until they covered her black, fingerless gloves and rubbed at the edge of the table. When she went up to bed Dad would come out here and he and Mum would whisper about her. She used to creep to the top of the stairs to listen. Lately she hadn't bothered. Well, she knew what

26

they'd be saying without having to hear it. Dad didn't seem able to whisper for long, he forgot, and spoke the odd word out loud before Mum reminded him by frowning him quiet again. Melanie had never quite caught the gist of it . . . just the odd word when Dad forgot — 'patience', 'phase,' 'I realise it's harder for you'. They were worried, they hoped it was a phase. For Janey, Melanie thought, it was yet another delicious punishment.

When she went upstairs tonight, Melanie would take another five pound note from David's wallet and, with a beating heart and a feeling of guilt that was almost sexual, add it to her mounting collection.

'Haven't you got any homework?'

A quickly-escaping laugh, a sneer. 'I did it yesterday.'

A silence as Janey wondered when yesterday. 'Are you sure?'

'Well, I'm not lying, if that's what you're saying.'

Janey was merely trying, deviously, to banish her daughter from the one room where she felt safe. And Melanie knew it. So Melanie refused to leave the kitchen. There was nothing for it . . . Janey would have to sit down opposite, or defrost the fridge again. She was tired, so she sat down.

They sat in uneasy silence for a while. Melanie, determinedly still, noticed with a kind of numb anguish the way her presence made her mother fiddle with patterns in the cloth. Janey's confusion mirrored her own. The difference was that Melanie dealt with it inside, adept at not letting it show. Don't let her start talking about the boys again, please, please. Don't make her try and include me in this grown-up collusion of women.

'That's a nice jersey Nana sent you. The zip would look better up at the neck.' Always the sting in the tail. Janey was aware of it, but couldn't stop herself.

'I'll zip it up if I want it zipped up. This is how I like it.'

Normally, when David was there, the relationship between Janey and Melanie was easier. It was easier because when he was in a room it was impossible not to think about him.

He shambled into the kitchen now with television eyes, and with derision Melanie noticed anxiety wrinkle her mother's forehead. She wore that weak, 'We're all right but how about poor old you', secretive smile.

Her father wore a cardigan buttoned over a cowardly narrow chest. He wore it like a sense of failure handed to him over a jumble sale counter. Seeing it there, he would have fought the crowd to buy it, because if he didn't have enough shit in his life he seemed impelled to go in search of it.

David was needy in a way Melanie was not. His inner life was in tatters. He was always talking about his melancholia. He spent pounds on therapists and counsellors but it never got him anywhere. And, young as she was, Melanie knew why. There was some parasite living inside him that gobbled up happiness.

'When Daddy's better' had been the overplayed qualification of her childhood. 'Not now, perhaps when Daddy's better.' 'Why do I have to be quiet?' 'Only till Daddy's better.' Melanie was furious that she had, for so long, been taken in. She was furious at Janey for inventing the lie and for trapping them all within it. She didn't want to feel sorry for her father . . . it was no way to love anyone. Janey had thrown herself into it so wholeheartedly that Melanie suspected she must enjoy it. But Melanie felt angry and cheated. David Tandy was as he always would be. Better or worse didn't come into it. He was as he was, and that was that.

'Hi Podge,' he said out of his hang-dog expression. Janey passed him on her way to straighten his chair, pick up his newspaper and empty his ashtray.

'Hi Dad.' The jokey camouflage of the uneasy between whom nothing real could be said. She would not make him a cup of tea. She would not!

'Been out?'

'Only in the square.' She did not notice her own fingers fiddling with the patterns in the cloth. They poked from the ragged edges of the fingerless gloves she refused, even in summertime, to take off.

29

'Anyone about?'

'Is there ever, in Meadcombe?'

David sniffed and wandered over to the kettle, picking it up to judge its weight. He was expecting it to be empty, and he sighed as he discovered that it was. That's life, his every movement always seemed to suggest. It didn't matter that it was the same for everyone, but other people didn't take it all so bloody personally.

Melanie took her darkness from him, although no one else in the family was quite as dark as she. With his cheerless interior, he had no right to his outward good looks. At forty-two his hair was mostly grey, but where it wasn't it was jet black, and thick and tough like oriental hair. He wore it too long down a neck that was pinkly naked at the back like a little boy's. It went with the shabbiness of his home clothes. For school he went tweedy, with pale Viyella shirts and co-lossal shoes with stitching.

'I'm going up.' She was forced into it. The urge to help him gripped like a hard old rose root planted long ago inside her. It put out suck-ers, twisting and trailing along her arms and legs, weakening her reserve, swamping her with the spongy green leaves of guilt. There was no way to fight it, only retreat.

'What about your mug?'

It stood, much too big for its own importance, alone on the kitchen table. It was a sore on an otherwise spotless skin.

'I'll do it in the morning.'

30

'You know very well that when your mother comes back she'll do it.' His back was to her. He wasn't even man enough to face her. For an instant she despised him. The feeling rose like sick, warm and sweet in her mouth. He added, 'And she's got enough on her plate.'

'Yes,' Melanie said, accusing.

'Well, wash it up then, there's a good girl.'

Although he spoke abstractedly, the point was an important one. Melanie knew this because he had stopped moving. He was standing over the sink, poised, listening. He was waiting to see what she would do.

She could obey, and bang around the kitchen, nudging her hopeless father out of the way, finishing off by stomping upstairs to bed, banging doors and throwing black looks over her shoulder as up until now she had always done. Or she could be cool. She could absolutely refuse to touch that mug. The daring of such bare-faced confrontation made her feel weak. Her eyes shrunk until she could see the down on her puffed-up cheeks.

This was the way he solicited obedience from his classes. He made them feel sorry for him by stooping and being clumsy, by putting that hard-done-by look in his eyes and forever looking weary. He never spoke his name, but at the beginning of a fresh term he just wrote it morosely on the board. Every movement he made was accompanied by a small sigh. It was a way of making people fond of him. He had no other. He couldn't be sparkling or witty or forceful. But David's methods invariably worked. No! It was not in his interests to get 'better'.

Well, Melanie saw through him. She wasn't going to let him get away with it one minute longer. She would die before she washed that mug.

'I'm going to bed now, Dad,' she said softly. 'And I'll wash the mug in the morning. Tell Mum to leave it there.'

She was about to go out of the door when she heard him say, equally softly, 'Melanie, I want you to come back here and wash that mug up now.'

She stopped in her tracks, itching with unease. This was between him and her, and when Janey came into the kitchen bearing a trayful of his leavings, Melanie grew hot with resentment. She had been on the point of giving in. She couldn't give in now she had a biased audience.

Janey walked slap into the tension, and a bruised look of nervous anxiety covered her face as quickly and as brutally as if she had walked into a stone wall. But she hadn't been hurt. Why did she have to react like this? Why did she have to take on his battles every time? She raised quick eyebrows of enquiry.

Casually, as though there was nothing going on, David lightened his voice and said, 'Melanie is just going to wash her mug before she goes up.'

They both turned round and looked at her at the same time . . . straight in the eyes. Melanie stared back defiantly, lifting her chin a little higher and crossing black, leather-jacketed arms. The hot smell and the slight crackling of it gave her courage. She was the unmentionable disease, the pus in the finger, and the white-coated doctors were looking across at her with barely-concealed horror, brandishing their syringes.

With exaggerated reasonableness and a sickly smile, Melanie explained, 'I've told Dad I'll do it in the morning, and I will. Now I'm going up, if nobody minds.'

'You're not going anywhere, Melanie.'

For God's sake, bastard, don't make such a big deal of this! Don't you see you've got me cornered? There is no possible way I can keep the new self that I am fighting for *and* wash that mug. You cretin . . . can't you see?

And she could tell that Janey, too, white-faced so that her whole body looked pinched and cold, would have preferred a softer approach.

The question was, what would David do if she did just walk upstairs and, for the first time in her life, openly defy him? It was the question all three of them asked themselves as they stood there, positioned around the kitchen like characters in a bad play, hanging on to their appointed parts in life with grim determination.

'Don't worry, I'll do it.'

David stopped his wife with an upraised hand, palm flat like a police signal. She stopped dead in mid-movement, expelling the now unnecessary breath.

Melanie leaned back against the wall. She would have put her hands in her pockets if she could have reached them. But they were under the leather, in the tight blue jeans that gripped her legs. And they were always hard to get into. It wouldn't have been the careless gesture she needed it to be. So she kept her arms crossed, and put a little half-smile on her lips instead. How long was he prepared to keep this up? Her posture said that she didn't care. She had all the time in the world.

'Come on, Melanie,' said Janey in her chummy voice. 'It's not much to ask.'

Melanie rolled her eyes and kept smiling.

'Are you going to wash that mug, or aren't you?'

'No, I'm not.' She answered her father in the same challenging tone. She was frightened but she wasn't sure what of. And she was enjoying the fear. It was exhilarating. It was something tangible for her anger to feed off.

Janey's head, twitchy as a chicken's, bobbed from one speaker to the other. Finally, unable to bear it any longer, she stepped forward and picked the mug off the table. David's arm flashed out and knocked it from her hand. It broke into three sharp parts on the kitchen floor. The noise of the crash, like a gunshot, released them from their traps of immobility. As did this piece of shockingly uncharacteristic behaviour.

'You bastard!' Melanie drew back with bared teeth. 'You fucking, crazy bastard!'

'Don't! Don't!' Janey stepped forward and slapped her daughter's face. Then stood back with her hand across her mouth, stupefied by what she had done.

David, choosing this moment to come out of a lifetime of lethargy, clutched at Melanie's arm and clumsily tried to drag her to the sink. Appalled, she felt this weak man's fingers hard around her arm, but they slipped on the leather and she pulled away. She screamed as she headed for the door, screamed to fill the awful atmosphere with something of her own before she left.

'I hate you! I hate you! I've always hated you! I'm getting out of this sodding place and I'm never fucking well coming back!'

Janey should have been angry. The hatred she had often lately felt for Melanie should have surfaced with all its powerfulness. But it didn't. Instead she felt tears flooding her eyes. She had never felt such compassion, not for David, not for anyone. Her chest heaved with it. She had never wanted so badly to pull Melanie close, to rock her and comfort her, pat her back and stroke her hair. Poor, poor, frightened little girl . . .

The door slammed so hard it made the windows shake. The silence afterwards was wrathful.

'She'll be back.' David said with withering scorn.

But as Janey bent to pick up the cup, she found she couldn't see the pieces for the bulging tears that filled her eyes but wouldn't fall.

And when, eventually, she could stand it no

longer, and David had gone to bed, Janey opened the door and called out softly. 'Melanie?'

She saw the Plague Stone looking blacker than ever, pricked by silver dots of frost, staunch and silent in the square, watching. She closed the door quietly and went to ring Sonia because she knew that Sonia kept late hours and she needed to talk to somebody. Paul answered and told her Sonia wasn't home yet. Janey would have gone to Marian's, but Marian would probably be asleep.

She glanced outside once more before she went to bed. The Plague Stone stared back at her through the window. And with a foreboding that made her shiver, she knew that her daughter would not be back tonight.

CHAPTER THREE

I sympathise with Marian Law. Everyone sympathises with Marian Law. Perhaps that was the trouble. For self-esteem drowns in sympathy, and there's something so pitiful about being called a 'brick'.

Constance Law is not in nappies — yet. About half past eleven, on her way to bed, her daughter-in-law, the widow Marian, will wake her and take her to the toilet.

But until then Marian turned on the television and sat empty-minded in front of it waiting, in the house they called *Dunoon*, for her children to come home. Her well-balanced children and their escorts, unnervingly contented with their provincial lives and their evenings playing darts in the public bar of the Weary Ploughman. On Friday they will baby-sit for Constance so that Marian can have her night out at the drama group.

Not a flicker of rebellion had ever furrowed the brows of Lloyd or Sally Law, not a day of worry had they given their loving parents, not like Melanie Tandy, and Marian secretly, righteously believed that the answer lay in the way they had been brought up, the way they had been loved. Of course, she never told Janey Tandy that, but she and Roger used to whisper about it smugly in bed at night.

Marian Law had a very big face on which to display her feelings, a flat, Mongoloid, pin-board of a face which she tried to reduce by bringing her hair forward. The moon-round face was a local feature found almost nowhere else. Generations of people who looked like her lay in the village churchyard. The Law family was well-represented there, too. Back in February when it happened, when they put him in the ground, Marian was comforted by the fact that Roger would not be alone or a stranger in that dark place.

There used to be an old Meadcombe resident, dead now, who firmly believed that men had never really landed on the moon. No amount of reasoning would convince him. He was ridiculed and called a fool.

'If you believe all they tell 'ee, you'm a bigger fool than I took 'ee for,' he used to say, leaning on his gate as he spoke, his ranks of chrysanths behind him.

Now she remembered him well, because Marian had never totally believed that beneath her head was a skull, a skeleton, tissue, gristle and bone, so she hadn't believed that Roger or she would ever die . . . not really.

So she was astonished when he did. Suddenly, resolutely and decisively he died for ever and left her alone, betrayed.

Other people she knew in her life had died, of course they had, but they could have been invented by her and Roger. Roger and her were the only ones she felt she could prove.

She still felt indignant with surprise and shock at the way life went on. The weather men still talked about what it would be like tomorrow, as if nothing had happened . . .

Sometimes, when she was alone, hoovering, making beds, her mind stuck around nonsensical couplets as if it had nowhere much else to go.

Roger Law will live no more. He dances headless on the graveyard floor,

and

I'll tell you a tale about Roger Law. His head came off in a mess of gore.

As hairy black flies heave and buzz to free themselves from tacky fly paper, so bits of Marian's mind floundered on vehicles of disrespect, and died there. Sometimes, lately, she feared that she was going mad.

A lorry had jack-knifed on the A5 and taken off Roger's head. It had jack-knifed on ice . . . yes, and Marian had always been fond of ice. Constance, of course, was belted into the safe seat in the back of the car at the time. She'd survived in a kind of a way, despite the dicky heart she had always liked to make so much of. Even her hat had emerged without a dent. Roger hadn't. They had cut her out of the car and scooped her to safety, perfectly cool and pale like a lychee on a spoon. Marian blamed her. How else was she expected to feel? Roger had gone to pick her up and bring her to Meadcombe for a holiday. The woman always refused to take the coach which would have dropped her off at the door. She always said that coaches were dangerous.

Oh yes, she was always very careful with her life, was Constance, as those with the least to give often are.

Overcoming her hostility, Marian had taken Constance in as a last futile gesture for Roger's sake. To make amends? To make up for the times she hadn't loved him as she'd wanted to? People called her a real brick. Back then, when everything was crazy and the pain hadn't gripped, she saw it as a way of staying close to him. And Constance hadn't immediately lost her mind. To begin with she was very quiet and sat in corners looking pathetic, in shock the doctors said. But the accident had triggered off some chemical in her brain that caused a quick-creeping senility. Marian imagined it the sickly fawn of pea and ham soup . . . this chemical. It had taken only months for Constance to acquire that do-lally beam in her eye, to argue like a child, to wander about outside inviting herself to strangers' houses for tea and to wet her knickers.

More and more the people of Meadcombe referred to Marian Law as a brick.

Marian moved forward in her chair to look round when she heard the key in the lock. Here were the children, coddled, cherished and over-protected, happy now as they surely had no right to be.

And she'd always been so afraid of becoming bitter.

Marian was forty-three, so she had perfected the knack of welcoming people to her house, wrinkling her eyes and putting a glint of fondness there whether she was pleased to see them or not.

'We're back, Mum.'

'God, you've got that television on loud.'

Funny, Marian hadn't noticed. Now she got up, embarrassed, to lower the sound, afraid to be thought of as peculiar by her daughter's posh boyfriend. She liked him . . . oh she liked him very much, but he was a Blogg and she was a Law, and there was a well-defined social structure in Meadcombe.

'Is Gran asleep?'

'Yes, she went straight off tonight. Must have been tired.'

'Poor old soul,' said the boyfriend. And Marian felt the strongest urge to slap his superior face. He knew nothing! Let him carry the water upstairs and wash that poor old soul's bottom in the morning!

She had to force herself to concentrate to hear what they said. Sound of mind, trivia still interested them, whereas she could only listen from the edge. They continued some conversation they had brought back with them from the pub while they stood around waiting for the kettle to boil. They were so big in the low-beamed living room that was identical to the Tandys', her children and their friends. The two-seater floral sofa creaked as if it were too frail to take them. She knew that because she was there they were having to be different . . . they spoke more loudly . . . leaving out in-jokes, dirty jokes, they kindly referred to her, trying to include the outsider in the conversation. And she knew that as she grew older this feeling of not belonging would get worse. And she didn't have anyone of her own any more.

Self-pity. Janey was always accusing her of it. And she was the last to talk! 'You've just lost yourself,' Janey told her last time they drank wine together. 'It's understandable. But you won't always feel like this. It will get better . . .'

She didn't trust Janey with her sharp-boned face and the witchy hair that fell in ringlets round it. She was her best friend. But Marian had always been the wise one, Janey the fool, and that was how they'd related. Now the worm had turned and Marian didn't like it. She suspected Janey quite enjoyed this sudden volte-face. She could be happy because she still had her man. Marian had just lost hers.

Janey apportioned her time unfairly. Marian sometimes needed more, but she never liked to barge in on the Tandys' evenings . . . because, she supposed, there was a man in the house. But it was evenings and night-times when she needed someone most. And she didn't like to burden the children who were being so good, so supportive. Marian didn't enjoy being dependent on Janey.

'But will I ever find myself again?' she had asked. Nowadays she tended always to talk about herself. Other people's problems seemed too tame to contemplate. Before the crash they had talked more about Janey and her struggles with the difficult Melanie and the manic depressive, David. But they'd always seemed to be *enjoyable* problems, brought on and controlled by Janey herself. She had watched Janey critically through the stains in an empty wine glass which distorted the world like fairground mirrors. Through them Janey appeared smaller, with an enlongated chin. It was how Marian preferred her to look. Oh, round and round went their uneasy friendship, entwined in a crazy dance like clothes in a washing machine.

'You see Janey,' she had moaned on, stabbing at a crumb on the polished table top, breaking it into a surprising number of pieces. She wanted to demonstrate the depths of her unhappiness. She wanted to convey it dramatically, leaving no room in Janey's mind for doubt. If Janey believed her, if anyone believed her, perhaps, just perhaps, they could relieve her. 'You see,' she confided, a little tipsily. 'I don't think I want to go on living.'

'Think of the children,' Janey had trilled, as once Marian might have done. 'Suicide is the most selfish way out. How can you bequeath guilt that size on to your children . . . and all your friends?'

The 'all' was climbed like a high hill. Janey came down off the word with accusation glinting in her eyes. She gesticulated wildly with her thin arms into space as if to embrace all these mythical people. There was nobody there. How shallow Janey was!

As if to make amends for the lack of friends, Janey had added, 'And everybody envies you your children. They are lovely . . . just the sort of children everyone would love to have.'

In and out of the option of suicide her mind had wandered, in and out as casually as dancing through those dusty old bluebells. Suicide, the quiet, beckoning eye in the hurricane of grief. If only she could believe in something . . . the after life . . . reincarnation . . . the spirit world where, for a few pounds she could retrieve some of Roger, go to the butcher's for a piece of his scrag end, a voice from the silence. But she didn't believe in anything any more. She went to church as she always had, but she didn't believe.

'Mum! Mum! Coffee?'

Marian jumped. There was impatience in the voice, and she realised that Sally had been trying to get her attention for some time.

'Oh, yes dear, please! I was miles away!' And immediately Sally looked down on her mother with concern. Yes, they were lovely children. There was no getting away from it.

Sally had her mother's distinctive flat face, but with her long, hay-coloured hair and her big blue eyes, it was attractive. Nineteen, and she'd been going with the Bloggs' boy, Harry, for four years. They would get engaged. They would get married. They would live in the converted barn in his father's field. They would never lack for anything. Marian had never felt easy in his presence . . . nor he in hers. Theirs was a sort of enquiring relationship . . . they asked each other questions all the time like, 'How's the farm?', 'How's your mother?', 'How's the drama going?', absurd questions laced with bright smiles which filled silences but didn't require answers. And they never seemed to get any further with it.

When Roger was alive he and Harry used to chat about hardware. The Bloggs had always been good customers. They believed in supporting local businesses, even if they did have to pay a bit over the odds. But then, they could afford to.

Her own son, Lloyd, twenty-two, had followed his father into hardware. The Laws owned the local hardware store. Now he brought her coffee, and put it down on the low table by her knees, presenting it like a wise man bringing a gift to the baby Jesus. He was only trying not to slop in the saucer. She smiled a thank you, and he sat on the protesting sofa next to Donna Wright.

Lloyd would never leave her. He would marry Donna Wright and move out of her house but, in spirit, this son would never abandon his mother. Lloyd had always been a responsible boy. Pretty Donna, the carpenter's daughter, whose hair shone with the copper tone of the brasses above the woodburner, was perfect for him.

'Sonia was in the pub,' he said, thinking it was a titbit of interest his mother might like to hear. 'She was having a meal with old Mr Hanaford.'

'Oh? No Paul?'

'No, I didn't see Paul.'

'Funny. I thought she couldn't stand Stanley.'

'Well, she was all over him tonight.'

'She'll no doubt tell us all about it on Friday.'

'How is the drama group going, Marian?' This was Harry. She felt like standing up and taking down her knickers to shock him. But at the same time she felt sorry for him. He was trying his best. He couldn't help it if, like her, he found small-talk hard going. He was being kind. They were all being wonderfully kind. Perhaps it would be better if someone would start being nasty for a change.

Marian was glad when they started talking among themselves, allowing her to scuttle back to her thoughts. She was safer thinking when there were people around. She could pull herself out more easily.

With shame she remembered her self-satisfied treatment of Janey when Roger had been alive.

46

Janey, who attracted disasters, disastrous events and disastrous people. There was always something going wrong in Janey's life. Marian recalled the times she had pretended to be out, leaving Janey ringing the doorbell, ridged in rejection like a piece of limp, corrugated paper. And all those glib alibis. It was easy to invent an alibi when there were two of you.

And Roger had encouraged her. 'You're not helping that woman, you know. By listening to her tales of woe you just make it easier for her to wallow. Anyway, you've got your own problems.' But she didn't have. She couldn't think of any when he'd said that . . . not problems like Janey's problems.

Ah, but things were different now.

Marian knew that in spite of their relationship, in a strange way Janey hated her, too. And no wonder. She'd been jealous, and Marian hadn't realised until later. Janey used to say, 'You're so lucky you've got Roger,' but, insensitive to the last she never gauged his true opinion of her. 'You know where you are with Roger,' Janey used to say, not knowing Roger at all.

Then there was Janey's phase of ghastly poverty, and the money they lent her which was never returned. David was in hospital trying to jolt himself from his misery with ECT, and Janey took to coming round on Sundays and Bank Holidays which, to Roger, were sacrosanct, a fact Marian had never felt able to tell her.

But, give Janey her due, she had been the first

round at the house after hearing the news of Roger's death.

Marian was relieved when Harry and Donna stood up to go. She had to face the fact, she was only ever genuinely relaxed when she was alone with her own flesh and blood. Flesh and blood, she could think that now and believe it . . . those pathetic bits of grey fur lying squashed on the road, that is all anybody really was . . . nothing more than flesh and blood and fur that was warm and smooth to stroke for a while . . .

She sensitively stayed out of the kitchen so they could say their demonstrative goodbyes. Their arrangements were neat — Harry would drop Donna home on his way past. Marian didn't want a late evening so she got up and started clearing the cups.

'Leave them, Mum, we'll do them.'

Marian nodded. 'I'll sort out Constance before I go to sleep,' she said on her way upstairs. She rarely griped about Constance to her children. The last time she did so Sally had said, 'Don't be unkind, Mum. She can't help it. She's old.'

But the crux of the matter was that Marian suspected Constance could help it. There was something vindictive in her senility, in the convenience of her deafness, and in the way the old woman ate, smearing her moustache with margarine before putting bread in her mouth. There was something sinister in the way she was always *watching*.

48

Through a crack in the chintz curtains the stars pricked the darkness. And the room felt colder than usual. The musty smell of sleep was missing.

Her heart bulged in her throat when she heard Constance's breathing. She hurried across the linoleum floor, nearly sliding on the gay red mat put there to make the room more cheerful.

Jesus Christ! Constance was lying flat on her back, her neck stretched oddly back over the pillow as she gasped for air through a flapping, toothless mouth.

Marian turned and instinctively made straight for the door. She must call the doctor immediately. Constance must have had a stroke, for one side of her face was horribly not matching the other. And her mother-in-law had gone a liverish yellow. Then she stopped, squeezing her hands hard together, and looked back at the body in the bed over her shoulder. The spectre of nappies and rubber knickers loomed before her. The spectre of Constance Law, getting worse, loomed like a ghost stretching rubber glove fingers and wading in faeces.

It would be a kindness to leave her and let nature decide. It would be cruel to prolong a life already such a burden to its owner as well as to everyone else. Not by any stretch of the imagination could anyone call Constance happy. What would be the point of calling the doctor?

She stood at the door, afraid of her thoughts, afraid of approaching the bed in case one terrible eye might open, and knowingly accuse Marian. Because Constance knew all right, Constance knew what nobody else did. Constance knew that Marian Law was not a brick, not the nice, open-hearted country woman she liked to make herself out to be. Constance saw right through her . . . always had . . . right from the start. Constance would know why Marian hesitated to call for help, and that reason was nothing to do with kindness.

Marian wanted to ascertain that Constance was not in pain. She couldn't have left her in pain . . . that would have been something else. It was hard to tell. There was an occasional moan, but it came from very deep, as if Constance was in coma, or definitely somewhere far away.

She crept towards the bed, hugging her cardigan round her, stretching to see over the top of the covers. She remembered that this was how they'd delivered the Christmas presents when the children were little, tip-toeing in in the guise of Father Christmas, terrified in case they woke them up. Afterwards she and Roger had gone downstairs and toasted each other with sherry, genuinely unnerved by what was really a game. But it hadn't seemed like a game . . . it had seemed more like this . . .

Marian grasped the cold brass bedstead, her thoughts whirling. Her heart was going like a pile driver. She cleared her throat to give Constance a chance. The woman in the bed didn't respond. She just kept on breathing as if every rasping gasp might be her last.

Marian heard hot water move round the pipes. Lloyd and Sally were washing up. What would they think if they knew what was happening upstairs, if they knew their mother was contemplating murder? Because it was murder, wasn't it? She was killing Constance by doing nothing as surely as if she was pushing a pillow down over her face. She was committing a murder . . . now . . . even as she stood there deliberating, because every second wasted might count.

Tense, tingling, she began to think like a murderess. Cunning, not adrenaline, coursed through her veins. She must cover herself. She would change Constance's hot water bottle and say she hadn't the heart to wake her because she was too deeply asleep. This meant thrusting an arm into the bed, retrieving the bottle and taking it downstairs. This meant facing people, immediately, with the new-born lie. Could she do it? Was she ready? She swallowed and her throat felt ulcerated.

Carefully Marian untucked the bottom of the bed, keeping one eye firmly directed on the end of Constance's chin which was the only part of her face she could see. Cautiously, quietly, she lifted the covers and squinted under, into the rank darkness. She saw the bottle, a palid red resting next to the mottled legs. She stretched out her arm, fingers splayed, and brought them together on the little rubber hole at the end. Accidentally her probing fingers touched a leg. It

51

was flabby as the cold hot water bottle. But cold as it was, it seared her fingers. Still watching Constance's chin, she pulled the bottle towards her. When it arrived and she gripped it with both hands, it was damp. For a second she wondered if it might have leaked, and ridiculously she had it upside down to test it. What did she care if the bottle leaked? She was about to leave the woman to die, wasn't she? Then she realised that Constance had wet the bed. She was lying there helpless, in saturated sheets. And she, Marian Law, was going to leave her there.

She passed Sally on the stairs. 'Leave the light on, Sall. I'm going to get Gran a fresh bottle. She's sound asleep. I can't bear to wake her. I'll just have to clean her up in the morning.'

'You go to bed, Mum. I'll do that.' Sally was so fresh-faced . . . so pretty.

'That's all right.' It was hard to sound casual when you had to bite your lip in order to keep your chattering teeth together. But Marian was surprised at how sensible she sounded. 'It won't take me a minute. See you in the morning. Sleep well.'

'And you, Mum.'

In bed. In the double bed, under the forget-me-not sprigged eiderdown she had shared for twenty-two years with Roger. Keeping to one side of the bed because she hadn't managed to adopt the habit of sleeping in the centre.

Marian quickly put out the light. No reading

tonight. Because she was too excited. She curled up into a ball with her eyes wide open in the darkness. She couldn't wait for the morning, although she feared it. She wouldn't get a wink of sleep tonight.

It was a relief to be alone. She was a sly old fox, back from its kill and safe in its den once again. Like a fox she licked her lips, and listened. She had to keep listening. She didn't know what she was expecting . . . some cry . . . some strangled scream for help from Constance's room? Or worse, limping footsteps on the floorboards . . .

Her temples throbbed. She was suddenly a different person. She was the type of woman she read about in the *Daily Mail.* Did it show? Would she look different when she got up to dress in the morning? Inadvertently might she choose a red dress, or scarlet lipstick . . . forgetting that she must be careful . . . oh dear God let me not break down and confess. Marian had never done anything terrible before. All she could think of now, as she thrust her hands between her knees for comfort, was the time she had peed in the bath when she was little. Interesting, how she could now compare peeing in the bath to murder. It must be something to do with the disgust she had seen on her mother's face, and the fierce, slapping reprisal. No, she felt no more repentant tonight than she had when she'd peed in the bath.

She made her lips form a smile of wicked pleasure. She had forgotten the wish she'd made earlier that evening. But now she made another one.

'Please, please, for the sake of my children, let no one ever find out what I've done.'

CHAPTER FOUR

The further I go the more I rely on speculation. Speculation backed by diaries, letters and gossip. Gossip was rife in Meadcombe. Information-gathering there was similar to visiting the library. You only had to ask to be pointed in the right direction. And everyone had an opinion. An hour in the Weary Ploughman was the equal to an hour poring over a book.

Sonia Hanaford was reported by all to have been an acquisitive, superficial woman. But so simple? Simplicity daunts me. There is no such thing as a simple human being, nothing more dangerous to correct interpretation than a caricature.

Friends. Janey, Marian and Sonia are all good friends together. Confidences pass between them like baby birds in hands . . . but selective confidences. They would never have grown so close had it not been for the Meadcombe drama group. It is a leveller, like a jury service, like a laundrette.

Sonia Hanaford blushed with self-disgust. Her cheeks burned. She feared she would be ill. But it was too dark in the car, thank God, for Stanley to see. Then she blamed her discomfort on the extreme parochialism of her friends. There was no need to feel bad about what she was doing. This was not incest. But their petty-mindedness, their fear of the unseemly, their small-minded village consciousness had been getting to her lately. Poor Janey — all kirby grips and worn-out sandals. And stoical Marian, so down to earth she was being trodden in.

The more 'O Ds' on that damn bank statement, the more vulnerable Sonia seemed to become. The overdrawn signs were like crosses down the mean strip of paper of a school arithmetic test . . . they made her ribs tighten with dread in the same way . . .

Her legs were crossed and cased in calf-length patent leather. The sovereigns clinked at her wrist. Nervousness moved her pulses and sprayed expensive perfume, like the behaviour of some intriguing insect carrying unspoken messages, out into the darkness. She was starting her forties, like her friends, but her hair was chestnut without a suggestion of grey. Janey Tandy's was showered in it. Marian Law's was blonde so it came through silver and was hardly noticeable.

Stanley's bangled hand touched the tape machine, and more country and western music flooded the gold Mercedes. In the dark his cufflinks glinted against the pink of his shirtsleeves. She noticed how carefully rounded the nails were on his stubby finger ends. Moneyed finger ends.

'I could have walked home,' said Sonia. 'There was never any need for a lift.' And there was never any need for them to be parked here by Dolan's pond, on the sloping willow fringes of the water. Never any need at all. How on earth had it happened? Well, Sonia was very drunk. And Stanley had a very high opinion of himself. But they had both used the same excuse — there was no privacy in the Weary Ploughman and they needed to 'talk'.

They were here to talk, she reminded herself. Hell, he was her father-in-law, and sixty years old! She was doing nothing wrong! This was her last chance to keep her house, to keep her clothes, to keep her lifestyle, to keep her credibility intact. Without her riches, Sonia often wondered what she would be like. How would she cope? Would anybody like her if she was poor?

When Stanley moved his head nearer she could smell the garlic on his breath, and a vague, cough-drop sweaty smell that mingled with fresh ironing. She thought of Beryl, but felt no shame, because they were only here to talk.

She said, 'Is there a light in here?' and Stanley flicked it on. She unclipped her smart handbag and took out a paper, unfolding it under the light. 'We've written down what we owe,' she said, holding the paper at arm's length in order to read it. 'And what we need if we start afresh, which is what Paul is eager to do. One mistake, Stanley, that's all we made. One mistake. It seems extremely unfair that you could abandon Paul and condemn him to failure after one mistake. After all, he is your only son.'

Stanley said nothing so Sonia continued, 'Of course we realise that you would want some sort of control over any money you might lend. Paul would be more than willing to allow you a major shareholding . . .' It was hard to concentrate on what she had planned to say . . . it was hard to focus on the paper. She only wanted to giggle, to turn the music high and to slap Stanley's face with the wretched piece of paper and then stick it into his fat-lipped mouth. Her words were articulated with the care of the drunk, eased out of her mouth one at a time as if she were blowing smoke rings.

She heard Stanley's arm move like a groan across the leather. It was up over the back of her seat. She leaned forward to avoid it.

'You could work,' he told her. His speech was slurred. For a second she liked him. She liked his sensible, positive side. It was something that Paul lacked.

'Right. Let's concentrate on that for a moment, shall we?' Humour him! She was in danger, briefly, of allowing her distaste to show. 'What could I do? I haven't worked for twenty years. I'm not trained at anything. Any money I might earn wouldn't even pay the grocery bill. And I like being at home. I enjoy the things I do.'

'You could help Paul run the business. Take a part in it. Stop playing the lady of the manor. Stop being so damn negative.'

She felt impatience scuttle across her forehead like a leggy spider. 'If you're determined to take this attitude there's no point in talking to you, Stanley. If you're going to reduce our conversation to a personality thing . . . I'm talking about the money we need to get *Hanaford Galleries* off the ground again . . . not a little two-bit typing job which might make you feel better about me. You're always criticising me!'

Drink poured confusion on her cocktail of chaos and she sounded like a little girl again. She bridled, pulling the paisley scarf round her shoulders, safe with the familiarity of its perfume. Stanley's car smelt unsafe. Stanley's car was beginning to smell revolting. The stench from the overflowing ash-tray began to reach her nostrils and make her feel sick.

She thought of her lovely house where even the toilets smelt of gardenia. Every time she went into the house she was overcome by its beauty. It was back from the road, and in the gardens was a breathtaking magnolia tree with a horseshoe drive wrapped round it. It was a large house, with twenty-two acres of land, mostly ancient apple orchards. It was thickly carpeted and taste-fully lit. Her house had everything magazine houses had. Her house, her house was slipping through her fingers . . .

'You've got me wrong. I'm not trying to put you down. There's an awful lot about you that I admire,' said Stanley, leaning closer and staring at her breasts.

She thought, with surprise, how very like a child he was! Beneath the coarseness, the blustering and the aggression, perhaps he was like this all the time!

Paul was a member of the two golf clubs and one expensive country club where he played squash and came home white around the gills. But he couldn't care less . . . he didn't care about anything so long as his 'tea' was on the table when he got home.

'Supper, Paul, please!'

'Tea!'

'Supper!'

And he always insisted on a slice of bread and butter with his meal, and he held his knife like a pen.

Working class . . . like his parents. And the things she used to say when Stanley and Beryl left after a visit . . . they were dreadful things. She was never angry, just cold, and bloody-mindedly quarrelsome. The commoner Stanley behaved, the crueller Sonia criticised Paul's parents afterwards.

'Unbend,' Paul said to her, often. 'You look as if you've got a stick up your arse. What does it matter if Dad wears a vest . . .'

'But it does matter,' she almost sobbed. 'It wouldn't take much for him to keep his shirt on . . . at meal-times anyway. And why does Beryl wear a hairnet during the day?'

'Why don't you just ask her?'

Paul was difficult to draw.

Sonia had a horror of the inadequate. She

watched them when she went out shopping . . . watched the legs of the failed and the sick as they trailed along behind the successful in their trodden-down shoes worn previously by somebody else. She watched them in motorway cafes, hating to sit amongst their litter . . . she watched them in craft shops as they leafed their way though plastic garbage and plaster of paris souvenirs. Mobile homes and three-wheeler cars made her shudder.

The trouble with Sonia was that she still had one leg stuck in the back to back with the primitive sanitation in Bristol where she had been born. Try as she might, she could not extricate that traitorous leg. Sometimes she used to say to herself, 'Sonia Doris Burridge — Sonia Doris Burridge,' over and over again until it made no sense. She would squeeze up her eyes and stare into the mirror to see if she could conjure up the fat, pasty-faced child, poor but happy, that she had once been. Thankfully she could not. Then, cakes and chips meant love, but they cost money. Well-loved, Sonia Doris had been given lots of cakes and chips. Now, the well-groomed, thinned down lady of the manor looked back at her wearing a superior smile. She was Mrs Sonia Hanaford . . . no middle name at all, and she would do all in her power to stay that way.

But Stanley Hanaford was perversely proud of his beginnings. 'What can you expect,' the easy-going Paul used to say after one of her vitriolic tirades. 'He used to ride round the countryside with a horse and cart calling Rag'n'Bone . . . that's how he started.' Sonia's toes curled. She knew he did. She hated to hear that story. It was too hideous to contemplate.

'But he's not doing that now,' she would argue, all reason gone. 'Yet he insists on living in that squalid little house of his in the new town, filling it with white leather and parking that flashy Mercedes outside. He'll pick up a brass bedstead and sell it for peanuts, while he sleeps in that ghastly purple-backed monstrosity with the nylon bedspread . . . he's got no taste . . . no sense of style . . .'

'And yet he makes money hand over fist,' Paul reminded her. Paul's business had grown out of pickings from Stan's warehouse. So she couldn't pretend he didn't exist, like she did her own family. The better stuff, the stuff with style, they labelled antique and sold to discerning people at staggering prices. The mistake they could not afford to make had been the shipping of one princely order to Dubai . . . one of their biggest orders ever. The address was fake, so was the cheque. The Manor was mortgaged, their outgoings were huge.

One of the most important things in Sonia's life was that the twins were at Murrayfield. For her that was a tussock in her quick-sand life of peril. When she met a stranger, this fact was one of the first things she used to say about herself. And she encouraged Flora and Phineus to bring friends home to stay so that they would rub a little gilt off on the family she felt were not quite really there. The thought that they might have to leave Murrayfield filled her with terror. It came to her in bed at night before she slept, and made her wriggle and squirm and kick the sheets in a childish, frustrated temper.

And she couldn't bear the bank manager, with whom she was on first name terms, to know their awful secret. And if it came out . . . oh God . . . if it came out . . . they all would know — Janey, Marian, everyone at the drama group, everyone in the village shop. Oh God, oh God, oh God . . .

People were wary. There was a ruthlessness about Sonia.

Stanley put the light out. As his face came nearer Sonia saw that something was happening to his features. They were melting, slipping off a horror film face, fusing at the edges. In her drunkenness it looked as if his face was being burned by fire from within, a mask disintegrating and the plastic oozing out.

She had to watch, horrified, fascinated, until it came so near she could not focus and then she felt his lips touch hers. Just a fleeting, gentle brush. There were beads of sweat on his upper lip below his ridiculous moustache, she tasted them and he eased himself in his seat to accommodate his new position.

'Stanley,' she said petulantly. 'Please don't.'

Now his teeth, which she knew were false, were nibbling away at the top of her ear, his drooping whiskers tickling her neck. And he was whispering words in a new, thick voice, words she had never associated with him before.

'Stanley.' Trying to sound matter-of-fact she eased her arm away and looked at her watch. 'It's late. Paul will be wondering . . .' She fought her way through the blanket of booze.

'Come on . . . come on . . . there's a good girl . . . come on . . .' And he had to stop to suck in his slobber.

There must be something she could do or say. She couldn't just sit here tolerating this grossness! But then she thought of her house. It stopped her from slapping his face, from opening the car door and slamming it with disgust.

'You want that money, don't you, darling? Well, be good to Daddy and we'll see . . . we'll see,' he crooned as his hand stroked her breast. She caught a glimpse of a red-veined eye. His rough skin caught on the soft jersey material of her dress. He whispered more lewd words. They alarmed and shocked her.

She closed her legs firmly to stop him thrusting his hand up her skirt. She closed her legs, she closed her mouth, she closed her eyes and she sat, rigid.

But all the time she thought to herself, 'Should I let him? For the sake of the children's education? For the sake of Paul's business? Should I let him?'

It would, at the end of the day, be no skin

off her nose. In her heyday Sonia had had more men than hot dinners. Well, she'd had to climb the ladder, hadn't she? If she hadn't detested Stanley, found him so repulsive as to actually raise goose-pimples on her flesh, she wouldn't have asked herself. She would have done anything for the money, anything at all. She tried to forget who was touching her. Tried to forget whose hand it was that was squeezing so clumsily at her breast, first the right one, then the left, while his face hovered not inches from her own. It was like sitting in the dentist's chair, eyes closed, wincing, waiting for the tweak on that exposed nerve.

When it happened, it was so vile that it decided her. He caught her hand and brought it across to his lap. He pushed it down on the bedraggled penis that flopped, ridiculous, out from his fly. A quick look, and she saw that in the half-light it had taken colour both from his shirt and from his denim trousers. It was a terrible pastel purple . . . and the texture of pasta stuck in a plughole.

It was not difficult for Sonia to feign horror. She snatched back her hand, rubbing it where it had touched the thing, and sat right back in her seat.

'Stanley! How could you? When I agreed to accept a lift from you, I thought it was so we could talk about money. Not for a minute did I expect this!'

His bug-eyes bulged, and discomfited he stroked back his silver hair. But the thing still flopped. She could see it out of the corner of her eye. Silly, but she imagined she could smell it, too — seaweed.

'There is no alternative but for me to tell Paul what has happened,' she said, clutching her bag in womanly self-righteousness.

'Don't be silly . . .'

'Stanley, I assure you I am not being silly!' She said it with all her authority, swallowing a hiccup.

'Fucking prick-teaser. You knew damn well why we came here!'

'Stanley! All I can say is that you have read me terribly wrong! Not for one second would I have considered coming out here with you if I'd known this sort of thing was in your mind. I never thought you were that kind of person. I can only say I am sorry for Beryl, and I feel she should know what sort of monster she has married!'

'You're not serious!'

Sonia turned to look him straight in the eye and show him just how serious she was. 'You have left me no alternative, Stanley. After this, I can't just go home and say nothing. I don't know how I can have you to the house again . . . and the children!'

'What has this got to do with the children?'

'Everything, Stanley. Everything.'

'Cow!' Again, he reminded her of a little boy. He wore a little boy smirk on his face.

'It's useless you flinging insults at me. You have already insulted me enough by assuming I wanted to indulge in this sort of hanky panky with a man like you. What possessed you to think of such a thing, Stanley? I can still hardly believe it!'

Stanley looked out of the window while he zipped himself up. He took a packet of cigarettes down off the dashboard and lit one, pulling the smoke well down. He breathed out slowly, and continued to stare out of the driver's window as if he could see something fascinating out there in the darkness. Sonia watched the glow on the end of his cigarette, watched it brighten as he pulled on it and thought.

Through clenched teeth he said, 'You're going to do this, aren't you?'

'Yes, Stanley. I am.'

'And of course I will deny it.'

'And of course Paul will believe me!'

'Will he, Sonia?'

'You know he will.'

The silence was long and as pernicious as the cigarette smoke. Finding the ashtray full, and not wanting, she supposed, to spill the ash on her skirt, he pressed the button and the window opened with a whirr, letting clean air in.

'You can't lose, can you?' he said as he flicked the butt outside.

'Not really, no.'

'I've been a fool. I've underestimated you.'

'Yes.' She was waiting for his decision.

'Of course, if I gave you a cheque you would feel able to let the matter go.'

'Probably.' She put the light on herself and pulled down the mirror. Opening her handbag she took out her lipstick and unscrewed it. 'We'd have to see.' Her smile was deadpan as she applied the red. 'I think something could be sorted out.' She pressed her lips together, screwed the lipstick back and dropped it into her bag, smiling about her pleasantly.

'Sonia, dear, I have to hand it to you . . . you've got nerves of steel.'

He wrote out the cheque with a shaking hand. She took it, and after a quick look at the amount, snapped it in her handbag.

'Now what?'

'Now you take me home.'

'Shall I come in?'

'No need for that. Drop me at the door. Paul will understand. After all, it's very late.'

'And you're going to leave me like this?' He looked down pointedly at where the denim trousers bulged over his belatedly erect penis. Something about her behaviour had turned him on! He liked to be treated badly! He liked a nasty lady! He wasn't ashamed. He wasn't embarrassed at all. She might as well have wanked him off . . . she had given him a pleasure all his own. She turned her rather stale picture of Beryl over in her mind and wondered about her hidden depths.

'There are things you can do about that, Stanley,' she said with a laugh. 'And I'm sure you don't need me to tell you.'

68

'Not just a quick one? Show your gratitude?'

She snorted. 'Come on, Stanley, I've had more than I can take already tonight. Drive me home.'

'I'm desperate, Sonia,' he pleaded. 'I'm dangerous like this. I could . . . I could do anything . . .'

She looked down at him with revulsion. He was enjoying himself, crawling. 'Take your dirty self home. Stop being so disgusting.'

Stanley Hanaford drove the car dangerously. Obediently he dropped her at her vast front door. She noticed that his hands were still shaking. The erection, too, was still obvious. His breath was coming fast and hard, and when he turned his eyes towards her, she saw a desperation there . . . a desperation she didn't like.

'Go home, Stanley,' she whispered through the window to the man with the mournful moustache. 'Go home to bed. We'll forget any of this ever happened.'

He didn't reply, but whimpered like a little beaten dog. 'Pervert,' she said to herself as she rummaged in her handbag for the door key under the porch light.

Before he had gone she was already thinking about how she would tell Paul, seeing the delight in his eyes as he read the amount in his father's bold, ungainly writing.

She was imagining how they would post off the unpaid school fees to Murrayfield. How she would walk into the bank in the morning and pay the two hundred and fifty thousand into her account as casually as if it were a hundred.

And how, if she were given the part she craved, she would play Phoebe in the Christmas pageant planned by the drama group this year. With what style! With what abandon! Confident once more with her money stacked behind her!

She didn't look round. She didn't even hear the car as it crunched away over the gravel.

CHAPTER FIVE

I'm sure that Marian knew for certain that Constance was dead long before Sally called her in the morning. Unable to stop herself, she had got up in the night, put on her dressing gown, and padded across the landing on cold, cold feet.

It had taken some time for her eyes to adjust to the darkness in the silent room. It was the silence that told her that Constance was dead. A big woman, slightly asthmatic, you could always hear Constance's breathing. Not now.

She didn't turn on the light. Avoiding the bed, shivering a little, she tiptoed over to the window and raised the curtain. She was surprised to see any movement in the square at this late hour. But right across, beyond the Plague Stone, she saw the shadowy figure of Melanie Tandy leaning against a large, parked car. The only sign of the driver was a moving cigarette end. Remaining hidden behind the curtains, Marian watched for some time as the girl chatted to the man . . . she assumed it would be a man. What was she up to, Marian thought to herself? What trouble now? She looked at her watch. It was two o'clock in the morning. Surely poor Janey would be frantic with worry. What a time for a fourteen year old to come home!

Were the lights in the Tandy house still on? She couldn't see from here. There'd be trouble, that was certain.

Eventually Marian had turned and walked across to the bed, surprised at the calmness of her feelings. That, she supposed, was that. No more Constance. Thank God it had been quick . . . whatever it was. A mercy. A release. She leaned over. There was no doubt about it. Constance's eyes were blank as a pike's, and bulged from her head to stare starkly at the ceiling. Marian had to restrain herself from closing them.

Now all she had to do was get back to her room and the deed was done. There were no sounds from the house, none but the pat pat of her own feet as they headed back to the bedroom that overlooked the garden, the double bedroom, Marian and Roger's bedroom, Marian's bedroom.

Still she lay in bed, sleepless, waiting for morning, waiting for Sally's call, for it would be poor Sally who took Constance an early morning cup of tea. Marian was relieved that Constance didn't look too frightening. It would be shock enough for Sally to find her grandmother dead in bed, let alone distorted and dishevelled. No, there was no fear of that. Constance, for the first time since she'd known her, had looked quite peaceful.

Bright, busy, breakfast time in the Tandy household. Daniel, Justin and Janey, but no David

72

yet. No Melanie. A toasty smell tops the coffee. A milky smell, reminiscent of babies, tops the cereal.

'Mum, the doctor's round at the Laws'.'

'Coffee or orange juice . . . Daniel! Coffee or orange? Answer me! Come on, you'll be late.'

'Doctor Crawford's round at the Laws'.'

'Save some Krispies for Justin. You know he can't eat flakes.'

Janey, with a weight on her heart, peered forward over the sink to try and see out. 'And did you hear your father? Is he up yet? I hope he hasn't gone back to sleep. Justin, run upstairs and give him a shout, will you?' Janey was annoyed. What right had he to sleep, unconcerned, when he was the cause of their daughter's disappearance. Her weak, muddle-headed man. To start with, years ago, she had tried to be competent, to do well so that he would notice her. Now she did it to save the family from going under. Someone had to cope with it all. She banged away in the sink, unnecessarily loudly.

'Where's Mel?'

'Mel went out last night and hasn't come back yet.'

Daniel paused with the cereal spoon halfway to his mouth. He watched his mother with big, surprised eyes. He delved into his crispy breakfast, trying to sort something out in his mind before he spoke. Then he said, 'Are you cross with Mel, Mum?'

Janey waited, listening for sounds from upstairs.

'No, Daniel,' she replied wearily. 'Not cross, just worried.'

'Something bad might have happened to her.'

'Act your age, Daniel,' she snapped. 'Melanie can look after herself.'

Hurt, the boy concentrated on burying every last Krispy under the milk. 'How do you know?'

'I'm afraid you have to take my word for it. And I don't want you home again today,' she said quickly, before Justin came back downstairs and started interrupting. 'You're either ill or you're not ill, and I'm fed up with this pretending.'

He considered a reply and decided to let it pass.

'He'd gone back to sleep, Mum.' Justin, ten, brought the news downstairs with some satisfaction. After all, he didn't go back to sleep when Mum called him, did he? He was normally first downstairs and today he had set the table. Sometimes Justin's great love of life, his sing-song voice first thing in the morning like a little, dark lark, amazed his mother.

'Where's Mel, Mum?'

Daniel scowled at him. Justin scowled back and repeated innocently, 'Where's Mel? Are these all the Krispies left? Where's Mel?'

'Gone,' said Daniel solemnly, speaking for his mother while he watched her. Justin raised childish eyebrows, pulled a funny face and dismissed the subject. He grovelled in the now-empty cereal packet searching for a blue hippopotamus. He scattered bits on the floor round his chair. Steam rose from the sink where Janey was rinsing plates. Carelessly she stared out of the window, just able, from there, to see the back of the doctor's car. It could only be Constance . . . her heart . . . When the children had gone she would pop round and see.

Janey had slept badly. She had left the door unlocked in case Melanie came back in the night, but really Janey knew she wouldn't. This morning she had gone, nearly gagging with hope, to look in her daughter's room before she'd come downstairs. No Melanie. Well, she hadn't expected it. All sorts of fears and horrors had twisted themselves round in her head last night. All the worst things, the things you dread. Melanie was sensible, but Melanie was only fourteen.

Secretly, Janey expected her to be in school this morning. She was going to telephone after nine o'clock and have a word with the headmistress. If not, she was going to search through her daughter's bedroom to see if she could find any clues as to where she might be . . . who she might have gone to.

And she wanted to talk to Marian. She hoped there hadn't been trouble next door . . . she needed Marian to listen to her and help . . . Cold, distracted, she could only think about her daughter.

Janey blamed herself. It was unfair of her to blame poor David. He couldn't help it. She would always blame herself, whatever happened in life. It was the way she was. She suspected that Melanie had not been given enough love. Worse, she suspected that other people, particularly Marian, thought that too. It wasn't fair! Janey's love had always had to be split, and therefore weakened. David, hopeless, miserable, always needed it, had always needed it, even when the children were very little. What else could she have done?

She remembered a conversation she had had at breakfast, once, with Melanie. 'If God's so great,' Melanie had pondered in her little girl voice, 'how come He made Daddy so unhappy?'

'You shouldn't talk about God like that,' Janey had replied, too busy to bother. 'He has His reasons. Not for us to reason why.'

'Will God strike me down if I reason why?' Melanie, Janey remembered, had been stuffing her satchel with her packed lunch.

'Probably,' Janey had answered, again without thinking much about it.

'And is it God, then, Mum, who made Daddy unhappy?'

'Lots of things make people unhappy, Mel. Not only God.'

'Perhaps it's you,' Melanie had said directly, levelling her dark eyes at Janey. And then, more softly, 'or perhaps it's me. Perhaps it's not God at all.'

'Well, whoever it is, nothing can be done now.' Janey had hurried her daughter out of the door in case she missed the school bus.

That evening she had come home with an answer. 'Mummy, I know why Daddy is unhappy.'

'Do you?'

'God made him unhappy to punish him.'

'Oh? And what has Daddy done to call for such a terrible punishment?'

'Not loved anyone but himself.'

Janey had, for once, stopped what she was doing to turn and consider her little daughter. There she stood, her black wool tights rucked round the ankles, her bottle-green blazer, too big for her, wide on the shoulders, her sombre eyes dark with the thoughts that had haunted her all day.

'Nonsense, Mel,' Janey had started to say. But Melanie was shaking her head, making the wide brim of the hat, held on with elastic, emphasize the point she was not about to give way on. 'How can you say that? Daddy loves us all, of course he does.'

Then Melanie had spoken to Janey as though she was a fool, too ignorant to have worked out the simple truth. Sweetly, she spoke with compassion, afraid of hurting her mother as she explained. 'If he loved us, Mummy, he would be happy.'

Janey remembered now how she had turned to butter the bread, unable to find an answer. How old had Melanie been then — eight, nine? Something like that. Now, for the first time, that remark rubbed a blister in Janey's mind and she wondered about that childish argument. Silly!

David was ill . . . it was nothing to do with love . . .

And then, a couple of years later, Melanie had chopped off her hair. Had come down in the morning with ugly tufts where the smooth sheen had been, looking as heart-breakingly spoilt as the doll whose hair Janey had hacked off when she was little.

'I wanted to make myself prettier,' was all Melanie would say.

Janey had bustled her round to the hairdresser's, embarrassed and unsure what to say.

'Naughty girl,' the hairdresser had said. 'You've turned yourself into a turnip! Such pretty hair! What a mess!'

Melanie, sulking even then, Janie remembered, had watched under thunderous eyebrows as the woman tried to repair the damage.

Janey, seeing her child damaged like that, had felt as if she herself had been mutilated. The shocking aggression in the act had seriously frightened her.

'Don't ever do anything like that to yourself again,' she remembered saying over her shoulder on the way home. She had spoken over her shoulder because at that time Melanie refused to walk along the pavement with her . . . with either of her parents . . . as if she was ashamed of them, embarrassed to be with them, or something. Hostile. Critical. Angry. Impossible!

Now Janey was trying to behave as if she was

78

not afraid. She didn't want to worry the boys, or David.

Melanie would be back, of course she would. Lots of children must storm from their homes in temper, to return when they are cold or hungry. And the nights were closing in . . . a cup slipped from Janey's hand and landed with a splash in the water. Her face was wet, and Justin's laughter spattered her with irritation.

Forgetting that she liked to make a happy breakfast, so that David, coming down, would have a pleasant start to his day, she turned and shouted, 'Damn you Justin! That's not funny!'

The boy covered his mouth with his hand, stupidly thinking that this covered his crinkled eyes, concealed his shaking shoulders.

'I said that's not funny!' She flung the dishcloth on the table, wanting to hit her youngest child yet not able to do so.

Daniel was sitting still except for the fingers which plucked at his bottom lip. 'And you!' Janey was appalled at the harshness of her voice. A shrew, a fishwife, that's what she sounded like, and it was, as usual, all Melanie's fault.

'I'm not doing anything,' Daniel whined. 'It's him!'

'It doesn't matter. Just hurry up and get yourselves ready. I can't help you this morning . . . I can't . . .' She stopped. She was bringing herself to tears. It was no use behaving like this. Once you let the control slip you were finished! She shrugged her shoulders and tried to smile in an effort at self-protection. Justin, relaxed, removed his hand and played instead with his blue hippo.

So the kitchen, if not a happy place, was a homely one when David Tandy, stooped, studious mathematician came down to have breakfast with the remains of his family.

'Just coffee, Janey . . .'

'You should eat . . .' Now she covered her mouth as Justin had done and equally hopelessly. But she was not trying to cover amusement, she was trying to cover caring — the sort of cloying, nagging caring which she daily heard in herself but was always unable to curtail. Sometimes she could see it annoyed David, could see the corners of his mouth twitch as she heard herself go on and on, mothering, smothering . . . so afraid that if she didn't love him enough he would be ill again . . . break down again . . . go to hospital again . . .

Now she went to fetch the paper from the mat, and brought it to the table, stopping herself this morning from opening it out for him.

Through the window they must have looked like an ordinary happy family, the sort they use in advertisements. Nice, cheery kitchen, lots of reds and yellows . . . Brillo-bright-bottomed pans hanging on the wall next to the Rayburn that always kept the room cosy and warm . . . but it wasn't real. Melanie was missing . . . again Janey stopped herself and went to hide at the sink.

'The police are round there now.' Daniel, on

80

his high stool, missed nothing.

Janey stretched forward to see. The police car was parked in front of the doctor's. What was going on? Perhaps she should go round? Her heart sank. This morning of all mornings she didn't want Marian to have distractions of her own . . . Melanie was what was important. If Marian was busy then she would have to see Sonia, and Janey didn't really like Sonia.

She could not prevent the boys from opening the door to have a snoop . . . not without shouting, and she was too fragile to shout any more.

'Time for the bus,' she said instead. It was ridiculous, but although they were going in the same direction, David had never taken his children to school. 'I like to have that time to myself,' he had said many years ago when first setting the precedent. 'I like to hear the news and get myself composed to face the day.' And so the children waited in all weathers, snow sometimes, at the bus stop with the rest, and watched him warm his car up and pull away from the square, sometimes with a wave, sometimes not. And not one of them thought it peculiar.

'She's dead!'

Janey's heart nearly stopped. Why was she thinking of Melanie?

'The old lady's dead.' Daniel's flushed little face was uncertain as he poked it back through the door and watched his mother take the news. Outside the door a cluster of children waited like ghouls for pickings of information.

'Martin Farrier said she died in the night . . . of a heart attack . . .'

'Poor Marian!' Quickly, for the sake of the children she amended her remark to 'Poor Constance . . . take your coats, it's misty this morning — and shut the door, you're letting the cold in.'

'Kiss?' Justin's arms stretched up to circle Janey's neck. No one from outside was allowed to see that he still liked a kiss in the mornings. Janey obliged, straightening his collar and giving his school bag a little pat. 'Be good!'

He made another of his funny faces and she smiled back. 'See you tonight,' she said. 'Bye Daniel!'

She edged the door closed, determined not to join the noisy throng outside. She would call round later. Never before had she noticed that the children didn't bid David goodbye. She supposed she hadn't thought it odd because she'd always assumed they would be seeing him later at school, so it wasn't strictly necessary. But with a jolt she realised they wouldn't. He taught the sixth forms, housed in a different building to the rest. He parked in a different place. He ate in a different place. They would not see their father until tonight . . . and yet they never said goodbye. Melanie hadn't either, when she'd been here . . . oh, let me not start using the past tense . . .

'The police?' David was getting up to go.

'Yes, there must have been an accident at the Laws'. I'll go round later.'

'Poor Marian. She's got enough on her plate.'

Was he really going to leave the house without saying anything? And what about her? Was she going to let him . . . for the sake, he would say, of his own sanity? She couldn't play his games, not this time.

'The police, David. I think we should inform the police.'

He raised his eyebrows and looked at her absent-mindedly. The paper he thrust in his pocket to read at breaktime.

'Yes,' she persevered. 'We ought to tell the police that Melanie's missing.'

He flinched as surely as if Janey had hit him. She was quick to make him better. 'Yes, even though we know she's all right and that she'll probably be back tonight . . .' Janey Tandy even managed to make herself laugh. 'I still think we should tell them. She's only fourteen, David . . .'

'Well, if you think . . .'

'Yes, I do. And David . . .'

'Yes?' He was unwilling to turn round and hear more. 'Will you have a word with Mrs Gibson. Melanie might go to school, and I want to know immediately if they see her.'

She knew this was an imposition. David went to school to work, not to carry with him the everyday burdens of family life . . . heavy as they were. His crumpled feelings hung on his care-worn face, but this morning Janey didn't respond as she should.

'Can't you telephone?'

'I will phone anyway. I just want you to have

a word . . . to explain to Mrs Gibson what happened.'

'I'll see if I have time.' He gave her her morning peck on the cheek. She closed her eyes against it, wanting to pull away.

'Try and make time, David. It's important.'

When they were gone, when she heard the school bus pull away, throbbing and fuming out of the square, she made herself a coffee and sat, staring at the milky eye in the centre.

She looked up at the kitchen clock before she went upstairs to make the beds and check through Melanie's room. Eight forty-five. And Melanie had been gone for nearly ten hours.

CHAPTER SIX

The behaviour of women intrigues me — their machinations, their conversations and their relationships with each other. Without the hormone to provide them with man's aggression, and yet the same capability to anger, they seethe and bubble inside, seeming to always blame each other for their own vulnerability.

Friendship! Marian, Janey and Sonia. To know them, it wasn't necessary to raise a glance from their feet. Marian . . . Dr Scholls in summer, battered old wooden ones with chips in the soles and stains on the leather . . . motley sheepskin boots some friend had brought back from Australia, in winter. And for special nights out, not that there were many any more, a pair of black court, chainstore shoes with a cardboardy inside, cruel round the heel, the 'uppers' of which refused to fall in leather creases, softly with age, and that dated back to God knows when and still looked new and uncomfortable, and were.

And Janey? Thonged Jesus sandals through which most unattractive feet showed through. Feet with bumps and bunions and not too clean toes. Feet which could be associated with the sandy prints of Man Friday. Large, splayed, di-

lapidated feet. And in winter-time, a pair of battered Sixties knee-high boots with flat soles that
she wore over ankle socks so she didn't have
to bother with tights. No smart shoes at all.

One whole wall of Sonia's bedroom was given
to wardrobe space, and right the way along the
rail at the bottom Sonia's shoes were neatly rowed
like cars in a car park. And they shone, well-kept,
like cars in a car park, too. All colours, all styles,
a different pair for every day of the week, every
week of the year. Perhaps it was these that gave
her such a firm, quick step, and why her friends
were slower and softer, sagging a little at the
edges, unpolished and chipped on the bottom.

Marian just wanted to creep round her house,
quietly getting used to what she had done. But
that was not to be.

'So this is to be my punishment,' she thought
as Janey whittered on, stories about Melanie's
diary, Melanie's thieving, discoveries made within
the last twenty minutes, discoveries about a
daughter she had lived with for fourteen years
and felt she'd never known . . .

But Marian knew . . . Marian knew that something terrible had happened. Marian had seen
Melanie in the square last night, talking to a man
in a car. Her torture was that she couldn't say.
Without admitting to her own crime, without telling how she watched Constance die without lifting
a merciful finger, she couldn't tell anyone what
she had seen. The only room in the house, other

than the kitchen, that overlooked the square was Constance's front bedroom. Marian could not admit that she had been there, not without giving the game away. So she went on listening without hearing, head back, eyes closed, as Janey went on and on, stupidly convinced that Melanie was quite safe.

'Listen to me,' said Janey shamefacedly, mistaking Marian's silence for grief. 'Going on like this when you've had such an awful time this morning . . .' She shook her head, and then, to excuse her selfishness, 'I think I must be going insane . . .'

'No, really, it doesn't matter. Actually, it helps to take my mind off it all. But honestly, Janey, I think you should tell the police. I know it's unlikely that anything's happened to her . . . but best to be on the safe side.'

And would the police sniff round asking questions? And would she, Marian Law, be able to convince them that she had seen nothing, knew nothing? She felt more and more like a Lady Macbeth, murderess with blood on her hands. She felt her self-control slipping away.

They were into the wine by half past ten. 'Damn it,' Marian summed it up. 'I think this might be called a special day. We need a booster, coffee won't do,' and they drank in the way that friends do together . . . but they were no longer friends. Marian knew that. Janey didn't . . . yet. Janey's legs were slack in jeans under Marian's kitchen table. Marian was still in her ancient, quilted dressing gown. Both women leaned across the table top, supporting their heads on their hands.

'Thing is,' Marian confided, 'I can't stop shaking. I'm not sorry she's dead, I can't pretend to be . . . but look at my hand.' She held it out, and she was right, it shook.

'Shock,' said Janey. 'You weren't expecting her to die. And even if you had been, it's always a shock.' Janey resented having to comfort Marian this morning.

Both their thoughts went back to February and tried not to stay there. God, this kitchen table had seen some tears. They had sat at it then, but on that day Marian had not appeared to hear anything. Did she even remember it, Janey wondered? She had been so dazed. She remembered how Marian had once got up and started laying logs on the woodburner in the lounge, one by one until she'd banked it up high, roaring, crazed, frightening. This misty morning in September was nothing like as bad as that, even with the woman lying dead upstairs . . . not for Marian, anyway. Damn it, this should be Janey's day, and minute by minute she felt she was dying as her imagination played wild games with Melanie's whereabouts.

Marian thought, 'Why doesn't Janey stop talking and ring the police?' But Marian couldn't make her, couldn't tell her what she knew. Halfway through the third glass of wine and she told herself it didn't matter anyway. What on earth good would that piece of knowledge be?

'Come on. I'll stand next to the phone. All you've got to do is report her missing. Come on, you must!' It took a great deal for Marian to get that out. She had to root about with her tongue to make space for the words.

'They haven't seen her at school . . .'

'I know . . . but she might go in yet. She might just wander home tonight as casual as you like, not realising how worried you've been. You know what Melanie's like.'

Janey nodded, not quite sure what Marian meant, while she cooled her forehead with the wineglass. 'Yes. Yes she might.' But she didn't think so. And something was wrong. Apart from the obvious, bellowing things that were shrieking themselves to be wrong, there was something else. There was something different about Marian . . . she had distanced herself. She was not the same. Oh, rubbish! Marian had been through hell this morning . . . found her mother-in-law dead in the bedroom. Of course there'd be something different about her. What had Janey expected?

And across the table Marian thought, 'David's attitude . . .' Why was Janey moaning on? Why didn't Janey ring the police? Why was she sitting here going over old ground? David's attitude was David's attitude . . . he never changed . . . why was Janey so bloody surprised? Marian was getting angry. This ravaged-looking woman, this friend of hers was hopeless. What David needed was a rocket up his arse, he should be here offering wine and sympathy. Instead here was Marian acting the surrogate, when her mother-in-law had just died in the bed upstairs. No, she corrected herself, when she had made sure her mother-in-law had died in the bed upstairs. She was even manufacturing her own self-pity now. That was good. She must keep believing it.

'I'll dial,' she was forced into saying. 'I'll hand you over when they answer.'

'I can do it.'

'Come on then.'

'Nine, nine, nine?'

'No, the local police station number. Ask for Sergeant Marks. He's nice. He's the man who came round here this morning.'

Marian knew that by calling the police Janey was admitting to potential disaster. It was having to face what might be. She understood and felt worse about her betrayal.

'Sergeant Marks, please.' Janey's voice sounded pitiful, a little girl reciting in a school hall. Marian's guilty heart went out, and she gave her a wink.

'I'm ringing to report a missing person — my daughter, Melanie — yes, that Melanie — fourteen years old — wearing? Oh dear, wearing?' Her eyes asked Marian the question. Marian was careful not to answer although she could see Melanie now as she had seen her through the curtains . . . tight blue jeans and a baggy leather jacket, black boots with little heels. Petite, neat, dark as all the Tandy children were. Her view from the window had been a clear one.

'Do I know where she could have gone?' Janey begged for help again. Marian looked away. God forgive me, she thought, I just can't handle this. Janey went on, 'No, I'm sorry. I don't know. I thought . . . I hoped she might have gone to school today, but I rang the headmistress and she said she'd call back if she saw her — Meadowbrook — in the new town.'

Marian nodded. There was nothing more she could do except pour another glass of wine.

'My husband . . . David Tandy, he works at the school. Meadowbrook . . . yes . . . My name, Jane Candice . . .' Why do second names only come into their own at times when life malfunctions? Marian hadn't known Janey had a second name . . . nor had she seen her as plain Jane before. 'Janey' was completely different.

'No, I'm not home now. I'm with a neighbour. Next door but one, *Dunoon*, yes, D U N O O N.' Did the policeman laugh? Marian's house was the only one in the square with a name. The others all had numbers.

Janey put the phone down and rubbed her arm as if it were stiff. 'They're coming round for a photograph,' she said, and burst into tears.

This day was becoming more and more of a nightmare for Marian. Why didn't Janey leave? A hearse arrived at the door.

'I can't watch while they take her away.'

'You don't have to. Stay here. I'll deal with it. You wait in the kitchen.'

'Janey, you've got enough to worry about. I should have kept Sally or Lloyd home . . . they both wanted to stay with me but I told them there was no need.'

'Quite right. What can anyone do . . . now?'

Marian looked up furtively, stung by the remark. But there was nothing behind it. Janey, grips loose, sharp raindrops in a cloud of uncombed hair, was merely being consolatory.

'I just don't want her to be left . . . I want her to be seen out . . .' Marian sobbed, pathetic, as Janey carefully closed the kitchen door so she wouldn't see.

Janey was very aware of her breath when she showed the kindly undertaker upstairs. She was aware that she exuded drink and that she looked ravaged. They would think she was something to do with the deceased. She hastily explained that she was a neighbour. She had no need. Mr Sanderson knew her.

Respectful, that's how Mr Sanderson of *Sanderson & Tike* the builders behaved as she led him upstairs. Dark-suited, he looked more comfortable with his bottom hanging out of his trousers and a trowel in his hand. But he was trying . . . and somehow that made the occasion all the sadder.

Janey had never seen a dead person before. Her experiences of Constance had been brief ones. To start with she had resented her, always sitting, as she was, like a statue in the kitchen of her friend, disconcerting as a silent television set left on. But gradually, as Constance played no part, it was easy to pretend she wasn't there and treat her as part of the furniture after an initial, polite greeting.

As Constance's mind had gone, Janey, along with everyone else in the square, had obliged by keeping an eye open for her. The cottage kitchens all overlooked the square, so it was easy to see her when she wandered outside, half-dressed sometimes, to go knocking on doors. Mostly someone who was not busy offered her tea. She would sit, sipping silently, humming a little tune sometimes, and go quite happily when she was ushered out. While she stayed in the square she was safe, but when she strayed towards the main road someone would hurry out, wiping hands on dishcloths or with washed hair in towels, to guide the poor lost soul back home.

Marian was marvellous with her . . . a pillar of patience. Janey had never seen Marian angry — no, not in all the time she had known her.

Now she led Mr Sanderson and his man Burt into the dead woman's bedroom. The empty coffin knocked against the walls at the turn of the narrow stair, and Janey was careful not to comment.

'To you,' said Mr Sanderson. 'Right a bit.'

Out of her depth, and not wanting to appear ghoulish, she wandered over to the window while they put their coffin down and carried out whatever business it was they had to carry out.

She concentrated hard, so she wouldn't be enticed to turn her head. This room had the same aspect as her own third bedroom . . . the one Melanie used to sleep in. From it you could see the square quite clearly and everything happening in it. On the right was the church gate, next to that the Weary Ploughman, and one along from that the gaily-painted village shop. The rest of the square was made up of cottages.

The autumn sun streamed into the room, hazy, crazy with motes of dust. 'Come on me old dear, let's be having you,' said Mr Sanderson behind. And Janey shuddered. They were having some trouble with the slippery floor and Janey saw that it was very highly polished . . . painted, probably, with varnish. And just there, on the floor where the sun hit it, she saw a set of footprints . . . a perfect set of bare footprints . . . and she thought of Constance standing here, days ago perhaps, not knowing she was so soon to die. She must have stood here for some time to make such firm prints. Janey wondered what the poor, batty old thing had been thinking about. Or perhaps she had just liked to stand and watch the people going by.

She turned around in time to see Mr Sanderson and Burt lifting Constance off the bed. Janey closed her eyes and turned back to the window. Not fast enough! She would never forget that sight . . . because Constance was naked, and Janey had caught the disturbing sight of a pair of white moon, sagging buttocks and the pathetic soles of two distressingly large bare feet before she had managed to shut them out. All bare and scaly.

God! How awful! And Constance was such a funny colour. For the first time she saw Constance as a real person . . . like herself . . .

Unconsciously, with her brain tottering about for escape routes, she thought to herself that the footprints she'd seen just now were far too small to be Constance's.

'That's it, thank you Mrs.'

Leading the procession, Janey headed back down the stairs expressing what she hoped was an air of practical commonsense.

As Marian would have wished she escorted the body through the door and outside to the hearse, standing back like a sentry while they loaded it into the back. Uneasily, she looked up at the window and imagined Constance standing there on monstrous feet watching her own wake.

Mr Sanderson raised his black hat, as he would his cap, and bade her a subdued good morning.

Back in Marian's kitchen, more 'grown up' than her own which was full of childish knick knacks and done out in primary colours. No, Marian's kitchen expressed her naturally homely character . . . floral wallpaper put up by the expert Roger . . . window sills rubbed down properly, and sanded by a man with the right tool. Not like her own, daubed in quick red because David had always refused to do it, had never taken any proprietory interest in the wellbeing of the house.

And Marian's children were grown. There was no sign, now, of children's pottery bits and pieces that asked to be ashtrays but couldn't be put to such disgraceful use, turned wooden bowls that held to the last meal's smell, and unwieldy salad servers. There wasn't much out on the shelves. The normal accumulation of kitchen junk was all hidden away. Competent, sensible Marian in her competent, sensible kitchen.

'That's done.'

Marian hadn't moved. Now she raised her head and said, 'I feel so bloody guilty.'

'You have nothing to feel guilty about.'

'I could have been nicer.'

'Constance wasn't easy to be nice to. She was . . . ill, most of the time.'

'I treated her badly.' Marian's eyes were empty. She took her wine glass on a tour of the table.

'Everyone knows that's not true.'

'Do they?'

'If you hadn't taken her in she would have lived a very lonely life in that flat in London.'

'I suppose.' The wine glass came to a halt and tapdanced on the spot.

'It's true, Marian. You know it's true.'

'What a bloody day! There just seems to be one blessed thing after another . . . you must feel awful!' Marian shook her head and squeezed her eyes closed. 'Absolutely awful!' It was almost better to think about Melanie than to think about Constance. Why didn't Janey *leave?*

Earlier, in the tiny hall . . .

'A heart attack . . . it could have happened

at any time. There was nothing anyone could have done.'

The doctor's verdict had rung silky in Marian's guilty ears. She could have knelt at his feet and kissed them, half-demented with gratitude. She'd watched Dr Crawford's face very carefully. It was businesslike, matter-of-fact, and showed not a hint of blame or suspicion.

'Time of death? Hard to say. I'll put it down as some time in the early hours of this morning . . .'

'Perhaps if I'd got her up to the toilet . . .'

'No good thinking like that,' Dr Crawford had told her. 'There's not much anyone could have done. After all, Mrs Law was nearly eighty, wasn't she?'

Marian had nodded, childishly accepting in the face of the doctor's greater experience.

Why didn't Janey leave? 'I'm trying to keep myself together.'

'Janey, you're doing fine!' Marian squeezed her arm, while inside resentment squeezed her guilty heart.

'Even if Mel comes back . . . when she comes back things can never be the same. Not now I've read what she thinks about me in her diary.'

'You can't take things like that literally. Diary feelings change from day to day. No one expects their diaries to be read. You'd be unfair to read too much into that.'

'Such hurtful things, Marian. It was like reading a book by a total stranger. I wouldn't have recognised one member of our family.'

'None of us really know what anyone else is thinking.'

'And the fifty pounds! That little minx had been stealing money for months, stashing it all away in her make-up bag . . . fifty pounds! And David can't have realised . . . Oh, Marian — it's not as if we kept her short. We always gave her money when she needed it.'

Marian *wished* Janey would leave. They were right out of conversation. She wanted to be alone to nurse her precarious position, rock it like a baby and discover its strengths and weaknesses, and it was hard to sit before Janey, knowing about the car, knowing about the man. She feared the words she dreaded might come out in a minute, come gushing and tumbling off her tongue, leaping and spitting like the spluttering sherbet space dust her children had loved to tip from packets into their mouths. She was sure that if one of her children were missing she would be far more upset than Janey appeared to be. But then Janey didn't know. Janey, innocently, still believed Melanie might be staying with some friend . . . David had gone to work, for Godsake! Where were the police? She hoped Janey would take them back to her own house for the interview. She felt sure they would see that she was hiding something. They'd only have to look at her to know . . . and she wished she hadn't drunk so much wine. What did they say about drink, that it loosened the tongue? She hoped not!

'What's this?' Janey took the book off the top of a pile.

'Oh . . .' Marian shrugged. 'I was having a tidy up. *Magic — An Occult Primer*,' she read.

'Is it yours?'

'I picked it up in a junk shop way back . . . in the spring . . . when I was looking for some meaning . . .'

Janey opened the dog-eared paperback, mainly for something to do. Where were the police? She wanted to leave. She sensed that Marian wanted her to leave. There was something about Marian this morning that made her uneasy. She was jumpy. She was distracted. She was definitely different, although Janey couldn't be more exact than that.

'Interesting,' she said, laying the book down and stretching. She couldn't stop yawning this morning, either. It must be nerves. 'I wonder if there's anything in it?'

'Oh, I'm sure there is,' said Marian, foolishly, as the doorbell rang.

It was an important morning. It was the last time they were ever to function, outwardly, as 'friends'.

CHAPTER SEVEN

It was a peculiarly English affair, this disappearance of Melanie, played out with such stiff-necked rectitude within the village within the hills of the sleepy shire.

Where were the black-garbed, keening women, wringing their hands and tearing their hair as they mourned the lost virgin?

Sonia, detached and two hundred yards along the main road, knew nothing of it. On this sunny, damp day that smelt of rotting apples and white woodsmoke, she had walked the short distance from her house to the village, made brisk by the exhilarating sharpness of autumn . . . the trembling herald of all things dread. Now, cushioned in a half beer barrel seat at the Weary Ploughman she listened open-mouthed as the news sunk in.

Something terrible had happened. The shadow that moved across Marian's face made Sonia think of Stanley. A great redness possessed the room, a pulsating redness that encompassed everything between the low-beamed ceiling and the patterned carpet. Guilt. Gnawing, embarrassing, torturous secret shame. The highly-polished glasses that hung behind the bar gleamed like knowing eyes. The brasses in the fireplace glinted with menace, licked by the flames of knowledge. Surely, surely Stanley hadn't gone and done something . . . Nine out of ten murders are committed by people known to the victim, and yes, Melanie had known Stanley, only vaguely, but she had known who he was.

But Sonia chastised herself for being so silly, rallied and said, 'I'm so sorry about Constance. What a dreadful shock for you.' Marian accepted the condolence, so formally given, with a look of annoyed resignation.

They were waiting for Janey who was still with the police. Sonia blinked. The day that had started so well was ruined. She had come to lunch, dressed bravely in zigzagging beiges, with nothing more on her mind but to sort out the Phoebe thing. Every year Mrs Henley, the local writer, who had once written scripts for a TV soap from the scalloped pavilion-cum-conservatory in her hollyhock-bordered garden, wrote a play for the Meadcombe drama group to perform. Every year there was discussion, unknown to Mrs Henley, as to whether they might prefer to do a different kind of play . . . a well-known one, as the vicar put it. Something a bit more well-tried, as the director liked to say. But they were voted down by the cast because nobody wanted to kick Mrs Henley in the teeth like that. As everybody knew she was a busy, successful woman, and doing them a favour for charity's sake in her spare time.

So every Christmas the drama group put on

a Mrs Henley play, and that worthy woman always tried to hinge it on some particular aspect of local interest. This year the play was about the Plague Stone . . . and it would be performed outside, come rain come shine, in the square.

Lady Phoebe Grey was the star. A good, if rather naive woman, with a cad for a father who spent her life searching for righteousness but came upon evil instead and ended up being burnt at the stake. And from the moment she heard about that, Sonia was determined to play her. But now this . . . She listened in dumbfounded silence as Marian, fuller and blotchier in the face than usual, filled her in.

'And I'm waiting for Janey now,' she said, giving a little chest shudder and looking towards the door. 'But when I came in here the police car was still outside her house.'

'I can't believe it.' Sonia stubbed a cheroot angrily in the centre of a large glass ashtray. 'I just can't believe it.' But her face went on the defensive, her pouty bud of a mouth went smaller and her little pointed chin stiffened. She should have known something would be bound to mar her day.

She could see that Marian was upset because she fiddled and fiddled with those old pearl earrings she seemed to always wear, and kept glancing towards the door in a more than interested sort of way. Sonia couldn't remember ever having seen Marian so nervy. It was catching.

'Have a short, Marian. Go on. On me.'

'I've been drinking all morning and I don't feel so good.'

Sonia felt a blip of jealousy. Why had nobody phoned her? She would have come round to help them both in their hour of need. She lived only just along the road. Why had they waited until the prearranged lunch date? They had been chewing the cud together all morning . . . she had been left out. She imagined them huddled up together by the fire, berating her as they poked it. She remembered her newly-acquired money and felt her plunging heart lift again. But then she thought once more about Stanley. It was painful to remember . . . she didn't like to remember. But if she tried it came back all right, almost too clearly.

He had been in a state when he left her. A terrible state? Yes, she would say a terrible state. Frustrated. Aroused. What had he done then? She assumed he had gone straight home to his space capsule of a bed and taken it out on Beryl. He was hardly in a fit state to drive round or go elsewhere. But had he? What would Stanley have done if he'd come across some young girl by the roadside . . . in the square as he passed through on his way home? What would he have done?

She told herself it was unlikely. She told herself this over and over again. But she experienced the most uncanny sensation of knowing. She remembered feeling like this when she was little, when they read the appallingly boring story of

Chicken Licken and Henny Penny to her, and that same daunting feeling of inevitability came to her now . . . she knew that, given time, no matter what she did, the whole rotten sky was going to fall with a bump on her head.

She remembered now how Stanley's face had changed, how even she had felt fearful for a moment or two . . . no! Stanley wouldn't do anything like that! He wasn't dangerous, was he? He was Paul's father for Godsake . . . grandfather of the twins. But what if . . . what if he had and everyone found out? Her part in the events of last night would not remain secret. Paul would know. Everyone would know how she blackmailed her father-in-law out of two hundred and fifty thousand pounds . . . and caused the death of an innocent child because of her insatiable greed . . . that's what they would say. She felt a hot stab of anger towards the hapless Melanie and an even hotter one towards the hopeless Janey. Some people attracted disasters . . . and pulled everyone else into the slipstream.

'What do you think has happened to her, Marian?' Sonia could hardly bear to hear the answer.

Marian looked round nervously again, like a conspirator, before she spoke. 'Between you and me I'm worried,' she said. 'I don't know why, I just am. I've got a feeling.'

Sonia picked up her glass and looked into it. This was unlike Marian. Marian tended to look on the bright side. 'It could just be that she's gone to stay with friends. It could be that she'll turn up again tonight bright as a bad penny . . .'

'It could be, yes,' Marian nodded slowly. 'But as I said, I've got this feeling. But poor Janey . . . really, Sonia I don't know how she's bearing it. She was such a help to me this morning with Constance and all that business . . . Oh Christ,' Marian suddenly bawled, 'it's horrible!'

'I don't believe it,' Sonia said again, not wanting to. 'You've had a real dose of it, haven't you? No wonder you're feeling queasy.'

'Too much wine,' said Marian, glancing round yet again. 'And of course that damn David is no help at all.'

Sonia's eyebrows arched. 'Well, that's no surprise.'

'It was his fault that she left.' And Marian launched into a critical description of the sequences of events that had led to the drama at the Tandys' house last night. Sonia chilled as she tried to picture it, and stopped herself at the point when Melanie Tandy slammed her way out of the door.

She toyed with the little pot of violets on the table. But all she could see was Stanley's purple-ridged cock. She pushed it away and picked up her drink.

The angles of Janey's head and shoulders signalled despair as she walked across the room to join her friends. But they, with their knowledge, forgot that she always walked like that. She was sniffling, a damp tissue held to her nose, and

105

looked as if she'd been crying.

'I could only find a photograph of Mel in a sulk on the beach at St Brelades Bay last year,' she tried to smile. 'They said it would do . . . but it doesn't really look like her . . . you know . . .'

'What else did they say?' Marian's strained face beamed rays of anxiety like a sickly sun.

'They said I shouldn't be too concerned . . . yet.' Janey sat down and started to worry the violets with bony, nervous fingers.

'What are they going to do about it?'

'They are circulating her description, and contacting the hospitals, stations and bus station. They told me how many children like Mel went missing every year . . . I can't remember the number. Marian, there were thousands . . .' The police had also told Janey, quite firmly, how many returned unharmed . . . the vast majority, but Janey, being Janey, wasn't about to repeat that fact.

A worm gnawed in Sonia's stomach. Marian paled. The sight of Janey trying to be brave, and the not knowing what to say made the silence uncomfortable. The gas fire with its false flames rhythmically leapt and tumbled upon itself, making no noise, pretending to be real, like they all were. There used to be a proper fire in here until three years ago . . . but it smoked too much.

'You just have to *brave* it,' said Sonia eventually. 'And believe that it will turn out right. After all . . . we don't *know* anything yet. It's silly to go thinking along *those* lines. It's very unlikely that anything bad's happened to her . . .'

'I'm trying not to think along *those* lines as you put it!' Janey's face was distraught. 'It's you two! You make me feel that way! You make me feel uneasy, as if there's something wrong! Something I don't know about!'

Sonia and Marian glanced at each other over the top of Janey's bowed and frazzled head. Sonia frowned and Marian wrung her hands. But each had seen the fear in the other one's eyes. And each, not understanding, looked quickly down.

Brightly trying to change the subject Marian said, 'I hear you were in here last night with "Hank".'

Sonia jumped. She wanted to pick her heart up like a naughty toddler and take it outside and smack it until it stopped leaping about like this. But she said, 'Yes, and Stanley was his usual horrendous self. Pompous, coarse, loud. I had to talk to him about a business plan of Paul's.'

'Where was Paul?'

'I thought I'd try a bit of my own persuasion. Paul stayed out of it.'

'Did it work?'

'Yes.'

Marian and Janey knew how Sonia felt about 'Hank'. And it was true he was not an easy man to like. Brutish, aggressive. His son, Paul, was so different. A giant, but funny and gentle. No one but a man with Paul's patience would have been able to stay so long with Sonia. They were her friends, but this is how they saw it. They were her friends, but they didn't trust her. Nor did they trust each other.

Now Janey studied her companions impassively for a few moments. Was there anything about either of them that she had ever really liked? There they sat, surrounded and protected by love . . . yes, even Marian, with Roger dead, was better off than she. Marian was adored by her children.

They were only here now because they pitied her. Sonia even had the gall to pass on magazines, old copies of *Country Life* . . . a sure sign of pity when people start giving you magazines. The terrible Sonia, who strode about like royalty, trailing along a cloak of expensive perfume behind her and looking down her aristocratic nose at her friends. Why did she bother with them, Janey often wondered. Why didn't she mix with the rich and powerful instead of slumming round with the peasants?

In Janey's eyes few people in the world suffered as she did. Janey Candice Tandy had always suffered, and always would. But there was inevitably someone else there to deflect the sympathy . . . mainly Marian. Even now people's feelings would be split between the suffering, abandoned mother . . . which is how she saw herself, and the woman next door but one whose mother-in-law had just died. And yet Marian never cared about Constance . . . she admitted as much in one breath, and yet managed to look the martyr in the next.

And in February, when Roger had died so horribly, the hearts of the whole village had gone out to the woman from *Dunoon*, and all Janey's problems had been pushed aside as if, miraculously, because Roger was dead they no longer existed. She'd had to pull herself together and pretend that all was well for Marian's sake . . . Marian, who needed her all of a sudden.

How hard it had been . . . how bitter Janey had felt . . . resenting Roger . . . resenting Marian . . . resenting the way she had to staunch the talking about herself for a change and concentrate entirely on the devastated widow.

What would Janey have done without the burden of David? Simple. She would have found another one, just as hopeless, just as demanding, to stick like a hunch upon her back in the space that was sculptured especially for it.

Janey was an obsessive. She craved to be utterly absorbed. In anything. To start with she had chosen love. She would have died for David, she would have enjoyed dying for David, but clearly David didn't want that. She was too useful to him alive. She had caught him by making herself utterly indispensable to him, and when love had failed to absorb her totally, she had thrown herself into the most important aspect of him . . . his illness. A woman of passion, she had wrapped herself round it like a desperate lover clinging to the knees of her hero. She had fed it, succoured it, mummied it, until, even if he'd wanted it to,

David's melancholia could never have got away.

David's illness was all-fulfilling. She'd never needed her children. When Melanie arrived it pleased her in as much as having a baby trailing along behind her added to her harassed image. Having to get up in the night accentuated the bags under her eyes.

Yes, marriage to David brought her the concern and attention she hungered for from her friends. It promised a lifetime's absorption and she wallowed in it. But there was one thing that stuck in her craw, one thing that she failed to understand and that sometimes drove her to distraction. Yes, she induced sympathy . . . her dramas attracted attention . . . but nobody ever called her a brick like they did Marian. She couldn't understand why people marvelled at Marian. And Marian hadn't the half of what Janey had to contend with. It wasn't fair.

Janey Tandy wasn't insane. Her behaviour was unconscious. But even her last big production, her abortion — interrupted so insensitively by Roger's death — had fed this obsessive need of hers. She had deviously allowed David to impregnate her, knowing full well his horror of having more children. She had watched her knickers, as the weeks went by, with a mounting excitement mixed with the adrenaline of dread that she craved. Nothing!

Even before the first week had gone, Marian knew. Before the second, Sonia. By the time the third week passed and no sign of a period, the whole village knew that poor Janey Tandy, with all her terrible problems, might now be pregnant on top of everything else.

Finally she had knelt before David's chair as a Catholic might kneel to a priest and confessed. Predictably, he had collapsed in a heap of nerves.

She had bowed her head in a agony of doubt. 'I don't know how it happened,' she had lied.

'I don't think I can go through with this,' David had said, greying, pulling his cardigan round him. 'What with Mel being so difficult at the moment . . . and for the first time ever the boys nearly old enough to look after themselves. Oh God, I don't know that I can face having a baby in the house.'

And he leaned forward with his head in his hands.

'Don't worry. You don't have to.'

So she was quickly at the point she had unconsciously looked forward to arriving at all the time . . . the point where she could thrash about in delicious dilemma with her friends around her, deliberating over whether she ought to have an abortion or not. Janey wouldn't have dreamt of having the baby . . . she could have gone and booked her place in the clinic on the night she had gone to bed without her cap. But she had to agonise over it . . . that was the whole point. But truthfully, none of this had been planned. She hadn't thought about it cold-bloodedly, hadn't schemed and plotted. It was just the way she was made. She could no more help being how she was than Melanie could help her sly habit of listening to everything that was going on or, being old enough now, at fourteen, understanding what was happening around her for the first time.

Then Roger had been killed, and Janey had had to cope with the clinic alone. David wouldn't take her . . . David wanted nothing to do with it. And Marian was in the process of quietly going insane.

One drama after another. And now Melanie gone. Janey was upset. Janey was truly concerned. But Janey was going to make it dramatic, whether it was or not. Janey was going to feed off this as she fed off every drama, milking the situation for all it was worth.

Nobody really wanted to know what Melanie had written in her diary. It was too private, too pathetic. It was like talking about the most intimate details of sex . . . just not on . . . not really . . . it was too great a betrayal.

But Sonia and Marian, the guilty ones, sat with fixed faces listening to the day by day revelations of a mixed-up, furious Melanie Tandy, read, pan-faced, by Janey, who was not going to let them get away without knowing.

'She knew about the abortion,' whispered Janey. 'Listen to this. "*Mum told Dad today. She is like a cow. She has no mind of her own. I would never*

112

kill a baby of mine." ' Luckily there was not much space for each day, so Melanie could not go deeply into her innermost feelings.

'And then she says, *"nearly thirty pounds now. Soon I will be able to leave this rotten hole and all the rotten people in it . . ."* '

'They're the scribblings of a child,' said Sonia. 'You can't take them seriously. All children write things like that, at that age.'

'You don't know that,' Janey was quick to react. 'Yours aren't old enough yet.' And in the sting behind her words lay the accusation of privilege and private schools, putting Sonia in a position from where she had no real right to comment.

'I don't mean my children or your children I mean *all* children . . . they all go through phases like that. You just can't take it to heart, that's all.'

But Janey was not going to be deprived of taking every word of it to heart. She flicked on, but was forced to put the diary down when she read a February entry with a start, *"Roger Law killed in car. Mum will be furious. No one to gripe to now."*

Melanie knew too much. Melanie was beyond forgiveness. Melanie was not a child, she was a woman, and thus to be feared.

And so, for Janey Tandy, a truth was perceived, a truth about herself that stung as sharply as a piece of grit in the eye, planted by a childish hand on the end of a blunt pencil, and rubbed in by the knowledge that she had never properly

113

loved her daughter. They were all guilty, all three of them, as they sat in a ring of dumb discomfort each with their own dark thoughts.

'Let's get drunk,' Sonia suggested. 'Let's get drunk or have something to eat. Anything, only let's do something! I can't bear to sit here getting more and more miserable like this.' She was impatient to leave. She wanted to go home and ring Stanley. What would she say? How do you ask a man if he's a child molester?

Janey flashed her a malicious look. Sonia missed it and tapped the table top with her fingernails. Sonia's nails were long so they curved, like a witch's.

Marian ought to lend her her book about witchcraft, thought Janey. Marian, wearing a dispirited smock every bit as lifeless as her house coat, just looked sad and studied her thumbnail. Her pie face was closed and drawn. Huddled round the pot of violets, Janey thought how right the two of them would look round a cauldron . . . stirring . . .

Marian and Sonia were hot in their secret condemnation of Janey. If she'd been a better mother her daughter would not have left home and they would not, now, be having to sit here like this nursing their awful suspicions. Their silent hostility crackled through the air like an electric storm, all the stronger because they were trying to conceal it.

Nobody else would have picked it up. But Janey was ultra-sensitive when it came to the attitudes of her friends. They were together in something. Janey was out on her own. The realisation brought shock as cold as a bucketful of water. What was it? It could only be to do with Melanie.

Janey tried to puzzle it out. Melanie had run away from home. She'd been gone only hours. Sergeant Marks had been almost dismissive. Janey had come here this morning expecting to have to battle to take the stage from the bereaved Marian. She hadn't had to. Why were they so distressed? They were pretending not to be, but it was obvious that they were . . . both of them. What did they know?

CHAPTER EIGHT

Friday night was drama night. The Meadcombe Drama group still meets on a Friday to this day in spite of all that has happened.

It smelled a bit like Marian's house in here — damp wood and lavatory cleaners. It was the absence of central heating that did this to places.

'It's fresh in here,' Sonia said instead, hugging herself. 'I can see my breath.'

The village hall was a flimsy building hung with fluorescent tubes on chains. Its thin, creamy walls were studded at regular intervals with a monotonous pattern of rivets which held the structure together. It belied any effort to make it anything other than what it was . . . even at party-times when people set about to deck it with streamers, balloons and subtler party parapher-nalia like red paper tablecloths and candles. It absolutely refused to respond. It was a glorified shack, and a glorified shack it would stay!

Today it was in its starkest state . . . naked and waiting like a woman with wet hair sitting dull and expectant before the stylist.

'I didn't know whether or not to come.' Janey didn't appear to feel the cold. Her bird's nest hair was all over the place. She wore faded jeans that had once been flares but now just hung with all the extra material round her ankles. Her rainbow sweater had been washed too harshly and the real wool hadn't taken kindly to it. She was staring, crook-necked, at a horrible picture. Remnants of an exhibition by a crazed local artist still covered half the walls. In the room that was empty save for canvas chairs, the pictures had the same eerie quality about them as the women's voices.

'We seem to be the first.' Sonia was embarrassed. She hadn't seen Janey since lunch-time yesterday, hadn't rung her, hadn't gone round. And no wonder.

'David said I should come.' Janey backed away from the picture and walked towards another one, less agonising, less charcoal-daubed. 'Life must go on, Melanie or no Melanie. We can't just stop . . .' Her fingers tore through her hair, as if she was trying to get to grips with either the picture or her situation, it was hard to tell which.

'Is Marian coming?'

'Yes. She won't miss the first meeting.'

'I'll light the stove. And we could start putting out the chairs.' This was the trouble with being first, but Sonia liked efficiency. 'Let's hope Jeffrey remembers to bring the coffee.' Sonia channelled her energies into activity before she asked, because she was forced to, 'No word yet, then?'

Janey turned round quickly, defensively. 'No,' she said, staring at Sonia, half-expecting contradiction. 'No. No word.'

'It's early days.' Sonia clattered away with the chairs. She squeaked round the floor in compulsory plimsolls. This room was too big with only two people in it. She fought with a dilapidated card-table. She was relieved when Nancy Blogg and Jeffrey the vicar came in together, sparing her more of this irrelevent conversation. Because any communication between her and Janey must now be irrelevent. Sonia knew, beyond doubt, that Stanley had done something terrible. Sonia had nearly not come tonight. The reason she had forced herself was because, if she hadn't, it would have attracted too much attention . . . she had not missed a drama group meeting in three years.

Strange. Because even now she knew something had happened to her friend's daughter, she didn't feel sad. She hadn't known Melanie that well. All Sonia felt was fear . . . fear of being found out. She would give anything, now, to take back time. If she could she would have said a firm goodbye to Stanley outside the Weary Ploughman and walked off home to cope, somehow, with her crippled financial straits. Sonia hadn't imagined that anything could be much worse than losing your money. If asked, before, she might have said ill-health, or death. Never fear. Now she knew otherwise.

She had to admit to herself that she had deliberately egged Stanley on. She hadn't said anything . . . or done anything . . . but she hadn't had to. Her intentions were in her demeanour, in gesture, movement and slant of the eye. Nothing she could be blamed for . . . was there? Yes, there was.

'Beryl?' She had phoned the moment she got home after that fateful, depressing lunch, when no one had eaten a thing but her. And she hadn't really enjoyed her Stilton ploughman's.

'Yes?' Beryl had shouted. Beryl, who still couldn't cope with the telephone, couldn't cope with any sort of socialising whatsoever.

'I'm ringing to talk to Stanley . . . about a deal we discussed last night. Is he there?'

'Stanley didn't come home last night,' had said Beryl in that same toneless voice. 'He left a message at the office to say he'd been called away.'

'When was that, Beryl?' Damn the woman! It was like talking to a cactus topped with thin, baby-white, peroxide hair.

'He left the message on the answering machine at work. They phoned me this morning to tell me.'

'And has nobody any idea where he is?'

'I don't think he said where he was going.'

'When did he say he'd be back?' Sonia held the receiver tight to her ear and blew a stray hair up over her forehead.

'He didn't say. But I know Stan . . . it could be anytime.' You know Stan . . . you know Stan . . . Sonia sneered. She rang his office but they had no more information than Beryl.

Later, she talked to Paul, Paul, who had been walking tall since the night his graceful wife

119

walked in brandishing the cheque that would save his business. 'It was easy,' she had told him that night, all innocence. 'Well, Stanley didn't want to see *Hanaford Galleries* go under, did he? He's your father, after all! I think he was touched that I went to talk to him . . . glad to know that we were in it together. It was a good idea of yours to try it that way. No, no strings . . . just a straight loan. So it looks as if we can breathe once again!'

Paul was such a simple man! Uncomplicated. Every feeling he had he showed on his face . . . never covered anything up or left a question unanswered. He had been thrilled . . . had wanted to ring Stanley.

'Not now, Paul.' Sonia had had to stop him, gently chiding. 'He'll be in bed. Wait until morning!'

But Paul had spent the morning smoothing things out at the bank, and it wasn't until after lunch that Sonia had been forced into tracking Stanley down . . . and not to thank him . . .

'Where could he have gone?'

'Anywhere.' Paul wasn't worried. Like Beryl, he thought he knew his father. Never the type to tell anyone what he was doing . . . a genuine cowboy with a 'don't fence me in' mentality. He would take up and go without letting anyone know. Not that he made a habit of it. It was strange enough behaviour, in the circumstances, to confirm Sonia's worst fears.

Now her time was increasingly governed by

portents . . . this morning she had read her stars . . . this afternoon she had told herself that if it rained Melanie would have turned up by tonight . . . if the sun shone her body would be discovered in some ditch tomorrow . . . covered in Stanley Hanaford's fingerprints. It did neither . . . after the bright morning the afternoon stayed dull, brooding, like she was. She prayed several times in her spare time . . . please God if You let this pass, I will sin no more . . . that sort of thing. Sonia had never been a religious person, not like Marian.

She picked up a photograph of Stanley from the sideboard. He had had it taken one Christmas and doled it out to his children . . . gift-wrapped, as a present. Paul had four sisters . . . and that was the sort of father Stanley was. She had picked it up, jumped when the gilt frame slipped in her fingers, and stared at the man whose eyes watched her from the centre of the square. Yes, he looked like a murderer all right, whatever a murderer looked like. She could see him on the television screen, dotted and blotchy and put together to form an impression. He looked like a photo-fit, anyway. He had a perfect criminal face . . . his mouth under the moustache was cruel. She remembered how it had come down on her lips, and even in her own sweet-scented living room she could smell the garlic and nicotine on his breath . . . and seaweed . . .

Perhaps no one would ever find out. Stanley was not, despite his appearance, a stupid man.

Perhaps he would have covered his tracks, hidden his evil deed like a dog scuffing over its dirt. After all, some children disappeared and were never found . . . not that she wished that on Janey . . . but it would be better than . . .

And then again, perhaps it was all in her imagination. She tried to convince herself that her worst fears were, after all, most unlikely. But in that case why had her mind gone straight to Stanley? Why had he been the first thing to come into her head when Marian told her? Oh, where are you Stanley, for Christ's sake!

Stanley had been mad when he left her . . . rampant . . . a disgusting great brute of a man used to his own way. She had bested him . . . he'd enjoyed that in his own perverted manner, but it hadn't satisfied him, not by a long chalk.

And she wasn't the only one to be fearing the worst. Marian was, too. Marian knew something.

Jeffrey sucked on his long teeth and tried to look naughty as he introduced Mrs Henley. He was hawing from the chair about how risqué the writer was getting.

Risqué . . . thought Sonia. If this is risqué then *The Little Red Hen* is pornographic.

He managed to annoy everybody. Jeffrey always did. He giggled, cleared his throat and looked embarrassed. Nobody helped him. Nobody smiled. Get on with it, was the unspoken message from the floor. And yet, from the pulpit on a Sunday he hammered out his message with the ease of a Shakespearean actor. Possessed, Sonia supposed . . .

This was quite unnecessary. He was summing up the history of the drama group using wide, feminine gestures. You could almost see his fat wobbling. Everyone present knew the history. There were no new faces in the hall.

Sonia rustled her script. Hearing the door open, she turned round, smiled, beckoned to Marian, and waited for her to come and sit down beside her. Marian was late. Why did the woman refuse to wear make-up? Marian reminded Sonia of the village hall.

Marian's face reflected the level of her suffering.

Constance had appalled Sonia. The fact that Marian had dealt with her, lived with her, nursed her, took Marian on to a high pinnacle in Sonia's estimation. Sonia assumed that Marian must be extremely relieved to be rid of her.

There had been times when Sonia had visited Marian's house around lunch-time. She had watched Constance eat with her fingers, play obscenely with her food, missing her mouth as often as not, dribbling, spilling and generally making a disgusting mess.

Constance had been a large woman, and in the months with Marian she had grown fatter and fatter until the buttons in those floral dresses she used to wear refused to close. She had worn her false teeth less and less, and when without them she took on a horrible, secretive look, her lips smacking together as if her mouth was stuffed with unmentionable things that tasted too juicy to share.

Sonia used to hate it when Marian went out of the room and left her sitting alone in the kitchen with Constance. She was forced to either sit in silence, which to Sonia was too rude to contemplate, or to make conversation with the person in the corner seat by the Rayburn.

'How are you this morning, Mrs Law?' Sonia had once asked cheerfully, resenting Marian's absence but determined to make the best of it.

Constance, instead of answering, had raised her little finger high in the air, closed her face up even further so her nose almost touched her chin and her little eyes nearly receded altogether, and winked at her.

'Well . . . that's fine.' Sonia had prickled under her arms, sweating in the heat of the impossible situation. And she'd been frightened . . . yes, actually frightened. There'd been absolutely no reason for her to think that Roger's senile mother might suddenly rise up out of her chair and attack her, but that hadn't stopped her feeling terrified that she might.

Sonia had turned to sit sideways on to Constance, fearing to turn her back on the mad woman, staring hard at the design of a tile above Marian's sink. Constance had not moved, but had made little gurgling noises in her throat which had upset Sonia, and given her the most peculiar feeling that Constance was intentionally trying to make her feel uncomfortable.

When she'd told Marian about this afterwards, Marian had said, 'Oh don't mind Constance. She's quite harmless. You get used to it.'

And Sonia had said, 'I think you're wonderful. I couldn't do it.'

And Marian had looked at her levelly and said, 'Oh yes you could, if you had to.'

Sonia knew otherwise.

She'd gone, only once, to visit her father in *Moorview*. And once had been enough.

The director, Grant Fitch, with whom every woman was in love and who was the reason many of them were here tonight, got up to welcome them and take over from Jeffrey. Blond and fluffy like a baby, womanly, he was certainly not interested in them.

Sonia had a friend on either side of her, and money in the bank. A new play to get her teeth into, and Paul, who would pour her a whisky and lemonade when she got home. She had everything a woman could wish for.

But where the hell was Stanley?

She looked to the left of her, and smiled encouragement at Janey. She looked to the right, and gave Marian a cheery nod. For a fleeting second she feared contamination. She smoothed down the rather eccentric smock which she had chosen as suitable for her thespian image, and felt the chunky metal earrings tug at her earlobes as she turned to face the front.

She had wanted, very powerfully, to kill her father when she had seen him screwed into a chair at *Moorview*. She wondered if Marian had ever felt that way about Constance and thought not.

The nurses, she'd quickly decided, were no more than high-level patients themselves. And this must be the reason why everyone in here was scared. Her mother, small by her side, was scared. Sonia was scared. And there was fear on the faces of everyone she looked at.

A television set, high on the wall, behind a wire screen, was on and loud. Her father was in the room and yet with his back to the television, unable to watch it. Bravely, tearing her eyes from a man who appeared to be having a fit and threatening to burst from his chair, she'd turned her father round. Her mother had looked even more scared.

'Do you think you ought, Sonia?'

'Well, there's no point in him sitting here looking at the wall,' she'd replied.

Why were men so much more pitiful than women when they finally tipped over the edge? Was it because, in the main, they tried so hard not to? Those who were not screwed in would get up every now and then to shout obscenities at the screen . . . or wander around the room with the little army of shufflers for whom wandering was a full-time activity. Some, like her father, didn't really seem to watch TV at all, but just sat there, with some part of them shaking. With Sonia's father it was his head.

A muscular, taciturn woman came round with a trolley of drugs during the visit. Sonia had tried to talk to her in the pause when she stopped calling, 'Medication!' The patients made an elaborate show of taking their pills, opening their mouths grotesquely wide, holding up the empty plastic containers as proudly as olympic medals.

'Tender loving care,' said the nurse. 'That's all he wants. He's no need to be in here really. He'd do quite well at home on drugs.'

And yet it was patently obvious that he couldn't go back to the chilly little house in Bristol with the outside privy. He was incontinent. He was heavy. His wife would not be able to cope with the fetching and carrying. Her back was bad. She was almost an invalid herself.

But Sonia ought to be able to cope. Sonia could take him back with her to Meadcombe and easily convert the old playroom on the ground floor into a sickroom. She could afford a nurse once or twice a week. And together the old couple would manage far better at the Manor than they would at home.

She'd looked at the father who had loved her to the point of spoiling. She'd remembered him taking her round the docks on his back and telling his workmates so proudly, to her embarrassment even then, 'This is my little girl.' She'd looked at the hands that had tied her dressing gown cord after a thousand goodnight stories . . . sometimes a rabbit's ear, sometimes a butterfly's wing. His lips through which such magic came were scabbed with scum.

With a pang of pain she'd remembered newspaper reports about *Moorview* . . . they cropped up regularly as bowel movements . . . about how the local residents resented having 'nutters' living on their doorsteps . . . It wasn't nice to see them trying to shop . . . or sitting muttering in the park . . . and warnings that one day one might break out and rape wives, daughters. She'd looked at her father . . .

Did he know? Dear God, did he know? A man at the end of his rope . . . swinging . . . taking a long, long time to die. A good man, a gentle man, with an integrity she knew had not been passed down to her. He smelled medicinal, not like a man any more. His grey hair curled around a weary countenance. His large brown eyes rolled warily towards Sonia, no humour left in them, and she'd wanted to kill him . . . then and there . . . and stop the jerking, because she couldn't, just couldn't do anything else . . . because of what she was . . .

They had gone down in the lift with a silver food trolley, all the people pressing back against the wall, giving it reverence as if it were a cadaver. It had stunk of old cabbage and mince. Sheep! They were sheep! They should have demanded its removal! Her father was a victim of the system because he hadn't the money to claw his way out of it. Sonia vowed it would never happen to her, Paul or the twins. She would never travel in a lift with a food trolley ever again. No matter what she had to do.

The wooden floor in the village hall had been buffed to a high shine. Their plimsolled feet squeaked as they moved towards the coffee table.

'That's the trouble with polished floors,' Janey said to Sonia. 'They mark so if you're not careful. While I was waiting for Mr Sanderson in Constance's front bedroom, I noticed a pair of footprints as clear as a yeti's in the snow. It's something to do with warmth and skin, you see. It sort of tears the top layer off.'

Relieved to be able to small talk and avoid the bigger issues, Sonia was encouraging. 'I prefer carpet . . .'

'Wooden floors look nice — with rugs. But they are cold for bare feet.'

'I thought Constance always wore those ortho-paedic slippers.' Sonia nodded to Jeffrey and chose a saucer without slops.

'Oh, they weren't Constance's footprints. Constance's feet were huge. They must have been Marian's. She must have stood at the window for some time to make such an impact on the polish.'

Sonia remembered seeing the lights of the Laws' going out as she'd sat in the Weary Ploughman with Stanley.

She vaguely wondered when Marian had been standing there and why. There wasn't much to see in the square. She hoped she hadn't seen her coming out of the pub and getting into Stanley's car.

'We were talking about polish and the foot-marks on your floor,' Janey said. Marian came to join them, glad to be stretching her legs and yet nervous of Janey. They had been sitting listening to Jeffrey, Grant and Mrs Henley for a good hour. Her hand went to her earrings and she raised her eyebrows enquiringly.

'Yes,' Sonia went on, stirring the gritty-looking liquid to try and turn it brown. 'Janey said your footmarks showed up on Constance's bedroom floor. We were just saying how easily it comes off . . .'

Marian, spluttering, could hardly breathe. 'I didn't realise the state of my house would prove of so much interest to Janey . . .' Cold! Sharp! Marian didn't sound like Marian any more. 'At times I wish you would mind your own business, Janey!'

Marian's huge face spread red, water colour on blotting paper. She wasn't used to talking like this. A look of pure malice shone from her pale blue eyes.

Janey quickly touched her shoulder. 'We were talking about the hall floor,' she said with an uneasy laugh. 'Don't worry . . . I wasn't criticising the cleanliness of your house or anything! Marian, don't look so upset. You know me better than that!'

Sonia's mouth dropped open as Marian deliberately turned her back on her friends and walked over to Nancy Blogg. She was left facing Janey, speechless.

'We upset her,' said Janey, pulling her lip like a child. 'She almost bit my head off. What did I say?'

Sonia shook her head, thinking hard. 'I don't know,' she said slowly. 'I think Marian's got too much on her plate at the moment. She's a bit touchy . . . what with Constance and everything . . .' But Sonia wasn't affected by Marian's cold shoulder. Already, Sonia had forgotten. To get through to Sonia one would have to be far more direct than that!

No. It was Janey, hurt, angry Janey who thought, always Marian . . . poor, hard done-by Marian. How did she do it? Marian wasn't the only one with too much on her plate . . . but other people managed not to be rude . . .

And they went to take their places for part two of the evening . . . the reading of the play. Janey, bristling with hostility, did not return to her chair, but sat at the back of the hall on her own.

Oh, guilt is a truly terrible thing, and makes us behave in wonderful ways.

CHAPTER NINE

I never told anyone this before, but I always yearned to kill my father.'

Awful words! Awful words! Why must Mrs Henley be so melodramatic?

'Louder, Sonia, please! I know Phoebe is supposed to be exchanging confidences, but we are in a church hall trying to compete with the coughings and shufflings of fifty-odd people.' Grant's voice was sharp, his baby edges all serrated as he looked reprovingly over the first two rows to where Sonia was sitting. What the hell was the matter with the woman? She sounded embarrassed! Of all of them, she never normally had to be told to speak up. Of all of them, she was a pro. 'Let's take it back, please, to Arthur's introduction . . .'

The tall young man who worked stacking boxes in Tesco and was playing the part of Arthur, turned back a page and started again. *'He's a wonderful man. You must be proud of him.'*

'I never told anyone this before, but I always yearned to kill my father,' Sonia repeated, loudly this time, hating the words which tasted lathery in her mouth. Her heart skipped as she heard Marian turn the pages beside her and she glanced down. Marian looked as uneasy as Sonia felt. Mar-

ian smelt of cooking fat. Her cheeks, despite the fact that it was evening, looked to be creased with sleep. The sheets of tightly-typed foolscap script were doing a dance of their own on Marian's knee. Her hands were shaking. She had one arm on one wrist, trying to stop them.

When she realised that Sonia's eyes were on her she brought up her doughy face and her lips twitched into a smiled excuse. 'Nerves,' she whispered. 'It's my turn in a minute. I always get like this.'

Sonia hadn't realised before.

So she had upset Janey. Well, there we are. Janey was too sensitive for her own good and who knows, maybe it was for the best. Marian found it impossible to relate to her properly anyway. Knowing what she knew.

For the first time in her life Marian hated being here. The world was conspiring against her. Did everyone know what she'd done, even Mrs Henley? It would seem so. If they didn't know, it appeared that they were going round with their noses to the ground looking for clues. This, after all, is what guilt does if you let it. Suddenly it was all implication and suggestion, as if no one was talking about anything else but the fact she'd killed Constance.

It had been hard to get away this evening. Marian had never imagined the absence of Constance could make such a difference to the atmosphere in the house, to the atmosphere in her head . . .

and Melanie, God oh God.

At one time, before Constance came, there used to be lots of laughter in her house. At tea time, when the children got home from school with their piles of homework, Roger would arrive and join in, laughing with that joyous yelp he had . . . sometimes Marian had even felt jealous of the relationship he had had with the children . . . silly, really.

At those times she had snapped and snarled, 'I do think somebody might give me a hand. Here am I, trying to feed four hulking adults all on my own and nowhere on the table for me to lay the dishes . . .' He had always come to her then, fooling about, arms round her waist, tickling, kissing, knowing how it was with her. Oh yes, they had understood each other.

How stupidly, sloppily affectionate they had been. Twenty-three years was a long time when you said it. Her life with Roger hadn't seemed that long. Every now and then, before the accident, she'd caught glimpses of how it was going to be when they were old together, fragile, fluttering glimpses delicate as dandelion seeds and butterflies.

They hadn't brought him home. There hadn't seemed any point. No, they had patched him up and put him in the Chapel of Rest and Marian had gone to visit him there, hoping against hope that they might have got the wrong man. They hadn't. It was Roger, a different sort of Roger, a waxen, white Roger, but Roger.

She had bent over to whisper. Perhaps he wasn't dead! Perhaps he was just asleep! He would wake up for her, he had to! She hadn't dared to touch him, touch his head, in case it came away in her hands although they said it was all right. But she hadn't touched him, just in case. She felt cheated by this, afterwards. He had smelt of lillies. In life he had smelt of sawdust and Gumption.

She would wake up at night and gingerly move her arm to feel across the space for Roger. Half in dreams, half awake, she would realise that he wasn't there and turn over with her back to where he ought to be in childish retaliation. Or she would hold her breath, trying to catch him out, listening hard for the sounds that he made in the night, her muddled, exhausted brain kidding her into thinking she could trap him back to life.

Months later, and whenever the door opened she thought it would be him and lifted her face towards it hopefully. It was all this hope that wore her out, not so much the grief.

She had taken happiness so much for granted. She could look back now, see herself as she was, and gasp with amazement . . . all that happiness she had taken as her right and had assumed would go on forever . . . Roger's arms round her at night, the children's health and sweetness, the security of the money Roger brought home from the store, sitting round the television in the evening or playing Monopoly in the circular pool of light cast by the standard lamp in the sitting room . . . she had just accepted it all so glibly . . . only now she knew how precious these moments had been, how precious and how fleeting. The magic circle of lamplight had been shattered. Everything had changed. Everything was cold and different now.

Now she hated the paraphernalia that had combined to lull her into that false sense of security and make her a fool . . . the two-seater sofa which they had bought, new, when they first married and where they had made awkward love before the fire during their first weeks together . . . the woodburner that Roger had put in during that chilly winter and he had let Lloyd think he was doing the work, father and son, flakes of plaster, and cobwebby cement in their hair . . . they had laughed . . . the family photos on the sideboard, smiling, laughing people with no idea what was going to happen to them . . . the house she had once loved had grown small around her, irritating, like a once-cosy blanket which had worn into a scratchy, hard crust of itself.

No, she couldn't stop herself, not for very long, from thinking of him.

Eight years ago, when old man Law died — Sam Law, founder of *Law's Hardware* — Constance had insisted on leaving the village and going to live in London with her sister. 'I'm not a village person,' she had said. 'Never have been. Never will be.'

Because she'd said this with disdain, suggesting

136

that to be a village person was to be something rather narrow and not very nice, Marian had wondered, then, if she was a village person. She supposed she was, born and brought up in Meadcombe by parents who had also been born and brought up here. She had never considered living anywhere else, and only knew that whenever she went away she was glad to get back. Marian felt at home in Meadcombe. She'd felt she fitted there.

She had tried to be nice to Constance when she had first arrived back in the village after the accident, tried to listen to her rambling on about her past and how things weren't as good as they used to be in her day. Children, she used to go on and on about children, clearly insinuating that Sally and Lloyd were included in her derogatory remarks about the youth of today . . .

'There's no discipline,' she used to say. 'Schools aren't the same. But I blame the parents. It's a different attitude of mind. Greed! Now, during the war it was quite different, people used to care then, help each other out . . . there wasn't such a thing as depression as it's known today, people didn't wander round being depressed all the time. Depression was something that everybody suffered, real hardship. Now look at your friend Janey, putting up with that long streak of nothing next door that calls himself a man. She looks worn out with it all the time and no wonder.'

On and on and on. And on the subject of work

she was unstoppable. 'Half of them just don't want to work,' she would start. 'If there were jobs they wouldn't take them. You can't tell me that there aren't jobs around for those that want them.'

Marian had tried . . . but it had been so different from the times when Constance stayed and Roger had been there and she could tell him afterwards or roll her eyes behind Constance's back or confide her impatience to him in the kitchen. Having Roger had allowed her to be kind, just because she was safe herself. Without him Marian was as she really was. Coping alone with Constance had been hard.

Then Constance used to like to talk about herself for hours on end. 'I'm not trying to show off,' she used to say, 'but I was a beautiful girl. The boys used to fight over me in the old days, they did! I could have had my pick of them all down Rammage Road . . . but there wasn't any hanky panky in those days. We knew what was right and wrong, not like today . . . with all these unmarried mothers and single parent families . . . got it too easy they have. Ordinary, married people can't get council houses any more you know. They go to the top of the queue, these people . . .'

And Marian knew she was being rigid and unkind by not joining in, not making allowances for Constance's age and generation . . . but somehow she couldn't, she just couldn't.

Lloyd and Sally could afford to be patient. They

138

weren't at home listening to it all day long, and they had their lives in front of them. Constance wasn't the threat to them that she was to Marian . . . the jump in age was maybe too great for them to feel an influence. Nor were they inhibited by her own generation's use of that kind of grotesque pretence of politeness. Most of the time they just ignored Constance, or humoured her, or joked and said, 'Oh Granny!' when she was outrageous. And they weren't bitter like Marian, all happiness gone, gone with its head knocked off on some grey, Godforsaken, unearthly bit of motorway between here and London. Sally and Lloyd had their futures. For them the lamplight beckoned.

Yes, many times Marian had wanted to murder Constance.

So gradually Constance had been left to talk more and more to herself, gabbling on quite happily even after Marian left the room. And as she stopped relating to anyone else in her speech, so she gradually stopped relating with her general behaviour, too, and once she'd started on the downhill path she seemed to move down it very, very fast. What with the shock of the accident and everything.

Normally on a Friday night it was hard to get to the hall on time. Marian had to give Constance her tea and clean up around her, making her comfortable and checking that the children were actually willing to stay in the room with her . . . not off upstairs or at the pub. She would have imagined that now, with the old woman dead, she would have just been able to walk out, easily, no responsibilities for the first time in years . . . just her . . .

But it hadn't been like that. Never had she found herself so disorganised. The place was in a mess. Constance's bedding half in, half out of the washing machine, trailing halfway across the kitchen floor. The kitchen stank of chips. Broken eggshells littered the draining board. The hoover, half-mended, blocked the hall and seemed to beg to have things hung upon its handle. Lloyd was on the phone organising something to do with Donna's car and Sally was thoughtlessly arranging flowers in the middle of all this mess.

No, it had been harder to get out this Friday night than any other she could remember. Funny . . . she was always so on top of things, normally.

'Just leave it, Mum, and go! I'll clear up. Go on!'

But Sally's clearing up was not her clearing up, and Marian didn't like to leave it. Silly really . . .

Yes, Marian really hated being here. And now it was her turn.

'Phoebe, Lord Grey's nubile young daughter, visits the witch's cottage in search of the truth.'

'Pessima, you're old. Try and sound old sweetheart, please, even if this is just the first reading.'

Grant could be wonderfully dominant when he had to be.

Obediently Marian put a wrinkle in her voice.

It would be interesting, playing an old woman, but she couldn't help feeling uncertain about Grant's casting. She'd never seen herself as old, or even approaching old age before. Grant obviously had . . . unconsciously Marian touched her cheek and let her hand run down it.

'*You shouldn't have come here, child,*' she read, not sure, at this stage, whether or not to attempt to broaden her accent. '*You won't find your father here. His wicked deed is done and he is in hiding. Take the money, take it and go. But remember . . . you are not blameless!*'

Beside her Sonia crossed her legs and her bangles jangled. Where was the wicked Henry Grey, and where was goddamn Stanley?

The cast for the play numbered twenty. Most of the people here tonight didn't want to be in it. They were artists, designers, dressmakers and teamakers. They were scenery shifters and people who wanted somewhere to go on a cold Friday night. Somehow Jeffrey would make sure everyone was involved and felt they were important to the production. He was good at doing that.

Mrs Henley, making full use of her artistic licence, had rolled the history of the Plague Stone into a ball, filled the stage with nursery rhyme type characters and given them space to kick it around the pitch together.

Nobles, peasants, witches, damsels, a Bishop, a Judge and all the King's men would make a colourful splash in the square on Christmas Eve. And the audience, no doubt stamping with cold and holding cups of cocoa, would watch the girl Phoebe move from youth to old age before she was finally burned as a witch. It was an ambitious endeavour. The play would take the watching villagers nicely up to midnight when they could go inside the church for the carol service and a warm up.

'*Weave that spell, sweetheart, weave that spell!*'

It was embarrassing for Marian to act such a drama sitting in a canvas chair two rows down, with Sonia fidgeting and thinking she could do better beside her. This would be the first play Marian had been in when Roger wouldn't be in the front row of the audience one hundred per cent on her side. When he'd applauded, it would have all been for her.

How he would have laughed! Marian would have gone back home and confessed she had been given the part of Pessima, the old witch. She would have acted hurt, a little upset, and he would have teased her. 'Well, I haven't liked to say but . . . yes, I thought if you weren't more careful it would start to show, and you have been looking a little peaky lately!'

She would have pretended to hit him, and told him how annoying Sonia had been, as usual. He would have rolled his eyes, tutted and sympathised. The children's attitude would be quite different. They would say consolatory things like, 'Just because you've been given that part it doesn't mean Grant thinks you actually *look* old . . . he thinks you are clever enough to *act* old, that's all. You shouldn't be upset about it, Mum. It's a compliment really.' They would somehow miss the point completely. She wouldn't say anything to them. She would miss Roger too much if she did.

An evil old woman, full of cunning and dubious wisdom, manipulating events round her bubbling pot of unspeakable things. Marian looked round the room and felt, again, that everybody knew. It was the perfect part for a murderess.

She looked at Mrs Henley whom she had known all her life. That middle-class lady, her spectacles on a chain lying on a flat, twin-setted chest, couldn't possibly know about Constance. Her eyes, bright as a bird's, flicked round the hall and she made important marks on her script with a gold biro. That, too, had a pleasing little chain on the end. Mrs Henley clearly liked chains.

Sonia nudged her, and Marian cast her spell for Grant.

'Brilliant!' enthused Grant. 'You were obviously born to it!'

And Marian blushed and felt all eyes on her as she turned the page again.

From her chair at the back of the hall Janey watched and listened and thought that Grant had chosen well.

CHAPTER TEN

I wonder if it's possible to put a marker at the point in time when suspicion turns to paranoia, anxiety to madness. Does the sickness creep about seeking entry indiscriminately, like a germ? Or is there a seed in some of us which, when watered with a certain kind of toxic misery, sprouts like a beanstalk up through the trellis of the system to the heart, to the brain?

Whatever, there were certainly many contributory factors which pushed poor Janey over the edge. But surely the majority of the rest of us . . . the sane . . . would not have ended up by acting as extremely as she did.

'From witches and wizards, and long-tailed buzzards, and creeping things that run along hedge bottoms, good Lord deliver us!'

Janey Tandy was cast as the narrator . . . a kind of village idiot who went round crouched, commenting, observing and moving things along.

It was an important part, but it only made her feel excluded from the action. 'It's just that you so put me in mind of Puck, sprite-like,' Mrs Henley explained. 'When I was writing the part I thought of you.' Janey persisted in sitting at the back and only half-listened to the general discussion that came at the end of the evening.

'It just seems a bit silly to have someone play the Plague Stone when the real thing is sitting there obligingly only yards away.'

'I wanted to give it life . . . I wanted to give it a voice. It is interesting to reflect on what sort of personality a thing like that might have.' Mrs Henley, although she asked for comments, never liked them when they came. She folded and laid aside her smile. She wore her spectacles, and the harsh hall lighting glinted off the glass and made her look extremely angry.

'But it isn't alive! That's the whole point,' said the boy from Tesco.

'I wouldn't mind dropping out,' hastened Jeffrey who'd been given the part of the Stone. 'I'll have to ring the bells on Christmas Eve because Gordon will be away, and I don't think I could cope with such a demanding part on such a busy evening.'

'It could be cut out,' the boy persevered. 'It doesn't actually influence anything.'

'It would be cutting out the heart of the thing,' said Mrs Henley, thinly.

From where Janey sat she could see, along the aisle, Sonia's dark head nearly touching Marian's blonde one as they peered to the front together. Although she had chosen to take the hump and go to sit alone at the back, Janey felt as if she had been banished there. Marian had nearly bitten her head off earlier on, completely out of character. People always felt they could bite her head off, chew her up and spit her out and get away with it. She felt as if she spent her whole life on the periphery. She could never really get in! And look, Sonia had been given the part of Phoebe. Typical. Some people seem to have beautiful lives . . . from start to finish . . . while others spend their whole time trying to be accepted.

She was grateful that Sonia and Marian were her friends . . . she was grateful to David for marrying her, and she found it hard to cope with all that gratitude. It made her bitter. It made her jealous. It made her suspicious. It came from her own low opinion of herself . . . and that had been dealt to her like a bad hand of cards.

Janey was a woman who harboured a secret within her heart. Her cheeks were hollowed with the knowledge of it, and her pale eyes burned with the intensity of it. Janey would never be fat, plump and contented. She had been given a chance, by marriage and motherhood, to purge out the charlatan that her mother was.

When she thought of her mother she went crazy with resentment and anger. For that cold and calculating woman had never held a child's head to her breast, had never made a home for any man, had never loved anyone in her life. Janey had set out from the start to be different. Even when very small she had tightened up her face, clenched her fists and whispered to herself, 'When

146

I'm grown up I will never do that!' And she hadn't.

She'd taken on the biggest burdens she could find so that she could prove herself a real woman, a giver, a lover, a carer . . . and she needed to be seen to be giving, loving and caring if she was to prove her point.

'You don't have to . . .' David used to say, when she complained about something.

'Someone has to . . . ,' she would enjoy saying as she wandered off to clean the toilet or complete some other menial task.

For months, before she knew him, Janey worshipped David from afar. She the sixth form student, he the newly-graduated teacher with the interesting, tortured eyes and the leathery patches.

The first thing she had done, when he married her, was give up her ambitions, her career, for his sake. She had given up the pursuit of excellence, having spied a more glittering goal. She couldn't wait to go and tell her mother what she'd done.

'What a waste!'

'I don't consider it a waste,' she had said indignantly, using the high-handed moral tone she always brought out for her mother. 'I consider it to be my privilege . . . to look after David and make a proper home for him.'

Her mother had turned and given her a condescending look. She lived alone now. A cold and scheming woman, long ago she had driven her husband out . . . and would have driven her children, too, if she could have done so within the law.

That same old condescending look — that look that said, oh no, not you again. Plain Jane . . . Jane Candice . . . we'll have to hope you catch a husband with your personality, for your looks aren't going to get you anywhere in life. And the green gin bottle lying on the floor. Her mother, in her night-before-clothes, sprawled on the sofa in the smoke-filled lounge, panting, out of control, awful, gasping the morning air as hideously as some old wet fish hauled up on the sand. And her father, pathetic, cooking breakfast for the children and attempting to make it home.

Janey, a Fifties child, had been brought up and bombarded by television images of Fifties families holding hands and walking together through pale pink hues towards rosy sunsets. There was no room on the screen in those days for anyone remotely like her mother, Isobelle. The Sixties might have been more forgiving, but by the time the Sixties arrived it was too late. Janey was a teenager and free, no, even encouraged to hate her mother . . . and hate her she did.

Janey buzzed around and dreamed of glory, turning herself into a homemaker. She learned to excel in the kitchen . . . but David had a tiny appetite. She filled her house with assorted knick-knacks, little bits and pieces she picked up cheaply at jumble sales and Women's Institute bazaars. She made jams and pickles and bought herself a stand-up pantry to store them in. It was doubtful that David noticed.

When the children came she gave them proper birthday parties and always made wonderful cakes shaped like houses or trains. She was the envy of other mothers who tried hard but could never outdo Janey when it came to a birthday cake. Every day there was washing out on Janey's line, and never did a pile of ironing accumulate to go crispy in Janey's ironing basket. And all this despite the burden of carrying David, who, at party times and washing times would go to bed and read, or take the television upstairs and watch it there.

And throughout it all she would go back to her mother at regular intervals and report. Her mother, always scathing, would give her that same look and not even offer her daughter one of her disgusting, herbal cups of tea.

Janey was glad to see her housebound. What a turnabout! When she was little her mother had never been home! Now she was housebound, not because of ill-health, but because she didn't have anywhere to go any more. They had closed the Bingo hall . . . and her mother couldn't work the new money machines which had replaced the bingo cards. And her old cronies were now all happily holed up with their families, cosy in old age, their gambling done. But not Isobelle. Isobelle was alone, abandoned, betrayed by her time, unloved by anyone except herself, mixing only with a few unpleasant people as bitter and strange as herself. And Janey was glad!

She hadn't been round recently. Not since Melanie started her difficult phase . . . Isobelle would only gloat and tell Janey it was her fault.

David's rumpled dressing gown, the tablets by the bed, the library of books dealing with depression . . . these were all Janey's challenges . . . the bottom line . . . and as long as Janey kept her balance on it, she was fulfilling her ambitions. As Melanie had grown older Janey felt resentful that the girl wasn't willing to help her more, didn't seem to recognise and accept the challenges as she did. She'd begun to worry, latterly, that Melanie might even have inherited her grandmother's cold, unloving nature. She thought she saw that same look of derision in her daughter's hard, black eyes.

'Sometimes I think I am paying you for all you do, not with the housekeeping money but with my life,' David once said to her.

Janey wanted to merge with David, but he wouldn't let her. Sometimes, even, he seemed to hate her like Melanie did.

David's misery presided over the house like a petty tyrant. When he was 'low' the children tiptoed and whispered. When the boys had their play fights Janey would rush from the kitchen to quiet them. When they were little and she'd wanted, on a rare occasion, to go out, Janey had paid a babysitter so that David could carry on marking homework, preparing lessons or being depressed. She had never asked David to do what she considered was her work.

But outside the house it was different. Janey wanted it all ways. Outside the house Janey made sure that everybody knew what battles she fought and what a gem she was. She never saw that it was she who had set the scene, that it was she who had created the monster. But she did absorb the blame for Melanie's behaviour. That, after all, was one of the penalties of being a proper mother.

But when they took David off to hospital Janey was devastated, feeling that she had failed him and been unable, like a bad mother, to kiss him and make him better. She also suspected that these hospital visits were deliberate attempts by David to get away from her. Times like those left her without a purpose, ignoring her children as her mother had before her, wandering like a lost spirit looking for a place to rest.

Times like these she went to Marian's house, and sat sipping wine, coffee and sympathy, as surely her drug as David's was Largactil. Times like these she resented Sonia's company, sighing deeply when she recognised her rival's car parked in the square. She wanted the attention, all of the attention, and she lived in agony in case Marian and Sonia grew to be close so she couldn't get in any more.

It seemed to be getting a bit like that now!

Oh, Melanie, Melanie, where are you? And how could you do this to me?

Someone had forgotten to put fifty pence in the slot and the lights went out. Conversation stopped, sucked itself in like a wave and came to shore on a crest of exclamations. Mrs Blogg, who was a smoker, led a wavering line to the meter with her petrol lighter. The fumes from the tiny gadget filled the hall as, with the light gone, the sense of smell quickly took over.

The lights came on and Janey felt she had woken from a Rip van Winkle sleep to find everyone sitting round her in this hall almost totally unrecognisable. She'd been daydreaming to the point of hallucination. Grant was saying, 'So everyone must take a script home and read the whole thing through before next week. Get to know your character, get to see where you fit into the whole and develop some ideas about how you're going to play your part. It might be useful for those who closely interrelate in the play to get together and practise some of their lines. Sonia and Marian, for instance . . . you two have a lot to do with each other.'

Janey was left with the cold, certain knowledge that all this was about nothing. All of it, she thought to herself, was trivial. Here she was, sitting at the back, lonely, unhappy, a mad husband at home and a daughter missing, and all these people were talking about the Christmas play as if it mattered . . . as if it had ever mattered. She found the situation shadowy and menacing . . . their casual voices full of ill-omen, coming at her from dark places. She sensed a kind of ungodly hallowedness in the ordinariness of the village hall.

'Effie is going to talk to the WVS about the urn for the cocoa. Doris is going to bargain at the hospice shop for materials. John thinks he can borrow the lighting from the college again and he's going to check up on that. And we're going to leave it to Jeffrey to work out who we should collect for this year. Now, can anyone think of anything else?'

'Isn't bargaining at the hospice shop a little obscene?'

'What if it's pouring with rain?'

'If it's pouring with rain we'll have to do it in the hall. But we'll only do that as a really last resort because we can't get enough people in here. Come wind, come shower, come frost, we are going to try and do it in the square . . . .'

'Publicity. We want the local rags to come.'

'Yes, that's not a problem. Mike is going to deal with that side.'

'A title. The play isn't called anything.'

'Ah, yes.' Grant stepped back and gave one of his charming little bows to Mrs Henley, dislodging a fashionably rustic forelock as he did so. 'That was something you wanted to bring up, wasn't it?' Everyone knew Grant's boyfriend would be waiting in the pub and that he was now eager to get away.

Mrs Henley took the chair, using two hands to hook on her glasses. 'I thought it might be interesting if we chose our own title as we got to know the play,' she said. '*The Plague Stone* seemed somehow too obvious. So it's up to all of you to think about it and then, a few weeks before the performance, we'll put our ideas in a hat and pull one out.' She gave a knowing little smile and added confidentially, 'It's a publicity stunt. It'll give the play a tiny bit of extra edge for the newspapers . . . I thought it was rather an eccentric little idea.'

Janey's hands were wet and she wiped them, as though trying to dispose of the evening. She caught a sudden glimpse of Sonia's made-up face. It was made-up to the point of stiffness, and from where Janey sat it appeared to be dominated by the Roman nose and the sharp, pointed chin. The unnatural profusion of dark brown hair round the face that should have been aging gracefully made it seem that she wore a wig. When had Sonia started to look so like a ferret? How strange that Janey hadn't noticed before.

And Marian, her friend and confidante. Why hadn't she come to sit beside her, realising her needs? Why had she abandoned her and chosen to sit with Sonia? Marian, with her book on witchcraft and the timely death of her mother-in-law. Janey thought of the footprints upstairs and considered them sinister. What had Marian been doing, standing peering out at the square like that in the middle of the night? It must have been in the middle of the night or else she would have been wearing shoes.

Perhaps she knew something . . . perhaps they both knew something. Were they sheltering Melanie? Did they know where she was? Where had

Sonia gone between the time she left the pub and the time she got home? Janey had telephoned in her hour of need and found her out. What had she been doing? Talking to Stanley . . . for all that time? Where? Perhaps she had seen Melanie.

Janey's imagination stirred from its normally safe, dusty place and went into overdrive so that even Jeffrey the vicar with his familiar pale, bland face seemed to take on the ominous profile of a narrow-eyed Mandarin. His voice rang in the hall with a kind of vinegary malice. And Nancy Blogg, who had come to ask her about Melanie with a horrible curiosity stretching her scraggy old neck. And Mrs Henley with her superstitious play and talk of Plague Stones coming to life. And if Grant Fitch, like Mrs Henley, saw her as Puck then she saw him as a devilish imp, weaving and spinning the threads of life and contorting them into an evil parody of make-believe.

Unsettled, Janey Tandy left before the meeting was officially disbanded. She crept out of the hall, head down, without anybody seeing her and made her way, disconsolately, home. Although her house was only a short walk away she found herself becoming frightened by ordinary sounds . . . two pieces of corrugated iron grating together in the breeze . . . the creaking of a tree . . . the sudden hooting of an owl making for its home in the belfry. Once she thought she heard footsteps following her. Everything was suddenly disqui-

155

eting . . . not as it was . . . unnatural. She walked in fear as she had never done before. She didn't want to walk past the Plague Stone and yet scorned her own nervousness, knowing she was behaving oddly but not knowing why.

'How was it?' David asked, courteously, as she walked in the door, her heart hammering as if she had just completed a marathon. Hot and breathless, she didn't know what to say. Her face was flushed, her voice was loud and her eyes were abnormally dilated as she replied, 'Awful! It was just awful!'

Surprised, David turned to look at his wife. She looked more harassed than usual. She always hid her feelings from him, she was hiding them now.

'Well? And what part are you playing in Meadcombe's grand tribute to the finale of the year?' He was always scornful of her activities with the drama group, almost as if he was jealous that he, because of his temperament, because of his sickness, could not join in himself. She didn't want to tell him what part she had been given . . . she didn't want to admit that she had been cast as narrator, neither here nor there, nobody in particular. And how could she confide to him her silly, manic thoughts? She couldn't. She shouldn't. She should disinfect herself of her dark ruminations and scrub herself into thinking clean again. Why was she allowing her normally dormant imagination to plot like this against herself?

She pulled herself together and gave him a potted version of all that had happened. He pretended to listen. She knew he wasn't really.

He, too, was different tonight. He, too, was conspiring in some way. Perhaps they all thought she was a bad mother and had taken Melanie's part against her.

After David had gone to bed she went to make herself a hot drink. Someone had left the jug on the sideboard and, picking it up, she sniffed it and discovered the milk had curdled.

CHAPTER ELEVEN

Misconceptions, misunderstandings. The most innocent of participants begin to play their parts. Together with the guilty, they must also take the blame for the final construction of the ghastly whole.

The days dribbled into October, too wet and sludgy to be passed through an hour glass. Still no Melanie. Janey, in a fit of pique, threw away her toothbrush and afterwards saw her action as a dreadful omen.

It must be winter because Janey wore her knee-length boots. It must be winter because the sounds of the distant goods trains grew louder on the air as if they no longer had to contend with the muffling effects of the leaves on the trees. It was wet and windy and the children of Meadcombe infant and junior school could not go into the playground because of the puddles, so spent many of their breaks in the classroom instead, much to the indignation of Mrs Spender the cleaner.

'Double the work,' she complained. 'There they are, unsupervised, allowed to get the art things out, making messes with paint and plasticine all over the place. And plasticine's a terror . . .

you can't get it off . . . nasty, grubby, grey stuff . . .'

And nobody argued when Mrs Spender had her sleeves rolled up because people were frightened of her and her caustic tongue, and nobody could clean like she could. To Mrs Spender cleaning was an art. She could whip through, doing the work of two lesser women in half the time. The subject of re-tarmacking came up again on the PTA agenda. They couldn't afford to lose Mrs Spender.

The nights drew in further. The children walked home in a cold halflight, twirling gloves on elastic.

Janey, haunted now, spent much of her time walking, looking for clues. She rarely went to Marian's house and Marian didn't invite her. Oh, they didn't ignore each other . . . they chatted when they met, chatted as if things were the same as always. But they weren't.

Marian had sobbed at Constance's funeral. Her children, standing so close to her they could have been on guard, escorted her home for cakes and tea and kept her friends from her. Which is what she wanted.

When Stanley finally surfaced from God knows where, and came innocently to the Manor one day with Beryl, Sonia told him about the missing girl. He said little, but Beryl, an insatiable reader of all things dismal in newspapers and a traffic accident freak, said, 'Dead . . . must be after all this time . . .' and Stanley didn't contradict her.

Murder. It was such a grotesque word, tolling like a black bell in Hell, music of primeval fears and dark connotations . . . murder. Sonia had looked long and hard at Stanley, fearing to ask the question, 'Have you seen her?' Instead she had said, 'Have another digestive, Stanley, and does Beryl want one?' Something about his shrivelled little wife made people want to talk as if she wasn't there . . . does she take sugar . . . but she wasn't a cripple, not in any accepted sense. Perhaps it was the way he overshadowed her.

Sonia was taking Oscar for a walk when she saw the glove on the floor of his Mercedes. A black, fingerless glove still scrunched up in the shape of a hand . . . or a hoof, more like, as it had no fingers. A glove belonging to Melanie Tandy. What had made her look in the car, because as soon as she'd done it she wished she hadn't. Who did she think she was anyway . . . some sort of goddamn Sherlock Holmes?

She looked obsessively round, certain someone must be watching. But no, no houses overlooked the private driveway of the Manor, and the gardener had wandered off to burn leaves in the back garden. Whispering warnings to an impatient Oscar, she had opened the heavy passenger door and, almost afraid of looking a second time, had groped on the thick carpet floor for the offending article. Shoving it immediately in her deep duffle coat pocket she had continued her walk, prickling with fear and silk-soft inside like the conkers she kicked in casual pretence with her booted foot.

She was now officially an accessory after the fact. She was in collusion with Stanley. She was as guilty as he . . . more so, because she had done her deed in cold blood.

She couldn't keep this most damning piece of evidence on her person, and because she was Janey's friend, she couldn't keep it concealed, either. Somehow it must be found . . . just so long as it wasn't found in the Manor grounds or in Stanley's car. If she put it somewhere she would be doing the police a favour, she would be helping in the finding of Melanie, not hindering.

So she walked along the country road towards the village with the glove burning in her pocket as surely as a charcoal-filled handwarmer.

It was a Sunday and, apart from a few leaping children, the place was deserted. She could nearly smell the Sunday dinners roasting in the ovens round the square. A line of cars outside the pub proclaimed the Weary Ploughman contentedly busy. She hoped Marian wouldn't see her, because Marian would expect her to call in for a quick sherry, as she normally did. She hoped Janey wouldn't see her. She wouldn't be able to face Janey.

'There!' Surreptitiously she let the glove fall from her hand as she passed the village shop. She didn't look down. She didn't look back. It was a blustery, petulant day and the wind would probably take it and place it properly. Leaves would cover it so that it looked natural. Melanie could have dropped her glove here at any time. She always wore the blasted things. There would be nothing to say the finding of a glove had any sinister connection. Sonia gave Oscar a tug and the cairn terrier looked peeved and tried to cock its leg against the Plague Stone.

'No, Oscar, don't do that, come away.'

The wind took up a bunch of leaves and whipped them into a sudden golden frenzy, blowing up her coat and stinging her legs from behind like a smack.

To Marian, sitting safe by her fireside, the sound of the wind and rain beating on her windows was pleasant. Her children were across the road in the pub as usual. She would put the chicken in at five o'clock. They would eat this evening.

The thought that she should visit the graves today nudged and irritated its way on to the pages of the book she was reading. Once it was there it was like needing to go to the toilet when you were warm and comfortable in bed at night — there was no way she could ignore it. Eventually it would triumph over her and try as she might she could not hold out against it. So, with a sigh, she put down her book and went to look out of the window. It would only take fifteen minutes to tidy round, put the freesias in the vases, step back, contemplate, and hurry back to the fireside.

Visiting the grave was something she did for others, not for herself. She felt further away from Roger when she stood by his grave than she felt anywhere else. It was the one place on earth where there was no sense of him at all. And Constance, buried there beside her son? If there was any truth at all in the religion they preached, the religion she had never been able to believe in, Constance would have told Roger the secret by now . . . would have rattled it across the ground beneath the earth from one grave to another. What would Roger say? What would Roger think of her? Marian shrugged. It was a good thing it wasn't true, wasn't it?

The freesia stalks were wet and smelly. She wrapped them in a brown paper bag, she wrapped her head in a scarf, and holding both herself and her flowers well down against the rain she battled across the blustery square towards the church-yard. It must be winter because Marian Law was wearing her sheepskin boots.

She saw the glove at the same time as a particularly harsh gust caught at her throat and nearly took her breath away . . . so she never knew whether it was the shock of her find or the wind that had affected her so. There it was, black, sloppy with water, accusing . . . in the very place where Marian had seen Melanie talking to the man in the car on the night that Constance died. Deliberately, Marian bent to pick it up and stood staring at it for all the world to see in front of the village shop.

There was no doubt about it . . . this was one of Melanie's gloves, dropped, no doubt, on that night. Horrible! Horrible! All her instincts made her want to throw it down. But she couldn't, not now she'd found it.

She would take it and put it somewhere more secluded. She couldn't leave it here like this. If the police found it here they might look for tyre marks, and how was Marian to know for how many weeks tyre marks could be detected, heavy tyre marks that had bitten deep and no doubt patterned the earth. If they found tyre marks they might be able to establish times and dates, and Marian didn't want that . . . these things passed through her mind as she made her way, bent-headed, into the churchyard.

God forgive me, the unbeliever let the prayer slip through and through her mind. On her way to the most recent graves Marian had to pass by her mother, her father, her grandfather, her grandmother, her great grandmother, her great grandfather, and any amount of uncles, aunts, great and great great great. Great was her guilt, great was her shame, but greater still was her fear of being discovered.

Meadcombe churchyard was not the sort of place that people only went to in order to throw confetti or get buried. Criss-crossed with pathways and hung with tiny bowers, it was a major route for pedestrians from the front of the village

164

to the back. In summertime children played there, made dens among the graves and indulged in glorious games of hide and seek. There were greens in Meadcombe churchyard that were never so green anywhere else, and lizards and all forms of creeping things basked and laid themselves open to being caught on gravestone sunbeds. Even snakes were to be seen, stalked and sadly, sometimes skinned by freckled-faced little boys experimenting with knives and sharpened sticks in Meadcombe churchyard.

Monday, and Lottie Marsden and Susan Bush passed through the churchyard on their way home from school as they always did. Neat in their zipped-up anoraks, hoods pulled well up by the teacher, they half-skipped, half-walked over the wet leaves, singing little snatches of song with some difficulty as they sucked and rolled their tender mouths round green boiled sweets.

From a pocket which held her dinner money purse and a crumpled note home that dealt with half-term arrangements, Lottie pulled out the plasticine doll. Susan stopped to look at it.

'You're not supposed to bring plasticine home. That's stealing.' Susan's eyes widened.

'No, it's not stealing. I haven't stolen anything.'

'They tell you you mustn't bring any artwork home unless Mrs Gandy says so.'

'It's not artwork. I made it in break.'

'Doesn't matter. You're still not allowed to bring it home.'

'No one will know.' Lottie was a clever child,

cleverer than her friend Susan, and more devious, too. Lottie had already learnt she could win running races by just getting on with it and not looking round. She could pass maths tests by looking back to see what they had done yesterday. She could get a second dinner by going to the toilet afterwards and not before the lunch-break. She knew now, that she should not have brought the doll out to show Susan. She knew as sure as eggs were eggs that Susan would tell Mrs Gandy in the morning.

'Well, if I throw it away no one will ever know, will they, Susan?'

'They will know if I tell them.'

'But if you tell them and I say I didn't they will think you are telling lies.'

Susan considered this for a long moment, rolling her sweet rather painfully from one side of her mouth to the other so that it clunked loudly over her teeth. She drooled over the sudden shock to her watering taste buds but recognised the truth when she heard it.

'But I wouldn't be telling lies,' she managed to say, keeping the sweet in her mouth.

Lottie took hers out to look at it and see if it had changed colour. It hadn't so she popped it in again after giving it a loving lick with a greenish tongue. 'No, you wouldn't be telling lies, but everyone would *think* that you were.'

'Mm. Well, you'll have to throw the doll away, won't you?' Lottie hadn't got away with it entirely.

'Let's look for somewhere nice to put her.' Friends once more, they searched around for a good, comfortable place for the truncated, grossly-shaped wedge of plasticine.

It had no legs but two discernible arms, and holes gouged out of its face for eyes and a sharp pinch for a nose. For hair, Lottie had used black embroidery threads which she had pressed into place with a crochet hook. The hair was quite cleverly done. If she had made it in art she might have been given a star for it.

'Somewhere where she won't get wet,' said Susan, looking up through dripping branches.

'Somewhere where she won't get kicked or walked on.'

'Oh, look! We can wrap her up in this.' Susan held out the soaking wet, fingerless glove she had found. 'It has a hole in the middle. It can be a sleeping bag.'

'She's camping out,' said Lottie, veering dangerously near the edge of a game, for they were under strict instructions not to stop and play on their way home.

Lottie tucked the effigy into its woollen sleeping bag, wrapping it tightly so that only its head showed. 'She's nice and warm,' she said, her tongue, finished with the sweet, flicking over her top lip in concentration, a habit that would cause nasty chapping before winter was over.

They made the doll a bed of pine needles, put her in it and covered her up with more. Now the boys wouldn't find her . . . an unspoken fear but one well understood by both girls.

'We'll check up on her every day to make sure she's all right,' said Lottie.

'We could even bring her food . . . sweets.'

Lottie thought this was silly so she didn't reply. She knew that by Friday they would have forgotten the existence of her little creation. She knew, too, that Susan was now too involved herself to tell. Yes, Lottie was a clever girl. As Mrs Gandy was to write on her report at the end of term, *'Lottie shows much promise . . . she will go far if she applies herself properly.'*

When coming to Billy Binns' report, Mrs Gandy would be more cautious. Sitting next to the old iron radiator in the deserted schoolroom, tapping her teeth with her pen, she would project him up into mind like a slide, that pupil whose brightness of eye belied the dullness of his senses. She would frown to herself as she saw his missing front teeth and his torn pockets . . . his untidy work and his one squinting eye, seeing him as clearly as if he stood before her.

In the end she would put, only half-satisfied afterwards, *'I know you and your family have been having problems lately, but I do feel that a meeting would be in order. We need to discuss Billy's present difficulties, and come to a decision over the best way to deal with him at home as well as at school.'*

Tired, weary, before she put the light out she signed it, *Sheila F. Gandy* and stuck it up carefully so Billy wouldn't be tempted to open it on his way home.

And it was Billy Binns now who, trailing home alone, caught sight of some unaccustomed autumn activity in the churchyard, and watched, his chin resting on the shoulder of a gravestone angel as Susan and Lottie put their baby to sleep.

After they had gone he crept up to the place to discover what they had been doing. He found the doll in its little bed of pine needles. He found it and he picked it up, turning his head awkwardly this way and that like King Kong trying to understand what his helpless plasticine victim was all about. His childish heart and hands were already too cruelly bruised to handle such delicate matters . . .

It didn't take Billy Binns long to decide what to do. He opened his coat, took out a toffee apple stick, and stuck it through the doll. He put it back, pinioned it to the earth, and covered it over once more with pine needles. He walked home with his hands in his pockets, whistling gleefully.

CHAPTER TWELVE

Perhaps, after all, she was her mother's daughter, because Janey Tandy had been doing quite insensitively well until next door's cat brought Lottie Marsden's effigy in through the window.

It was quite astonishing that, in such a time of trouble, the agony auntish Marian could turn her back on her neighbour like this. But turn it she did, and only she knew why.

These days Sonia's car was always in the square. The two women remained closeted together in *Dunoon* for hours on end — going over their parts, they said.

Janey spent much of her time squatting on Melanie's bedroom floor getting acquainted with the daughter she seemed to have lost long before she left home. She'd never wanted to know her before, now the knowing became a powerful need, an unquenchable thirst. Nothing must be overlooked, no ornament, no precious keepsake was too small to turn over, grasp, feel and study.

Janey had never realised Melanie meant so much to her. Had she been, in some indefinable way, dependent on her fractious teenage daughter? It would seem so, for with her disappearance whole areas of Janey's emotions had gone with her. Janey was left feeling strangely empty, and suspicious, and afraid, but as yet she wasn't sure of what.

Her search for discovery required her to ignore David. The weight of all her unhappy years . . . for yes, she saw now that she had been unhappy . . . pressed her limp like a flower between heavy books, made her sluggish and slow, and frankly she couldn't cope with David's ramblings and meanderings.

There was no doubt that Janey was hurt by Marian's behaviour, but Janey was changing, subtly and surely as each day passed. She was certainly not devastated by Marian's rejection as she once would have been. Her feelings seemed to be ebbing away as she sat there hour after hour on Melanie's floor, listening to her tapes, reading her books. Famous Fives and Judy Blumes and the last one, the one that had been left with a page bent back on her bedside table . . . *The Crucible.* Slowly, stealthily, she felt her heart was being anaesthetised. She wept.

Oh, why don't you write to us, Melanie, and let us know you're all right?

Maybe it was because of Janey's attitude, maybe he was due for one anyway whatever, David took one of his turns for the worse.

'Daddy is getting hard to wake in the mornings. I went in to him twice while I was cleaning my teeth and he *still* stayed in bed hiding his head under the covers.'

'But he's up now, Justin, is he?'

The boy nodded and sniffed. Janey reached for a tissue. She stopped herself from wiping his nose. He was ten years old, for Christsake. 'Hurry up, eat your Krispies. You're going to be late.'

Were the children as fed up with their un-swervingly boring mornings as she was? Some-times she felt she could stay in bed herself and put a tape recording on downstairs. Everything was mechanical. There was no gratification for her, any longer, in the simple knowledge that the Rayburn made the kitchen nice and warm for them in the mornings. Justin and Daniel no longer seemed to exist for her. They'd started having to ask where their clean shirts were.

This morning, over the sink, she had floundered back fourteen years to Melanie's birth, and the lemony washing up water mingled with a turgid smell of blood and milk that she couldn't re-member sensing at the time. She'd hardly both-ered with the child in the cot. All she could think of, back then, was getting home to look after David. And so it had gone on . . . missing, missing, missing, she had missed it all.

Now she tried with all her might to conjure back that baby. She closed her eyes tightly and tried to remember the colour of Melanie's new-born eyes. She couldn't, and this failure grew so big inside her it threatened to burst with the catastrophe of pure pain. All she could really re-member was the frustration of trying to keep a sanitary towel in place without the benefit of a belt or clips. All she could see were purple eyelids threaded with a crisscross network of veins. The baby had its eyes closed. *Open them, Melanie, and let me see what colour your eyes were when you were born!*

'Just coffee, please, Janey.'

So he had come down at last. David looked as drained as she felt.

'I didn't sleep,' he said lamely.

And yet he was not so anxious that he could do without sex. He had demanded his rights even on the night that Melanie disappeared. She had responded coldly, relieved when he finished and pushed the shrivelled flesh back into his pyjamas, out of sight.

Normally, when he came down in this state, she humoured him. Now she said, 'Nor did I. I haven't slept for weeks. And I've been dreaming terrible dreams.'

This response, this confession of weakness, and at breakfast time too, was so extraordinary that it caused all movement to cease for a moment round the Tandys' kitchen table. Six eyes stared at Janey's back. She felt miserably aware of them, and she knew an explanation for her outburst was in order. But she couldn't give one, not this morning.

When she handed David his coffee, fresh and black, she noticed his hands were trembling. But try as she might she could not make his manifestations of misery anything to do with her.

She didn't want to sit at the table with them. She tested the washing which hung airing before the Rayburn, holding it to her cheeks and finding the fresh, warm smell of it comfortably reassuring. Everything that happened, these days, she seemed to be seeing for the first time. Was she about to see David at his worst for the first time, too? Apprehension hit her square between the shoulder blades and she turned away from him to fold the clothes.

'I think I'll call in at the surgery on my way home to see if he'll give me some more of those tablets.'

'You've got a boxful by your bed . . . and the bathroom cabinet is overflowing with them.' She'd always considered it odd that David's doctors prescribed for him so freely. Sometimes he was suicidal in his depression.

'You shouldn't take old tablets. They can be dangerous when they're out of date.' And this from him, who was so disparaging about his life!

'Well, they should put a sell-by date on the boxes. And if that's the case, why do you keep them? Why don't you let me flush them down the toilet? I've always said how dangerous they are to have floating around the house.'

She wouldn't have dreamed of flushing them down the toilet. David collected drugs like some men collected stamps or Nazi memorabilia — but with a kind of dreary defiance. There were varicose veins on the backs of his legs. They stood out like bunches of wormy fish bait. And his back was covered with bright red spots. It always had been, ever since she'd known him. Why did

174

she think of that now? He was all covered up, dressed for school, his clothing hairy and thick . . . a tall, sensible dark man perpetually on the edge of the nervous breakdown he threatened but never actually had. And all the time, as far as Melanie was concerned, he was pretending that nothing had happened. He refused, point blank, to talk about Melanie. Why? Why?

There were things Janey had to do, had to keep doing regularly to reassure herself. Making the beds and opening the bedroom windows was one. Turning the calendar daily was another. If she turned the calendar she was still in control. Thirty-first of October . . . November tomorrow. Justin, happy little fluting Justin would come downstairs backwards tomorrow morning with his 'Pinch, punch, first of the month!' Melanie would have been gone for forty-two days.

It was as if Melanie had sunk in a pond and the family were closing over the vortex she had left in one, smooth wave. The boys asked about her occasionally, they listened avidly if Janey brought the subject of Melanie up. But otherwise . . . nothing had changed. They had one empty bedroom, one spare place at the table. That was all.

But for Janey it was the not knowing.

Time and time again she re-lived her coming through the door. Her own attitude varied, swung like a pendulum from one extreme to the other. One minute she would tearfully fling her arms around her . . . rush to the pub for champagne, welcome her home like the prodigal child. The next she would turn her back and walk away, closed and hurt. Most of the time she imagined herself reacting somewhere in between. She could not get over the fact that she had hit her, had slapped her daughter's face before she went. Secretly she believed it was that which had made her leave. She had never hit any of her children before . . . she supposed she had never really been that interested . . .

'You're well enough to go to work?' She asked it flippantly, but she didn't want David mooching round the house today.

'I'll have to go to work,' he said. 'Someone has got to bring some money in.'

Ah yes. Money. It was a subject he always brought up when he was on his way down. He would work at it like a scab, painfully pulling off the surface and getting to the suppurating core of the thing, scratching and irritating until he inflamed it and caused it to spread. Times she had come downstairs in the night and found him, with a sweater over his winceyette pyjamas, slumped over the latest bank statement with his head in his hands. Times they had sat up all night together, discussing cuts and economies. And out of his terror he had conjured up for her images of soulless hotels in cities of mills, drab streets, sordid, one-roomed flats with washing draped from end to end, communal kitchens and railway sidings. 'We could end up like that,' he would repeat, over and over again. 'Surrounded by asphalt, unless we do something quickly we could . . . we could . . .' In the end it always boiled down to the fact that she was a kept woman . . . a drain on the family resources.

It was coming, it was coming, she could scent it like a wary fox scents a pack of hounds.

After they had gone and she was left in peace and quiet, Janey sat sipping her coffee, holding herself back from the moment she would make a bolt for Melanie's room, draw the curtains, settle on the rug and start rummaging once more. It was becoming like a drug to her . . . this immersing herself in her daughter's illusiveness. It was a puzzle she must work out for herself or die . . . or go mad . . .

In Melanie's writings, in her school essays, her diary entries and unposted letters to her friends Janey read very little good about herself. But after the initial shock she accepted this, understanding, seeing herself through Melanie's eyes.

The rude drawings took longer to comprehend. Janey had the strongest urge to crumple them up and destroy them. They were vulgar and explicit. There was nothing beautiful or gentle about them. Surely this was not what her daughter had come to believe that sex was about?

She was going through a box of papers that had been hidden, shoved far under Melanie's bed, when she came across the pen and ink sketches. Heavy metal music throbbed tunelessly in the background and Janey's coffee, by now, was cold with a skin on top. With a start Janey realised that her daughter had been quite an artist, because the cartoons she was holding up before her were of local people, all of them easily recognisable. They were as she herself had seen them on the night of the first rehearsal . . . on the night she had left in a hurry . . . on the night she had felt so dreadfully frightened.

Here was Mrs Brierly who ran the shop, naked as a jaybird, cavorting in the churchyard with Jeffrey the vicar. Their private parts were grossly exaggerated, nothing had been left to imagination, but it was Jeffrey's eyes that made Janey gasp, not his michelin bumps and bulges . . . for they were narrow, slitted, sinister, the eyes of a macabre mutant.

Even to look at the pictures made Janey feel dirty like a voyeur. There was something intensely private about them, about what these people were doing. She felt a little as if she was undergoing some awful initiation . . . just by looking. She forgot they were by Melanie . . . some spiteful game to while away the time. They loomed large, larger than life and more than merely make-believe.

And here was a crone, smooth-faced, angular-bodied, brittle, pared down to little more than a skeleton with a wart on the end of its nose and a hump on its back. It was so like Mrs Henley it could have been a photograph . . . on the other hand, curiously, it bore no resemblance whatsoever. But Melanie hadn't written the names on the bottom, and recognition of this terrible haglike creature was instantaneous. She mated, in a way that had always embarrassed Janey, with a goat . . . no . . . it was no goat . . . it was Paul . . . or someone very like him. He looked much older. A silver-haired Paul with big ears, horns and a beard. And the look of bliss on his face was a look that Janey had often seen him wear when settled in the pub with a beer in front of him and his feet up on the bars of the phoney gas fire.

Oh, Melanie!

Marian looked more like a gnarled old tree than a woman, except for the face. The face was large and moonlike, it beamed with a menacing evil down upon the bony skeleton of her son Lloyd. She was doing unspeakable things . . . oh, God, no, unspeakable things!

David was cloaked in a dressing gown, holding it like an actor, swishing it on his arm as he stepped from grave to grave on long, pointed feet. His penis was long and thin and stretched to his knees where it came to a point like a carrot end. In fact the whole of him was pointed. He was a spear, a spear of destruction, and the tears that coarsed down his haggard face were spear-like, too. Janey staunched a terrible urge to laugh. Melanie had caught him just right!

There were more. They tumbled from the box when Janey let them, but she couldn't find a picture of herself. She didn't know whether to be relieved or sorry. She hadn't wanted to see herself, but why had Melanie left her out? Was it too terrible, even for Melanie, to envisage her mother in this way? Why else had she been excluded from this Black Sabbath dance? This devilish ritual in Meadcombe churchyard. And where, she worried, was Sonia?

The curtains moved and Janey jumped. It was cold in here. Time to go round closing the windows now that the smell of sleep had left the landing. Time to get dressed and go for her walk. She needed her walks like she needed her mornings with Melanie . . . or Melanie's ghost, whatever. She liked to get out of Meadcombe, to look down on it from the hills and get it in perspective.

Next door's cat had jumped on the wall again, and from the wall had leapt into the pool of temporary sunshine on Melanie's windowsill. Janey saw its tail move the curtains. A long, languishing tail striped in greys and blacks. She must close the window before it got in and went to sleep, as it sometimes did, curled up on Melanie's bed.

Janey stood up and went to the window just as the cat leapt from the sill.

'Out! Out! Go on! Shoo!'

From the corner of her eye she saw Sonia's car. So they were together again. The cat, surprised to find someone in the room, turned tail and fled, leaving its offering on the mound where the pillow raised the bedline underneath the counterpane.

'Oh Lord, not another mole.'

Janey bent to pick it up, looking for the tail.

She could only lift them by the tails. She couldn't bear to feel dead fur, or get blood on her fingers. It wasn't a mole. It was Melanie's glove. With a figurine inside, a plasticine figurine with Melanie's hairstyle. And a spike had been driven through her daughter's heart.

Sick! Sick! Sick! Her throat swelled and she feared she would choke. She lay back, faint, dizziness moving up from her feet and drying them like blotting paper. She shook . . . she shook . . . so her top teeth banged hard down on her lower jaw, jangling, bony in her head. Jesus help me! Jesus Christ help me! Jesus! Jesus! She rocked herself, bringing her knees half up to her chest.

Who was in this? Who was involved? The vicar? The police? Every single 'native' of the village . . . for there were no 'outsiders' like herself in Melanie's pictures. Just those who laid claim to the place in manner and attitude . . . the close-knit society of people who had known each other's families down through the generations. Jesus, help me Jesus. David?

She picked up the figurine and carefully put it in the box with Melanie's pictures. The police were coming this afternoon. They wanted to make more enquiries. What if they asked to see her bedroom, wanted to search it? What if they found these pictures? Guiltily, unable to throw them away, Janey stuffed the awful drawings back in the box and, clutching it to her chest, moved it to the safety of her own room. My God, they mustn't find these. Had Melanie inherited David's

181

instability as well as his dark looks? She must have done . . . to even imagine things like this, let alone put them down, for posterity, on paper!

Can't think about the glove . . . can't think about the figurine . . . mustn't think . . . won't think . . . must hide the pictures somewhere safe, somewhere the police won't look . . .

The glove was caught up with dusty pine needles. There were pine trees in the church-yard, the pictures had been drawn in the church-yard. The churchyard was where the witches danced, all of them . . . David, the Henleys, Grant, Jeffrey, the Spenders, Paul, the Laws, the Brierlys, the Bloggs and more . . . they were all here, in Melanie's box . . . all proof of what she knew . . . won't think, mustn't think . . .

Janey walked in the rain, holding up her face to let the wet drops cool her. She carefully laid out her thoughts as she walked. If she had more interests, if she wasn't leading such a dull, boring life, would she have come to believe what she was now beginning to believe? I doubt it.

Busy, busy, busy, she had always kept herself busy, doing things. This was the first time in her life that she had really stopped to think . . . and look where her thoughts were taking her! Perhaps it was dangerous for women to have time to stop and think, women like her with no mathematical brain, no logical mind, no interest in the 'bigger' issues of life like politics or religion. If Melanie hadn't disappeared she would never have given herself this time. If Melanie had died she wouldn't have been allowed it . . . people would have gathered round her, protecting her from this very thing — the dangerous act of thinking.

She paused, out of breath, and realised how fast she had been walking. She never normally enjoyed this sort of thing. She took her exercise mopping the kitchen floor or hoovering the stairs. She realised what she had been missing. Out here in the hills around Meadcombe she was herself, herself as she had never been before in her life. All the decisions about where she went were hers . . . no one was telling her which way to turn, which path to take, whether she should climb that hill or whether she *ought* to. But what had come of this new-found freedom? What exactly was she thinking?

She was thinking about black magic . . . that's what! The words, when she said them, when they were finally out, made her freeze. Down in the village she couldn't have made sense of them. Up here, among the beech woods, she could. Everything was combining together to tell her there were things going on down there that she didn't understand. It wasn't just Marian's attitude, or Sonia's, or David's mild reaction to the disappearance of his daughter. It wasn't the pen and ink sketches, or, worst of all, the effigy of Melanie with the stake through the heart. It was the whole, satanic atmosphere. It smelt bad, it smelt of decay, it stank of malevolent magic . . .

And not until she had started to descend, back to the village again, not until she thought she'd seen a green fog, a swirling, twisting excrescence rising up from the village square with its tendrilled centre focused on the Plague Stone, did Janey realise that tonight was Hallowe'en.

CHAPTER THIRTEEN

Now that Sonia knew the truth she felt extremely foolish. She had no reason to disbelieve Stanley's explanation. It sounded very reasonable to her.

'But why didn't you speak out when you heard that Melanie was missing?' Her question sounded softly sly in the padded silence of her drawing room.

'I didn't want to get the girl into trouble. She sat in the car for what . . . maybe fifteen minutes? She was upset so I gave her a cigarette and I remember now . . . she took off those funny gloves to smoke it. She must have dropped one. What is this all about, anyway? What are you thinking . . . that I raped her? Jesus Christ she's a child, Sonia. Just because I took a fancy to you doesn't mean to say I molest children! How extraordinary of you to think so!'

'But why were you in the square?'

'Calming down! Resting. I had to drive to Liverpool, don't forget. After that business with you I felt bloody whacked.'

God, he was repulsive! He had to keep reminding her of what he so matter-of-factly called 'that business'. Sonia turned away and reddened, wishing she had asked him earlier. Directness always paid. She had suffered for weeks as a consequence of not adopting her normal direct attitude. She'd been distracted by guilt, she supposed. 'Did Melanie say anything? Did she have plans, mention to you where she was going?'

'No, she didn't. Just that she had to get away. Couldn't tolerate living in Meadcombe any longer and I must say I couldn't blame the kid. She didn't look much like a Meadcombe type to me, old before her time, that one. She said she wanted some fun. I told her good times aren't everything. Anyway, we can clear it up now that we know what we're both talking about. It's no secret . . . one of your neighbours saw us, next door but one. Marian Law. I'm surprised she hasn't said anything. She was standing staring out of her bedroom window like a ghost at the curtain. I saw her clearly in my mirror.' How could he bear to sit with a cigarette hanging on his lip like that, so that it moved, Andy Capp-like when he spoke? Didn't he care at all what he looked like?

'No.' Sonia tapped her nose with a long, red nail. She considered herself in the mirror over the marble mantelpiece. She wore a green silk dress and her neat profile dripped at the edges with diamond earrings. The dress was tight. It rustled when she spoke, giving her words an agitated air. 'No. I don't think there's any point in saying anything. . . not now . . .'

So Marian had seen Melanie. Marian had seen and had said nothing. That partly explained her rather odd behaviour. What had she been doing in Constance's room at two o'clock in the morning? Constance would have been dead by then.

'But if the information might help . . .' Stanley narrowed his eyes when the smoke threatened them.

'No! It wouldn't help. And I still don't want Paul to know we were talking by Dolan's pond . . . it might come out, if you said something . . . he'd wonder why we went there.'

'You were late home. Where do you think he thought you were? Still in the Weary Ploughman?'

'Yes. They often ignore closing times. It's best he thinks that we stayed in the Weary Ploughman, talking.' Sonia still didn't like to think of her behaviour on the night when Stanley . . . but it had all turned out well. The money had saved their lives. The business was on its feet again and they had learned an important lesson. She loved Paul. Really loved him. But she wasn't sure how she'd feel about him if he went bankrupt. She needed to admire . . . she hated to pity . . . failure appalled her.

Long white hairs curled out through the sagging diamonds in Stanley's vest. Stanley was disgusting but he wasn't a failure. When he got up he would leave sweaty imprints in the brown leather of the Chesterfield. He was repellent. He was obscene . . . something about the baseness of Stanley excited her . . . she stopped herself from thinking further, dabbing at her powdered nose like a Victorian spinster needing smelling salts for succour.

'Out of Scotch, are you?'

187

'Oh, sorry, Stanley, I didn't realise,' and, bending over him to reach his glass and satisfy his rude request, she caught a whiff of seaweed. It was the smell of an old man.

'I would have given you the money anyway, you know.' He raised a pudgy arm and laid it across the sofa back, exposing yellowy, hairy wisps in his armpit.

He enjoyed this secret they shared, that time together by Dolan's pond. Now he thought he was safe he would use it, she was sure of that. Stanley was a clever man . . . he had an animal cunning . . . he was strong . . . she should have known he would have given her the money anyway. It was in his interests to do so. He sometimes used *Hanaford Galleries* as a tax loss. But he was not the only one to use the secret. Sonia used it, too, to fantasise when Paul made love to her. So horrified by the degenerate and yet so drawn to it . . .

'Ah, Paul! You look nice!' A theatrical entrance for fresh, clean cut, decent-minded Paul. In a dinner jacket he looked like a film star. An advertiser's dream with his square chin and his clear blue eyes and enough old Greek suntan to make him appear the outdoor type. But he couldn't escape the common touch, the smug stupidity in his face which was his country inheritance, not even dressed like this. Something, something so insidious that Sonia couldn't name it, gave his background away. Was it the way he stood, a little diffidently? Was it the way he moved . . . always so slowly? He was a man who took a long time to give his answers. He considered matters before he spoke. Stanley had it, to a degree. They all had it, the 'natives', this Meadcombe shadow. Unsophisticated, hardly read, he would divorce her if he knew what she was really like.

Stanley knew what she was really like. They recognised each other as rats from the same gutter. 'Very smart,' said Stanley to Paul. 'I suppose I better get myself together if we're both to accompany this lovely lady this evening.'

'It's a shame that Beryl couldn't come.' With that weight off her shoulders Sonia could begin to feel happy again. What a fool she had made of herself . . . if anyone had seen her with that glove . . . sneaking about and behaving like a character from the antique copies of *Girl's Own* she collected!

'Beryl has never liked opera,' said Stanley as he buttoned up his shirt, brushing off the stray ash as if he was dealing with Beryl.

'I'm rather surprised that you . . .' Sonia started, patronising.

'You'd be surprised at what I like,' he replied, hunching on his jacket and pulling down the sleeves. So this was to be their private joke. Dreadful though it was, it was true. The velvet collar, Sonia noticed with rising distaste, was speckled with dandruff. But dressed formally he managed to look quite dignified, with his silver hair and moustache . . . cowboy dignified. Opera for the people, imported, subsidised, for the new town. But the same old few always went. And when he caught her arm to escort her outside, for Paul had gone to get out the car, she felt another disgraceful ripple of pleasure. After all these years of sparring there seemed to be something between them after all, some inner beetle gnawing hungrily . . . Sonia was outraged by her own feelings.

Her friend, Janey, was behaving extremely oddly. Marian thought about this as she searched in her high cupboard for the bag of sweets she knew she had somewhere. The village children would call tonight . . . trick or treat . . . it was Hallowe'en. In the past they had never celebrated Hallowe'en. Bonfire night had always been the big one when her children had been small. Hallowe'en, Marian considered, was an American tradition brought to Britain by the greeting cards people in order to make more money. You saw it all in the shops now . . . witches' hats, rubber spiders, skeletons on elastic, and liquorice . . . why liquorice, she wondered. And told herself it was because it was black as she felt what she wanted and retrieved a stiffened arm. It was her first Hallowe'en without Roger.

Marian was fed up with inviting Janey round. When? She'd forgotten. Well, she never used to. Before Melanie's disappearance Janey had invited herself . . . had come round anyway whether it was convenient or not.

She was fed up with telephoning, too. Well, she never got an answer, even when she knew that Janey was in. She conveniently forgot she never let the telephone ring long enough for anyone to answer it. Janey would have had to be standing next to it to catch the phone before it stopped. Marian told herself there was only so much one could do. But she did feel uncomfortable about it. Janey must be distraught by now, what with Melanie missing for so long. Marian had seen the police go into Janey's house only this afternoon. They had stayed for over an hour. They, too, must be getting anxious now. After all, Melanie was only fourteen.

But it was difficult for Marian . . . with what she knew and couldn't say.

They had met the day before yesterday, in the shop. It had been a sticky little meeting, with neither of them quite knowing what to say. Janey had been jumpy as a cat.

'You weren't at the rehearsal last night!'

Janey had delved deep into the freezer, untidying it so much that it would annoy Mrs Brierly.

'I know my lines,' she had said. 'And I know when to say them.'

'It's a long part you've got, though.'

Janey had surfaced, her face red and her hair on end like a swimmer underwater for too long. Janey's hair was frenzied as the scribblings of a child. Marian had been certain she would have left grips in the freezer behind her.

'Yes, but I don't feel the need to go over it time and time again.'

Stumped, Marian had persevered. 'Why don't you come in, now, and have a coffee?'

'You'll be busy, rehearsing with Sonia.'

Marian had laughed. 'Well, we don't need to rehearse. Come on . . . it's ages since we've talked. I keep ringing and you're never in.'

'Oh? I haven't heard the phone!'

'Well, there must be something the matter with it then because I've been calling every day.' But it only rang four times before it stopped.

'You never came round.'

'I never like to come round . . . without phoning first.' Unlike you, Marian managed not to say. She could feel herself becoming more and more annoyed. What was the matter with Janey? Why was she so troubled? There was something stopping her from coming round. Something that Janey expected her to know. What on earth was it?

Without realising that she had relaxed, Marian had, over the space of time, put her guilt about Constance behind her. After all, she had not committed murder, she had committed a mercy killing, and there was plenty of that about. Many people would understand and applaud her for what she had done. At the time she had overreacted, gone way over the top. Her guilt, she thought now, had sprung from the fact she had never liked Constance, had not been able to give her the peaceful old age that she thought she could. The guilt was because she'd failed her in life, not because she had let her die.

And Melanie? Well! Marian tried not to think about Melanie.

She ought to try to make herself available to Janey again. She had been a little offish to begin with, but all things considered she saw that as understandable, in the circumstances. She had, after all, just been bereaved.

No. Janey was jealous of her friendship with Sonia and that was something Janey was just going to have to get over and learn to grow out of. At least Sonia was not forever sobbing and basking in self-pity. At least Sonia made her laugh. And Marian enjoyed learning her part with Sonia. It was a most companiable activity. It took her out of herself. It helped her to stop thinking of Roger for a while. They had not deliberately excluded Janey. And if Janey felt they had, well, that was Janey's paranoia, and something she'd have to deal with herself.

So the meeting at the shop had been a difficult one, and had ended on an unsatisfactory note.

'Well, you know where I am, Janey. Come in . . . any time.'

'I'm busy just now, Marian, thank you.' And Janey had stalked out without buying anything, leaving Marian feeling rejected and fragile. Even Mrs Brierly had noticed and raised her eyebrows.

Marian hadn't seen her since, not to speak to. If she hadn't known better she would have begun to suspect that Janey was avoiding her.

'Trick or treat!'

Warnings had been given about Hallowe'en this year. Dark warnings by churchmen who knew about such things. Warnings about the occult. Satanism was growing, that was a fact. Children were being used as sacrifices . . . evil was abroad.

Children in shadows. The light from their torches penetrated the tinted glass of the Hanafords' windscreen and Sonia winced. The car was only just out of the drive, crawling slowly along to turn the corner before picking up speed. Sonia had been miles away, deep in the back seat, lost in a maze of muddled thinking. If Marian knew that Constance was dead why didn't she wake everyone up and tell them? And why had she kept quiet about seeing Melanie? It was so unlike her.

'What do you mean, trick or treat?'

The children were baffled, not expecting to have their motives questioned. Paul smoothly whirred down the window and stuck his head out.

'Trick or treat,' the bravest started to explain, tugging on a python-like scarf and adjusting his demonic mask. 'You give us something or we do something nasty . . .'

'I know what you do,' said Paul, rifling in his breast pocket. 'I just wanted to know what it meant. But isn't stopping cars a little unfair? We're not very likely to be carrying sweets or cakes, now are we?'

'But you've got money, Mister Hanaford.'

'Here.' He handed them a couple of pounds. 'And keep away from the road. You'll cause an accident. Go on, stick to the village. Don't roam around outside it.'

And Sonia, who hadn't realised it was Hallowe'en, suddenly wished her own children were with this little cheeky-faced group instead of a hundred miles away at prep or choir practice. Were they missing something that was genuine and good by being away from home nine-tenths of the year? It was something she had really never considered before.

'Trick or treat!' Marian hadn't even read about the warnings.

Marian had been waiting for them. She stood at her door in her stockinged feet and the light from the kitchen circled the group of children and seemed to hold them in a protected ring of their own. Surprisingly, she felt the light embarrass her. Her feet felt broad and homely, her complexion sallow. She held out the large bag of assorted sweets and lollies, feeling she was using it for bait. What on earth was she trying to catch? They treated her with the respect they reserved for the mothers of older children . . . for people who didn't know them very well . . . for old women . . .

'I hope you enjoy them,' she said.

She tried to joke with them, tried to remember the sort of conversation Sally and Lloyd had been easy with at their age. But she couldn't remember, and anyway, she was rightly excluded from that honorary position. Her day was done. She was a sympathetic outsider, entitled to nothing else.

One tiny, leggy girl wore a Walkman, and her deadpan eyes were almost closed to the noise that filled her head. Another chewed bubble gum and wore a thoughtful expression of great concentration. Marian wondered if children still loved snow as much as she had done. After she'd closed the door she stood and listened as they shared out the booty into their individual Tesco carrier bags.

'One for you and one for me . . .'

Little boys' hair was kept so neat these days, Marian Law reflected as she wandered back to her television set.

'Trick or treat!' Janey believed the warnings.

Janey wouldn't have opened the door but Daniel went, slouching, hands in pockets, eager to show himself and emphasise the fact that he was too old for this sort of childishness.

Justin had done the rounds earlier and was now at a friend's house, doubtless scoffing the loot. Justin had lots of friends. Justin was easy as Melanie had never been.

David wasn't back yet. Janey hardly noticed his absence. He was often late, and tonight was the evening he went to his reflexology with Mrs Mason, or he might have called at the doctor's.

'Mum! Mum!' How wearying was that sound!

She responded to that universal call wherever she went, offering herself unconditionally . . . walking down the street . . . in the supermarket . . . she had brought her hot head out from the dryer in the hairdresser's once in mistaken reaction to it.

'Mum! Have we got anything to give this lot?'

Janey took a breath and replied reasonably, 'Oh, I think I can find something, Daniel.'

Janey jerked her chair back from the table and marched to the fridge like a puppet. With a shudder she took out a bowl and put it on the sideboard. The liver flopped out, only half in its paper, blood black, natal black, and velvety. How strange, it smelt of violets. She fetched a cheery paper bag and thrust the meat inside. At once it started oozing.

'Mum! Come on!' It was proving embarrassing for Daniel to be standing there for so long. Like Marian, he was uneasily bereft of the right sort of conversation. Marian shouldn't have worried, it was only a couple of years that built the barrier.

'Trick or treat,' the bravest felt impelled to repeat on spying the lady of the house. But the element of surprise was missing, and the words sounded silly. Two helium balloons bearing pictures of the Devil bobbed around their heads and conversed idiotically from a few short feet above the weird scenario.

'Here you are,' said Janey, thrusting the bloody bag into the leader's hand. She closed the door and abandoned the little group to amber torch-light.

197

CHAPTER FOURTEEN

Something happens, we open our eyes and find we hardly know ourselves at all. It would appear that I am overly partial to brown.

I am a studious man, and I live alone in a comfortable flat on the university campus. One day, not long ago, I stood back and realised that I had surrounded myself over the years, unknowingly, with brown. Comfortable brown leather chairs . . . friends to me now with cracks and creases in well-worn faces. Mahogany desk with its ebony-brass inkstand, pen-holder. And rows of brown-backed books, brown rugs on the floor. I draw the brown velvet curtain while clad in a brown dressing-gown. And when I sit and talk with friends, extraordinarily we smoke brown cigars and sip a gold-brown brandy.

Behaviour. Living alone as I do, allowed to absorb myself with thought, I sometimes find myself doing strange things . . . putting a casserole in the fridge to cook . . . going to the door for the milk and coming back forgetting it. People would call me absentminded. They're wrong. I'm not out of my mind, I'm in it!

Strange things. Oh God, she had started doing strange things. There was no longer satisfaction in watching the filthy water churning and slopping through the coloureds in her Bendix washing machine. Janey watched the action morosely through the round window, feeling like a prisoner in her house. Her hair itched. She sat watching the washing while she scratched her head. Lately she had not bothered to dress. She had stopped her walks. She was afraid. They were all against her. They had made a pact with the Devil and she was alone.

What had they done with Melanie?

The essential thing for Janey, now, was that she get up early. Why, she didn't know. But that area between sleep and wakefulness, when her imagination played havoc, was a dreamtime too riddled with menace to risk. The downstairs windows took on a three-dimensional lozenge shape when condensation tucked in the corners. Outside it was cold. She sat watching her washing while a wicked draught played under the kitchen door, disturbing the calendar on the wall. The kitchen clock drew out the minutes, and the Rayburn moaned as the wind gusted through its hidden, metal places. She could hear the rooks cawing from their messy nests high up in the churchyard elms.

Once Janey had taken Isobelle to meet the ever more wayward, ever more eccentric Constance. They had got on well together, these two women who had both retreated in different ways from life, neither taking the slightest notice of the other and yet managing to communicate all the same.

Ostriches, defeated, their heads in sand. In a strange way she now admired them.

Thinking about it now, Janey saw that they had been no threat to each other. Constance with her clots of wild, white hair, had been more normal than she'd been for a long time. Isobelle had behaved caringly towards the sick old woman. Janey was under threat from everyone . . . she was even uncertain about her children. No wonder she was withdrawn.

Only a place like Meadcombe could have affected her so.

In the summer, tourists came to take snaps of it. It was even featured on postcards. Idyllic, they called it. A slice of Olde England, untouched by time.

Meadcombe was a village of high, drystone walls, cemented in latter years, but still the same high walls with decorative, triangular tops. Covered in a flowering creeper that strove to subdue this battlement effect, the walls towered over little green patches of garden, hiding, protecting, privatising. The first comers to Meadcombe must have been a secretive lot. Maybe this was so because, in a village, privacy was so hard to come by. Everyone enjoyed a gossip, everyone knew and was extraordinarily interested in everybody else's business. Perhaps it stemmed from a time before wireless, before television, when, for sanity's sake it was essential to construct real life serials — soaps — from a time when no one went anywhere and people needed relief from the inordinate dullness of their lives. If this were so, then the villagers should have adapted to the circumstances of the present day by now. They hadn't. And they shared a kind of morbid delight in the misfortunes of others . . . more so than townspeople, with so much more going on around them.

But the cottages in the square had no protection. The people who lived in them were susceptible. It was possible to see what time the inhabitants got up, what washing they hung out, what visitors called, and, from the blue flickering television lights that came from their back rooms, even what programme they were watching. And there were people in Meadcombe who were interested in these things.

As in wartime, when a thrifty housewife could prepare a feast with a bit of corned beef or a dried egg, so, too, could the villagers of Meadcombe construe anything from the humblest hint or detail. Gossip flew, reputations were ruined overnight by a careless remark in the public bar of the Weary Ploughman. No wonder Sonia had been nervous. No wonder Marian had been jumpy. After living in Meadcombe for any length of time, it was easy to imagine eyes in walls and ears in ceilings. Everyone who lived there lived with a kind of sublimated horror that one of their many skeletons might one day be hauled out of the cupboard and jangled about for all to see. It had a way of making people secretive and guarded. It had a way of making them wary. It was easy for Janey to feel intimidated when she knew that so many eyes were on her, so many tongues were wagging. She liked to get up at dawn when there was nobody else about.

Last night David had come out of the blue with, 'I seem unable to maintain any sort of consistent level of happiness.'

There he was, propped up in bed while he waited for his pills to work, talking away endlessly about himself, blind to the misery of his wife, untouched by the disappearance of his daughter. Just the same old, dragging bore that he'd always been. But this time Janey didn't encourage him. She wished she hadn't found Melanie's cartoons, because she couldn't help seeing him as he'd looked in those — bug-eyed, wild-haired, devilish . . .

She listened while he launched attacks on himself. She was supposed to respond. She didn't. There were green stains on his dressing gown. He had been out night-walking again, something he'd always enjoyed, pacing manically backwards and forwards over the soaking lawn between the currant bushes in the back garden while he pondered on life. Was that really where he'd been? Could he have gone to the churchyard? What else had he been up to? Who had he met?

She quizzed her enemy with caution. 'David, where do you think she is now?'

He shifted his position in the bed, tearing his

imagination away from himself while he edged towards her with a cold right foot. She knew he'd nearly asked, 'Who?' but pulled himself back just in time.

'How can I say? Knowing Melanie she's probably gone to London. Knowing Melanie she'll be all right . . . she'll have found somewhere to sleep, money, some job washing up in a café . . . She's very self-contained, not like . . .'

She stopped him before he could manoeuvre the conversation back to himself. 'You don't think then, that she's dead?' Janey listened tensely for the answer, tracing the neat lines of patchwork. David knew what had happened to Melanie. He wouldn't say she was alive if she wasn't.

'Dead? No! Why would she be dead? She'll be back when she's ready.' He sounded resigned to this last idea, as though he wasn't too happy about it. But then he wasn't too happy about anything just now. 'You worry too much about her. You always have.'

Yes, Janey thought to herself. David had always resented the children. But how could he be so calm? He must know something . . .

'You're thinking the worst,' he said, a little querulously, for that was his prerogative. 'It's not like you.'

'Well, why do you think she hasn't rung?'

'Since when has Melanie considered anybody else's feelings?' David turned to her, suddenly angry. 'You're forgetting what she was like! Because she's disappeared you're turning her into a fantasy person . . . as if she was dead! You'll have to stop it, Janey! You'll drive yourself insane if you let yourself worry like this!'

Well! Of all the people to threaten madness!

'This whole thing is too much for me.' He rubbed a hand harshly over his stubbled chin. 'I can't take it, Janey, I just can't take it!' He started to sob and tried to bury his face in her breasts, using her as a mummy, the comforter she had always been. His face looked desolate, his eyes wide and searching for solace. She couldn't bear it. She pushed him away from her and got up.

'Where are you going?'

'I'm going to sleep in Melanie's room.'

'Janey, you're different . . .' His desperate voice trailed out after her on to the landing. How frightened he must be, cast adrift on his unsteady sea without her to balance him. He was frightened. And she was frightening herself with her own thoughts. Was the hopeless, inadequate David really part of a secret and sinister cult? Was he a man who could sacrifice his own daughter to some terrible rite? He was David . . . David whom she'd known for nearly twenty years. But he was unstable enough for anything, and weak. And did you really ever know anybody?

She hadn't known him the last time they had taken him away. Everything about him, even his smell, turned foreign. He'd taken to dressing in shiny black suits he brought home shamefacedly in brown carrier bags from jumble sales. All he could eat were tinned tomatoes on toast, covered with a thick layer of pepper. All he would drink was bottled water. He was convinced there was poison in everything. He prepared all his meals himself. He refused to call her Janey . . . he called her 'Heather' because he said it was her real name. 'And you should know that by now,' he had shouted at her. If a man could suddenly behave like that, a man could do anything.

Back then there had been times when she had been afraid of him. And she'd been afraid for the children, too. But she had the consolation of knowing she could pop round to Marian's any time. For Janey there was much solace in this. She spent hours there, wallowing in the misery of David's near breakdown . . . no . . . the doctors still said it wasn't a proper breakdown. David had failed, even in this.

Marian had helped her get him into hospital. Even Janey had reluctantly realised that he was now too ill to remain at home. He had gone too far. She was angry with him. She'd thought they had reached an unspoken understanding as to how far he could go, how manic he was allowed to become.

She confided in Marian, she confided in Sonia, she confided in Nancy Blogg and Grant Fitch. She confided in every person who stopped to ask how David was, until, in the end, the villagers were satiated by gossip and began to avoid her when they saw her in the shop or hovering in the square waiting to pounce. There was no room left for inventive supposition. The thing had happened. There was no mileage to be made of it. It was unsatisfactory. Nothing about it was secret. Nothing about it was precious. Everybody knew.

But Janey hadn't realised. Still didn't realise. Now she looked back on their offhandedness, their rudeness almost, and read into it a different interpretation.

Yes, they had all been acting against her then . . . just as they were now. No one really cared that Melanie was missing. People still avoided her, she was sure, when they saw her coming. It was all so contrary to village tradition. Not many people asked for news . . . well, they wouldn't, would they? *They all knew where Melanie was.*

But there was one person she could go to, she thought, on this chill November morning as she sat waiting for the day to begin, watching her washing spinning round. There was one person she trusted who didn't live in Meadcombe, who hadn't been included in Melanie's dire portfolio, and who could be counted on to be honest to the point of cruelty. And that was Isobelle.

Janey was filled with enormous, energetic excitement. Her mother's inscrutable face floated before her like a speech balloon. She squeezed the detergent dispenser so hard that it snapped. She scrunched it up, unseeingly, and put it in the pop-up bin. She would go to the new town today. There was no time to be wasted. She would go to her mother's drab little open-fronted house in the street in the middle of streets and she would tell her of her unhappy conjectures. She would tell her about Sonia and Marian, about how cold they'd been . . . about David's unnatural reactions, about the sinister play, Melanie's pictures and the awful effigy. She would ask, 'Could it be true? Tell me I'm imagining things! Wake me up from this dream, please, before I lose my mind.' And Isobelle, blunt and to the point if nothing else, would remove this dreadful weight from her daughter's heart. Would make it possible for her to go round to Marian's again so she could cope with Melanie missing. Would be a proper mother.

Later that morning, sure that people were watching, she waited for the bus to arrive before she left her house. Then, crablike, she scuttled to the stop and mounted the steps. A tuft of wizened grass which she passed on the way, peeping up alone between two flagstones, brought her to such an exquisite pitch of irritation that she almost had to stop to pluck it out. But she made herself go forwards. She jumped as the doors wheezed closed behind her, feeling trapped and unreasonably strange in an environment she hadn't entered for at least two weeks.

Various acquaintances nodded politely before closing their faces and looking quickly away. They hadn't the guts to face her! Janey kept her head well down and ignored them. She even cunningly bought a ticket to the town centre, ensuring a longish walk back to Hunters' Close which was where her mother lived. She didn't want anyone knowing where she was going. She carried a large shopping bag so they would assume she was visiting the supermarket.

The skin on the back of her neck prickled as Meadcombe was left behind, as if hostile eyes from the village bored into her. She reminded herself that she didn't have to go back. If she felt she was so unsafe she could stay away . . . stay with her mother and never return. No one had prevented her from leaving. She coughed and cleared her lungs of a thick, green phlegm which she wrapped with peculiar care, surreptitiously in a tissue. She felt lighter, as if that might have had something to do with her heaviness of heart. She knew it was an infection, something of Meadcombe that had been sent with her. Her eyes streamed with hot, sneezy tears. She hid her head behind the seat while she wiped at them frantically and then she turned to stare out of the window. Whatever it was they were doing to her was most effective. But she would go on. Nothing would induce her to turn back. If she had to be carried to her mother's house unconscious, then so be it.

The stomach cramps were fierce. They doubled her up and she felt her eyes bulging. She gripped the cool handrail of the seat in front and willed them away. She stared hard at the scattering of tickets on the floor. 'Relax,' she told herself, remembering her pregnancy textbook. Yes, they were as uncomfortable as late stage birthpangs. She tried hard to concentrate on the purring engine of the bus, on watching the monotonous movements of the driver's head as he turned it from left to right, from left to right while he smoothly turned the wheel.

Faces turned to watch her, no longer hindered by politeness. Janey heaved and groaned as she tried to stare them out through dizzying waves of pain. Meadcombe eyes . . . Meadcombe heads. She must look a mess. She had forgotten to do her hair and Janey's hair, at best, was a gorsey furze bush. She hadn't washed for days, and was aware that her face was greased and shiny. And with craven horror she realised that nor had she dressed. She'd been so intent on getting away, on remembering what ticket to buy, on remembering to take her shopping bag that she was still in her quilted dressing-gown and slippers. She had no knickers on. She rubbed the material between two fingers as she had rubbed a piece of silky blanket-binding as a child, and wished she could also suck her thumb.

'Janey! What the hell are you doing here?'
Janey had intended to stop and rest by Dolan's pond. She wasn't aware of the cold any longer. She wanted to hide herself, for a necessary few moments, behind the weeping willows in the little oasis by the side of the road. The flat pondwater would have been a solace for her sore eyes after the nightmare ride, after crossing the road in the

busy town centre and enduring a torturous five minutes as she waited, in her ludicrous attire, for the return bus to Meadcombe.

She'd tried to act aloof. She'd tried to appear as if she knew she had her dressing-gown on and that there was a good reason for it. A greyish nylon nightie that had once been baby blue trailed sadly beneath the riot of roses. But she hadn't succeeded in being able to ignore the nervous smiles and nudges of the people who walked by.

Afraid of being dropped off in the square where everyone would see her, she had asked to be put off at the stop before, affecting a breezy manner towards the nonplussed driver. From here she could quickly walk the two hundred yards of country road and get to her house through the back garden.

The Mercedes was hidden halfway down a rutted track that led to a ploughed field. No one but a lone pedestrian with nowhere much to go could possibly have stumbled upon it. But Janey had, and, with her thoughts elsewhere, she had not reacted quickly enough to withdraw before being seen.

'What on earth are you doing here? In your dressing-gown?'

Sonia was trying to cover her unbuttoned chest. A flesh-coloured Janet Reger slip showed through. Lipstick was smeared, clownishly, halfway up one cheek and damp mascara gave her a black-eyed look. She was shivering. Her teeth were chattering. Shock . . . that's what it was. Janey wished

210

she could do the same. It might have afforded her nerves some relief. But all she felt was sick.

Sonia came out of the offside back door, flustered and confused, long legs first, parted and ungainly, knowing, Janey supposed later, that she had been seen. Typical of Sonia to choose to face the music rather than try and hide, pretending she hadn't been recognised. No, Sonia got out and confronted Janey as if she was trespassing.

'What are you doing?' Sonia asked again, all fingers and thumbs as she tried to sort out the buttons while staring warily at Janey.

Incongruous with dressing-gown and shopping basket, Janey held the latter up, as if that might speak for her and explain what it was she was doing. 'I came to find some kindling,' was all she could think of to say.

'But you're not dressed!'

Decency prevented Janey from asking anything. It was blatantly clear what Sonia had been doing . . . and with Stanley! Janey realised she was shaking her head.

Sonia sidled closer, all done up now, trying to pull down her sleeves and straighten her skirt at the same time. She wobbled, finding her heels in thickish mud. 'Er, Janey,' she gave an embarrassed puff down her nose. 'Janey, I'd be grateful if you said nothing to anyone about this. I'd be grateful if you'd forget you'd seen me.' And in a high falsetto she continued, 'Stanley and I were talking . . . we have business problems at the moment and there are things . . .' She stopped

211

after realising how improbable she sounded. And went back to, 'And I'd be really grateful, Janey, if . . .'

Janey turned round and made her way back up the track. She longed to be back at her kitchen table jam-making again. Where had the days gone when she'd been safe in her head? Where was the woman who had gleaned so much excitement from labelling the shining jars . . . she had even painted intricate water colour pictures on the labels, blackberries, raspberries, gooseberries and blackcurrant.

Melanie had done this! It was Melanie who had turned her world upside down! Nothing was as it seemed any more. There was a pervasive wickedness all around, the smell of a bad bonfire. It was not coincidence that she had left home without her clothes this morning. Some menacing evil had caused it to happen, wanting to prevent her from talking to her mother. And Sonia, making love in the car of an old man she professed to despise . . . what powerful forces were at work there . . . what vile malevolence was motivating that?

Witchcraft. Devil worship. They were all involved. If she hadn't been sure before, Janey was certain now. There was no other explanation for this extraordinary event. She had no need to talk to anyone, not Isobelle, nobody. She knew what she needed to know and if she wanted to get her daughter back unharmed then she would have to act with far more caution and intelligence.

Janey slipped back through the back door and went upstairs to consult Melanie's pictures again, sobbing and laughing at the same time. Yes, it was as she thought. The goat in the pictures which had been mating so obscenely in the churchyard was not Paul at all. It was the old man, Stanley, white hairs, white whiskers, horns and all.

Melanie had found out. Somewhere they were punishing Melanie.

CHAPTER FIFTEEN

To be scrupulously fair, they should have destroyed all women back in the sixteenth century witchhunts, for women survive by manipulation, the stirring of pots and the weaving of spells. And even the Cindy dolls develop long noses, humps, pointed chins and toothless smiles at the ultimate end.

So when Sonia called on Janey for a confidential chat the following morning, to describe her as the most manipulative woman in Meadcombe, as many people would, must surely be intended as a compliment.

Because of a silly slip, Sonia saw she was in danger of losing everything she valued. Her safety now depended upon Janey . . . Janey, who, it was rumoured, was acting out a kind of wilful, solitary madness of her own at home.

Sonia supposed she was partly to blame. She knew that she had been monopolising Marian, and, despising Janey for the loser that she was, Sonia hadn't minded about this at all. In fact, she'd quite enjoyed watching the worried face at the window as she pulled her car into the square. Well, it added spice to life, didn't it?

And to Sonia, it must be said, these amusing

214

little pastimes were of no great moment, no more important, shall we say, than poking a stick into an ants' nest and watching the inhabitants dementedly scatter. She was a busy woman with bigger things on her mind than the relationship between Marian and Janey. She was a busy woman who sat on committees in the village hall where groups faced each other as calculatingly as the card players who met on a Monday. And Sonia Hanaford had a reputation to keep up. It wouldn't do for people to know she had been dallying with her own father-in-law in the back of a car like some love-lorn teenager down some tawdry local lovers' lane. It wouldn't do at all. And gossip like this spread like wildfire once it was given its head. Nor would it do for Paul to hear of it!

Sonia was one of the many recently arrived 'outsiders' who ran the village and lampooned the 'natives' for their lazy apathy. The 'natives' were only now waking up to the fact that these local organisations were to do with money and power and planning. Especially planning . . . a pernicious little issue that stalked the countryside with the gaunt insensitivity of a string of pylons. The people in the big houses wanted to protect their views and property prices. The 'natives' wanted work and cheap houses. A member of the Meadcombe Parish Council, Sonia also sat on the board of governors of Meadcombe school.

She hadn't realised these intense female relationship situations happened out of school, until she'd arrived in Meadcombe, and discovered that one half of the village was never on speaking terms with the other. Feelings ran high in small villages where, to be truthful, most of the inhabitants secretly despised the others, or feared them . . . one and the same.

Sonia came to Janey's house borne on the wing of a generously-cut trenchcoat that she liked to swing behind her.

'Hello, Janey.'

'Hello, Sonia. Well . . . you'd better come in then.' So, Janey thought, 'they' had sent someone to see her at last. She'd known they would. She grew tight with dread. Over Sonia's shoulder, as Janey closed the door, she saw the weathercock gleam gold, like a firebird, high up on the church steeple.

With the door closed a farty smell of old boiled egg instantly fugged the kitchen. Sonia and Janey sniffed it together. It seemed oddly apt for the occasion. Guiltily Sonia met Janey's expressionless eyes.

Sonia was aware she had a hard face. She spent hours before her mirror doing facial exercises, trying to soften it. She tried to soften it now, and only succeeded in producing a rather wry, malevolent expression, which Janey saw as a leer because Sonia's eyes did not change. And the way she dressed did not soften her image. She wore hard, smart clothes and her polished neatness emphasised the rigidity of her features. Her eyes glittered this morning with a furtive fire. Her

216

coat she pushed back with a dash behind her elbows, exposing a scarlet lining.

But Janey reminded herself of her resolution. It was vital she remain calm. Melanie, whatever was happening to her, depended on Janey to save her. Everything might hang on this morning's conversation. She must be careful . . . careful.

Her hand shook as she filled the kettle. Sonia must be an important member of the group to be entrusted as messenger. And where did Stanley fit in, she wondered?

'I haven't been here for ages,' said Sonia in a bright, busy voice. She settled at the table and looked around the room, re-acquainting herself with Janey's kitchen and wearing a queer half-smile. This was going to be difficult. If only there hadn't been this time of mistrust between them. If only she'd kept away from Marian, kept the threesome balanced and happy. But now it was important that rift was never healed. Sonia was clever at twisting knives. She was a practised manipulator. Sonia was always regretting past behaviour, and having to put her skills to good use. And now, because she was basically a believer in good fortune, she put her doubts behind her and pressed on.

Look at her! Poor Janey. She had relapsed into a kind of inadequate squalor. Her face was grey, her lacklustre hair had hardly any of its mouse brown strands left, and her brown eyes were watery and glum. Not dressed, there were stains down the dressing-gown that hung baggily about her. She had even lost weight.

'I though we might have lunch.' Janey looked as if Sonia had suggested an expedition to one of the poles. 'Not here . . . in the new town. A friend of mine has bought a restaurant . . .'

Cupping her hands round her mug, Janey sat down at the opposite end of the table. 'Why, Sonia?' she asked.

'Just because I haven't seen you. You're turning into a recluse, you know. Everybody is quite worried about you.' Sonia felt confused and gave a nervous little laugh.

Everybody? Are you representing everybody? Janey said defensively, 'I was at the rehearsal last week.'

'I know.' Sonia relaxed a little, and turned the mug slightly so she didn't have to sip over the chipped edge. 'But you didn't sit with us. I hardly managed to get to speak to you.' The steam softened Sonia's face, but through it Janey could still see the eyes glitter like the jewels in her rings.

Sonia's hands were gnarled, the long nails curved, and the skin rose in ugly bumps round her fingers where her rings went. Janey remembered that if you were young and you pinched your skin it would spring back down without indentation. It was a sign of age if it took time and left a mark. She knew that if Sonia's skin were pinched it would be left with a mark. And yet Janey, only a year or so older, didn't have old hands like Sonia's.

One of Sonia's hands was laid flat on the table

while the other toyed with the mug. She was picking her time. She had to raise the small matter of the 'incident', but she wasn't sure of her timing. Janey was a reluctant ally this morning. Janey was very reserved. She wasn't helping at all.

But Sonia was not stupid. Sonia had come bearing gifts. Lunch out had been the first one, and that had been rejected. The second she slapped down on the table now. It was a softener, it was the sweet before the pill. It was the fact that she and Marian were not really hand in glove at all. It was the fact that Sonia didn't trust Marian and never really had. She started out carefully, 'Marian misses you, you know. She talks about you a lot. She wonders how you are.'

'Well, why can't Marian come and say that?'

'She feels you might not want her to.'

'Don't be ridiculous. Why would she think that?'

'Because she says you've acted so strangely lately. She doesn't want to impose.'

Sonia skilfully appointed herself as intermediary where there hadn't been need of one before, thus virtually securing a perpetual state of estrangement between her friends. An intermediary with a difference, for with Sonia in the middle it was doubtful that the twain could ever meet. Not after she'd finished. The fact they had been discussing her at all would undermine Janey. It was part of Sonia's plan . . . trust me . . . don't trust Marian. I, Sonia Hanaford, am the one who is

on your side. She didn't want them coming together. If they became close as they were before,
she was certain Janey would tell Marian about
the incident with Stanley.

'Well, I do think Marian could come and see
me herself.'

'Well, you know what Marian's like. . . .' the
unspecific suggestion hung in the air to be mulled
over and interpreted in whichever way was de-
sirable. And a further little bombshell: 'She seems
to think you're behaving this way to attract attention . . . of course I tell her she's silly but
there we are. That's Marian . . .'

At one time Janey would have been hurt . . .
hurt that Marian would say such a thing to Sonia
of all people, hurt that she would think that about
her. Now she was numb, and wondering what
purpose lay behind Sonia's revelations. What else
would she say? Janey waited.

'She saw Melanie, you know . . . on the night
she disappeared. Oh yes, Marian saw Melanie in
the square talking to Stanley, but she never said
anything to you about it, did she?'

Janey had actually paled. 'The footprints?'

'Yes. She must have been standing there watching. I would have thought she would have told
you straight away . . . under the circumstances.
And she ought to have told the police, too. Who
knows? All these little bits of information, pieced
together, can be valuable.'

'But why would she not tell me?'

Sonia shrugged her padded shoulders and

hunched, wrapped in a sharp bout of disapproval. Through mascaraed lashes she watched Janey. She seemed to have managed finally to get under her skin. But it had taken her strongest card.

Janey was not worried about the breakdown in friendship. She didn't care about Marian any more. What terrified her, what made her head swim and nausea rise to her throat was the thought of Melanie talking to Stanley. For Stanley, she surmised, had a big part in the diabolical goings on in Meadcombe. She already saw him as some sort of satanic high priest. Melanie's pen and ink portrait of him had been the strongest drawing of all. But why was Sonia telling her this? Was there something she was supposed to understand? She didn't. She was totally confused.

'Marian can be very odd.' Sonia was waffling on, fairly certain she had succeeded in changing sides . . . or treading a careful central line, which was what she intended. 'She certainly has strange ideas about you.' And, as planned, Sonia proceeded to launch into a list of criticisms Marian had made of Janey, ending with the coup de grâce, 'She's a big critic of how you treat your children. Once, I think, if I remember rightly, she said she thought they weren't loved enough.'

None of this was touching Janey. Her thoughts were whirling. What does this mean? What do they want me to do? How can I get Melanie back? She nearly asked . . . just came right out with it in the open . . . in many ways it would have been easier to get it over and done with just like that. But she stopped herself. She must be careful, she must be cautious. It wouldn't do to act impetuously. The waters were too deep and too fearsome to jump into naked and unprotected.

Considering Janey to be sufficiently unnerved, Sonia leaned forward over the table and came to the point. 'I wanted to talk to you about yesterday.'

'Oh?' Janey hardly heard her.

'About yesterday, when you met us at Dolan's pond.'

Met you? Was that what I did? Her hair was itching again. So were her legs.

'It wasn't as it seemed, you know. There is nothing between Stanley and I.'

'No?'

'No.' Sonia was shaking her head, her diamanté earrings spun and caught the light like daggers dancing. As she spoke she lowered her voice to make what she said more awful. She lowered her chin so she had to look up at Janey through half-rolled eyes. 'No. It wasn't as it seemed. It was a ghastly mistake. That oversexed brute was trying to take advantage of me. I was never so glad in my life when I saw you there. God knows how far he would have gone if you hadn't turned up. It was like some frightful nightmare, Janey. Once he started I just couldn't stop him. But if Paul should ever find out . . . he wouldn't understand . . . and it would mean he would have to disown his father. Do you see? It would be absolutely awful! And I would feel as if I were to blame.'

Janey watched dispassionately as Sonia unclipped her handbag and took out a tissue. Her eyes were wet when she dabbed them. She wagged her head frantically as if to escape some awful torture inside. She linked saliva-slippery fingers and brought them up into a steeple. Janey had never seen Sonia behaving like this before. 'I couldn't bear it if Paul ever heard about it,' she managed to knock out her words in splintery little jerks. 'And I wanted to make sure you understood the implications of it . . . if you should ever say anything to anyone our marriage . . . our business . . . it would all be finished . . . finished . . . just like that.' She splayed both hands on the table to illustrate the finish of everything. 'Just like that,' she said again, gratified by her performance and waiting for some response.

Janey felt as if her throat had swollen shut. Her waxy pallor had turned to sickly. She twisted her legs round the kitchen chair as if that action might hold her to reality. She shook her unkempt head and at the same time realised this gesture was becoming a habit with her. This woman was evil. This woman was venomous. Even the words she spoke tumbled from her mouth in a froth of warm jelly so you could almost see them landing in glutinous gobs on the table. She felt a frantic desire to fetch a cloth and wipe it clean.

'What do you want me to do, Sonia?'

What was the matter with Janey? Sonia's head

223

sprung up at the hollow-worded question and she saw the distaste on the face in front of her with rising alarm. This soft reply was not what she had expected. She had wanted a rush of sympathy, an immediate understanding and a reassurance that the secret would be kept. Instead she faced a vacant-eyed, distressed wreck of a woman who looked no more capable of sensible interaction than Constance had when she'd been alive. What the hell was the matter with the woman? Was she in need of psychiatric help, like her blasted husband? Sonia realised, with disgust, that she had been pulling on broken strings.

Ah! While Sonia was regarding her with ill-defined horror, Janey was beginning to see the light. So it was blackmail. After yesterday's excursion 'they' were afraid she would tell. She would get Melanie back if she said nothing about what she'd seen or what she suspected. But who would she tell? Who was there who wasn't involved? The messenger this morning was warning her to keep quiet. She hadn't believed a word of what Sonia said and she hadn't been meant to. From what Janey had seen in one short moment at Dolan's pond, Sonia had been thoroughly enjoying her experiences with Stanley. Paul was just as involved as they all were . . . knew about it . . . everybody knew about it. Sonia had been acting all the time. No, this was a way of letting her know she must keep quiet if she wanted Melanie returned to her unharmed.

'You can tell them I will say nothing. I swear

on my daughter's life that is true.'

Sonia wasn't sure what she heard. Janey had spoken too softly. 'You will keep the secret? You won't say a word to anyone?'

'I won't say a word. You can count on that.'

'I can't tell you what a relief that is. As I told you before, it was none of my doing. The cursed man needs castrating. He's had his eyes on me for years but it's never gone that far before . . .'

'How long will I have to wait?'

'Sorry?' Sonia cocked her head like a bird. She was rustling, eager to be off now, as expansively as the coat that billowed where it touched the floor.

'Until she comes back? How long do I wait?'

'You are talking about Melanie?'

'Of course.'

'You poor thing! Here am I blabbing on about my own little problems and here are you half out of your mind with worry. Where is she, everyone is constantly asking themselves. The naughty girl . . .'

'She's a virgin, you know.'

Sonia was disconcerted. 'I'm sure she is, darling . . . but surely there's no relevance in that. She could be a raving nympho, it would be just as awful, wouldn't it?'

Janey bowed her head. 'I thought . . . I read that it was. I imagined that's why you wanted her . . .'

Sonia stood up quickly. Janey was clearly out

of her mind. 'Well, if you're sure I can't tempt you for lunch?'

Janey remained seated, so that Sonia made her own way to the door and opened it. 'Glad we had this chat. Will you be at the rehearsal on Friday?'

Janey looked bewildered, and shivered, suddenly frozen. 'What? Oh, yes, the rehearsal. Yes, I'll be at the rehearsal. And don't forget to tell them I won't say anything . . . they can rely on that . . . when I give my word . . .'

'Well, I'll close the door . . . don't want to let the cold in. Thanks for the coffee, Janey. I'll maybe pop in again tomorrow . . . see how you are. And if there's anything you want . . . anything at all . . . you know where I am.' She was talking, she realised afterwards, as the 'well' address the 'sick', with a sort of encouraging patronage. She was talking to Janey as she had talked to her father in *Moorview* just before the end . . .

Sonia tapped at the square with her high-heeled boots, rushing along like a frilly-necked lizard with spindly back legs and an absurdly straight back, to Marian's house. Hither and thither, hither and thither. You'd think she would be dizzy with it all, wouldn't you?

CHAPTER SIXTEEN

The horror, for me, as I continued my relentless enquiries, lay in the harrowing inevitability of it all.

Friday follows Friday follows Friday. And life goes on — as it must. Life, with all its urgency, all its banality, all its withering destruction. The true miracle, as wildly magnificent as any sunrise, lies in the fact that anyone gets up in the morning, let alone with vigour and energy as Grant did, as the vicar did — if only to fall straight down to his knees in praise again — as little Justin did, as Lloyd Law did, and as Janey Tandy always used to once upon a time. But maybe that's too cynical a view.

It is a pity Janey Tandy was estranged from her mother, Isobelle, for what she needed right then was a big, fat, comforting hug and a long, lingering looking after, which Isobelle, had they been in touch, would have been unable to give her anyway.

'But why is the WVS reluctant to lend us the urn? Surely they don't think anyone is likely to whip it?'

Grant, as great a lover of life as one is ever likely to meet, had smoothed troubled waters at least once already this evening. Now he leaned back in his chair looking tired. Let Jeffrey or Mrs Henley take the strain. The subject of costume had upset everyone. Chronology bored Mrs Henley so she took not the slightest notice of it. Everyone was in danger of being dressed in billowing Widow Twankie outfits, purloined on the cheap from the pantomime department at the technical college, everyone except for Janey who was to wear a hirsute Ancient Briton skin, appropriate, in Mrs Henley's eyes, to the weak-minded idiot she was to play.

'She's not supposed to be a hermit,' puffed the croaky-voiced Nancy Blogg through a veil of cigarette smoke. A stickler for detail, she had brought along some sketches of the sorts of outfits she had in mind for herself.

'No one will think she is a hermit. For one thing, she's a woman . . . and I've never heard of a female hermit although I suppose they must have existed. No . . . to make her appear to be timeless, she will not dress in rags . . . but skins speak for themselves. There's something very primitive and magical about skins.'

There was a short silence while this clue to the jigsaw puzzle of Mrs Henley's unusual mind was digested. Grant was supposed to be in charge. Mrs Henley was only the writer. Why wasn't he speaking out?

'The witch, Pessima, must surely wear black and go bent so she looks like a goddamn witch! It's not good trying to be subtle in Meadcombe.

No one will know what's happening if the characters aren't clearly dressed!' Sonia spoke up because she was afraid this was going to turn into a hideous modernistic effort with everyone wearing present-day clothes and no mystery about it at all.

'And what about you, Sonia? What do you think Phoebe ought to wear?' Grant, quite recently trained, did not like to impose his own views openly. He asked people first before manipulating them round to his way of thinking. It was a time-consuming but pleasanter process.

'Phoebe is the daughter of a Jacobean nobleman so she should wear early eighteenth century clothes . . .'

'From the pantomime department . . . just right!' Jeffrey seemed to be obsessed with the pantomime department.

'No,' argued Sonia. 'Too flamboyant. They must be sober clothes. They must illustrate her character. She is a serious, much-troubled woman. She takes to witchcraft in the end under the influence of Pessima. She is burned at the stake. Look . . . there is no room for clothing changes, and I am not going to be burned looking like someone out of *Cinderella*!'

'The boy, Nog, has his own clothes. He used them in *Oliver Twist* at school last year . . .'

Sonia sighed. Penny-pinching, small-minded, parochial, they couldn't see how important it was that the costumes should be just right. As long as they were 'oldfashioned' it was fine with Mrs

Henley . . . and Grant, who ought to know better.

Henry, Lord Grey, was going to look like a motheaten highwayman, particularly if they made him wear that pointed beard and the feathered hat that Mrs Henley was holding up with such proud aplomb. *'Humpty Dumpty,'* she squawked. 'Nineteen eighty-two. One of the king's men!'

'Well, we'll see what Pessima looks like in a moment. Marian has gone to try her things on in the back. If you feel you want something special, Sonia, you'd better get something together by next week and let us have a look at it.'

'I will do the same,' reiterated Mrs Blogg. 'Sally Law will make anybody's costumes for a small fee, she told me.' And so the costume argument was won.

'Lovely!' murmured Mrs Brierly occasionally. 'Lovely!'

Marian Law was sitting on a closed toilet seat in the unheated ladies' lavatory allowing her face to be made old by the village shopkeeper.

'It's better if it cracks,' Mrs Brierly said. 'It looks more effective.' As she concentrated on her task, her mouth moved this way and that, to the right and left, up and down, gruesome expressions of agony, terror and euphoria crossing her face in turn and meaning nothing.

Mrs Brierly smelt of BO and lily of the valley alternately, the smells coming as suddenly and profusely as her changing expressions. She loved this job. She was good at it. It was a skill she had discovered late in life, and as she said, 'I can't put make-up on my own face for toffee . . . look like a whore I do, if I try . . . but when it comes to making people look old or young or fierce or mad . . . well, I seem to have this flair. Pity it's just a once a year thing . . . pity I can't make money out of it . . .' She chatted on as she worked, only pausing when she pulled a face so terrible there was no room in her twisted mouth for words.

The make-up was cold. It came to her face on vast wads of cotton wool, clammily. The cistern, recently pulled, was dripping onto the cement floor behind her, making the atmosphere feel even chillier. Marian turned her eyes up when asked. 'Hold them there,' said Mrs Brierly. 'That's it, keep them open, just like that, hold it there . . .'

It was nice to be touched again, if a little roughly. It was something that Marian missed very much and couldn't get used to. Mrs Brierly was so confident, so skilled, it was easy to go into a trance-like state under her ministrations.

'Ugh!' said Mrs Brierly with immense satisfaction. 'You're going to look awful!'

It was hard to enjoy being made to look ugly when all your life had been spent trying to combat ugliness in one form or another. Marian would have preferred the part of Phoebe. But she suspected Grant had picked her for Pessima because of her large face, because of the scope available on such a wide canvas.

'I've ordered you your Christmas *Radio* and *TV Times*,' said Mrs Brierly happily. For some obscure reason these magazines had to be ordered from the village shop more than a month in advance. 'I didn't expect you to remember yourself.'

Marian Law didn't know what she'd have done these past months unless she'd been part of a village. People were kind . . . sympathetic . . . and when something really went wrong they formed a network of support, a bit like a fireman's jump net, so's not to let you fall. When people had known you all your life, and your parents and grandparents before you, it was no good pretending . . . you were as you were and they knew that and accepted you. Marian sometimes thought how difficult fitting in to this close-knit community must be for the newcomers . . . those who had arrived within the last thirty years. Sonia, for instance . . . and Janey. They were both outsiders even though their husbands were not. Marian was glad her children had grown up in the village. No matter what happened to them in life, or where they went, they could come back to Meadcombe and find people who knew who they really were. Roots — yes — roots were all-important.

Not that Sally or Lloyd showed any signs of going anywhere. Marian sighed. Mrs Brierly said, 'Sorry!'

'Oh, it wasn't you,' said Marian. 'I was just thinking.'

'Well, you know what thought did,' said Mrs

Brierly, conversationally, as she went to work on the wrinkles. It was to prove the understatement of the year.

Everybody knew about the liver, they'd been told about the outing in the dressing-gown, and they responded characteristically according to their own lights. Nancy Blogg, a forceful, earthy woman, applied the same motto to anyone remotely questionable, 'There but for the grace of God . . .' and came closer to Janey when she arrived and edged her way nervously through the door. She smiled more warmly.

Whereas Gerald Hope, a tight little man in computers, was genuinely worried by the rumours and sent scurrying glances towards poor Janey from the corners of his eyes.

It took a strength Janey didn't know she had to come to the Friday rehearsal.

Incredible, but it was possible to drag out from under the slime of despair if gripped by one of the two great levers, responsibility or revenge. Janey, having abandoned the first, had made a life raft of the second and grabbed it. Janey had made a special effort tonight. Having always considered herself a somewhat weak individual, she was surprised to find she had such power over her own debilitating misery.

Before setting out across the square into the cold November night she had soaked in a bathful of Body Shop bubbles which had been given to her last Christmas. She had washed her hair and blown it dry . . . not left it . . . so it was smooth in the parts she could get at, if a trifle rumpled at the back.

She looked a little better.

David, watching his wife's antics from his 'early night' position with the television perched on the chest of drawers, said acidly, 'This is a change, isn't it? A few days ago you were saying you didn't want to live! Now you're getting yourself up like a dog's dinner . . .'

'I do it because it makes me feel better,' she retorted, glaring at him through the mirror. 'I do it because I must go on. I'm not lucky like you, I can't just take that defeated attitude and give up. And I hope you're planning to get up to put the boys to bed.'

Silenced, he pummelled his pillows and Janey's too, and hauled the double bank of white higher up behind him. She watched him closely as she spread on her foundation . . . old, so the first blob from the tube had dried and came out in a crust on her cheek. David Tandy had not cracked, as he had signalled he was about to do. Strange, how he had rallied, in the absence of sympathy. She understood how, in the past, she had allowed him to indulge himself. She also understood that she had somehow needed it. She didn't need it now. This was no time for old and worn-out games. He was an evil man, he disgusted her.

After Sonia had left on Tuesday morning, having issued the warning, Janey had shuffled across

234

the room and gone to look at herself in the mirror. She had been appalled at what she saw. This old woman, this old, grey-faced woman that was her had given up as completely as if she knew that her daughter was dead and never coming back. But after Sonia's visit she knew better. Melanie would come back . . . eventually . . . if Janey behaved herself and kept quiet. She could either let herself go mad, accept the fact that she was beaten, or she could try and pull herself together and by doing so, defeat them somehow. One or the other. There were two roads and she had the choice of which one to take. She chose the road she saw as sanity. It looked long and difficult . . . but it was preferable to the other that seemed to drop off at the bottom into a kind of black limbo.

Janey could act. So she would act. As well as she knew how. Innocent no longer, she knew what was going on in the twilight village underworld, and that in itself was armour she hadn't had before.

Pale-faced, despite the make-up, she attempted to be natural and pleasant. Marian, who had been assaulted with innuendo brought to her door by Sonia, found it difficult to be pleasant back. But she tried to forget the things Janey was supposed to have said about her . . . after all, Janey was not herself if all she had heard was true. And Janey needed her more than she needed Janey.

Sonia smiled and pretended to be pleased to see them together. But she knew the pleasantries to be difficult and false, just as they did. They went through the motions . . . talked a great deal about old times . . . but underneath there was nothing there but anger. Janey's eyes were veiled, her fists tight at her sides. Marian was overly relaxed, too ready to laugh, nervous.

Marian, the only one to have her costume together was persuaded to try it on, and coaxed away to be made-up by Mrs Brierly. 'It'll be good for morale,' whispered Mrs Henley as they passed her. 'Give everyone a fillip to see someone looking dramatic after all the unwarranted criticism.'

'Where am I to find my skin?' Janey wandered over to Grant, trying to control the brainstorm that threatened to engulf her.

The paraffin heaters in the village hall were valiantly trying to fight against the cold. But as they succeeded, they put something of their own back into the soulless room, something that hadn't been there before . . . a limpish, yellowy heat that dried the mouth and tired the eye. But it was not that that was affecting her, Janey realised. It was something else, a cloying, sickliness of atmosphere that made her want to swallow, a cold beyond cold, a low-level, tinny, second-strata cold that affected not the outside of the body but the inside. It tasted of rusty nails.

All these horrible people . . . all these horrible people . . . and they had Melanie . . . somewhere . . . for what purpose she didn't know.

Mrs Henley pounced. 'The wolf,' she said

briskly. '*Little Red Riding Hood*, nineteen seventy-nine. We can adapt the wolf-skin, cut it down so that it fits like a toga, and it will do beautifully.'

'Am I supposed to be a savage?'

'No, you're supposed to be timeless.'

And Grant didn't try to explain because he didn't know how. He was in a state of despair. The thing was bound to go completely, totally and utterly wrong. He always felt this way as time inched mercilessly closer towards the day of production.

'Tarah!' Mrs Brierly opened her arms and emitted the feeble fanfare as she preceded Marian in from the back.

'Enter the witch!' With this introduction Mrs Brierly backed herself up and looked behind her.

Hunchbacked, with a tiny little head peering from a great black hood, Pessima the witch made her entrance.

'Magnificent!' Grant muttered to himself, and frowned. 'Extraordinary! Even the eyes are crusted!'

With the attention of the whole room upon her, Marian decided she had to do a lap. She knew she looked good. When Mrs Brierly had eventually held up the flyblown little hand mirror she carried in her make-up box, even Marian had shivered.

'My God! Is that really me?'

'Do you think I've got it right?' Mrs Brierly had asked, in the wheedling tones of one who knows she has excelled herself.

'Yes,' Marian, taken back, had replied, 'yes, you certainly have.'

Now she hissed as she went along, curling her hands towards her body, witch-like. *'Yes, you can come in,'* she quoted the lines that immediately came to mind. *'I will take care of you, child, until it's time to leave!'*

Passing Janey, and not wanting to exclude her over-sensitive friend, she stretched her neck and gave one of her special hisses, recoiling back under her clothes like a venomous rattlesnake.

Janey held her hand down hard on the surface of the paraffin heater. The hot tin seared her flesh but she did not move her hand. She let it burn until the two horrors met at a scalding peak and she knew she must pass out. At that point, she removed her hand and turned away from the spectre. Loathsome . . . evil . . . the embodiment of malevolence, and could no one else smell the stench that came from the black-garbed creature as she stalked the room? Excreta . . . and Marian wrapped in the browny-green skin of putrefaction. Automatically Janey lifted her hand to her chest in protection. The burn was livid, a raised scarlet weal from wrist to fingertip. But she felt no pain. The sensation was nothing compared with the realisation of what she knew.

They shouldn't play games like this . . . they shouldn't.

CHAPTER SEVENTEEN

We've all had our glimpses of Hell. I think we can all of us imagine, just a little bit, how it was.

Running.

Sniffing laughter.

Something that was animal hiding in the darkness.

Tapping branches on the window where there were no trees.

Whispers that reminded Janey of feline girls at school, ganging up together because she had stolen an extra bottle of milk and they were going to snitch to the teacher. The same sense of bewildered surprise . . . because she'd always thought they were her friends.

Janey had moved into Melanie's room, quite unable to bear David near her, but careful not to say so. Mustn't give the game away. Must keep sharp . . . one jump ahead . . . they didn't know how much she knew . . . they didn't know about Melanie's pictures.

'Cystitis,' she told him. 'I need to get up in the night. I need to be by myself.'

Lying awake, listening at night, her skin grew clammy like pastry from the fridge. She covered her feet with hot water bottles but it didn't

239

make any difference.

Sometimes she strained to listen and tried to make sense of the sounds. Sometimes she gave way to her fear and hid her head under the covers as she had done as a child. She would have liked to sit up and put on the light but she didn't dare move in case she made something happen.

Where was Melanie now, and what were they doing to her? She searched her head for what she knew of witchcraft, but it wasn't much, it wasn't enough to help her. She knew that Meadcombe had been rife with it a long time ago but she'd never really believed . . . just funny old women who liked to live alone . . . persecuted by fanatics and fearful men . . .

And all the time the fear, 'Is it me? Am I scaring myself? Is this what it's like to go mad?' And she'd try, once again, for sleep.

Sonia was frightened.

How do you speak about something that's wrong when you don't know what it is? Sonia tried when she went to visit Marian, using herself for illustration.

'When I look back at my childhood what I remember most is lots and lots of fear.' She didn't take her coat off. Sonia always preferred to keep her coat on in other people's houses.

Marian watched as a gold snake bracelet was slid urgently round her friend's slim wrist. Sonia was anxious this morning. There was something on her mind.

'Everyone has fear . . .' Marian poured the coffee and inspected it.

'No! Not like mine!' Sonia blinked nervously under long eyelashes. 'D'you know, I used to wake up in the night choking because of it. Maybe I was made nervous by the fact that we constantly seemed to lurch from one crisis to the next. There were the adult fears which I knew about and was supposed to join in but could not . . . the terror of the rent man, the awfulness of the electricity being cut off, the fears I paid lip service to . . . and then there were my own fears, the secret fears no one worried about but me. The dark, death, the big ones at school, teachers, arithmetic tests, dentists, not being chosen, not being liked, growing up and having to leave home some day. I even remember being afraid of not being able to pull my knickers up. So you can see how little I must have been . . .'

This was unlike Sonia. 'Everyone is frightened . . .'

'No! Not like me! And I'm still frightened, and my terrors are still my own . . .'

'Well, you never give that impression. Look how fearless you are in the play. You don't seem to get nerves like other people.'

Sonia frowned at the burning end of her cheroot. 'I don't show them, that's the difference. I'm frightened of losing things . . . losing Paul . . . losing money . . . losing the twins . . . losing face . . .'

'But we all are!'

241

'And I always thought I wasn't quite as good as anybody else, not as intelligent, not as pretty, not as sophisticated, not as able somehow.'

'But you know those things aren't true . . .'

'No, Marian. No, I don't know. I think it's different for you. You've lived in the same village all your life. You've never had to prove anything to anyone. You've always been surrounded by family and friends . . .'

'Friends? There aren't many people in Meadcombe who I'd call my friends.'

'Acquaintances, then. People who care what happens to you because you are part of their lives like the church is, like the Plague Stone, like the village shop . . . you're all part of it all. But I never feel that way. I feel alone. I feel frightened. And I can recognise that fear in others. And I know that Janey feels frightened of something at the moment. We ought to do something to help her. She's going dotty. She's frightened.'

'What of?'

'Of you. Of me. Of David, of everyone. Marian, why didn't you tell her you'd seen Melanie?'

Marian's face hardly registered surprise before composure made it merely interested again. 'Who told you?'

'Stanley. He had her in his car on the night she disappeared. He saw you watching from your window.'

'Yes,' Marian said. 'I know. And I didn't tell Janey because I didn't think it was important.'

Sonia sat back and stroked the smooth jersey

material that covered her knee, picking off invisible fluff. She'd said what she had come to say and had been given an answer . . . of sorts. She didn't like it. There was an inconsistency here. She didn't like the smell in Marian's house, either. She used to think it was a result of Constance's not too hygenic habits, but it couldn't be. A damp, Dettol-y sort of smell like the village hall, as if someone had tried to clear up a mess and not very well. Above it she could smell her own perfume. It was familiar and comforting.

Sonia said, 'I think this whole thing is pushing Janey over the edge.'

Sonia watched the face of her friend as she spoke. Marian's blue eyes were piercing, the same eyes as Lloyd's and Sally's and Roger's. Her hair was badly cut. She wore her ancient sheepskin boots. Sensible, care-worn Marian. Her friend. Janey's friend?

Marian's voice was unusually sharp as she contradicted. 'Janey is a very silly woman. She always has been and I'm afraid she always will be. This has nothing to do with fear. This is merely another of her attempts to attract attention to herself. In the past she's used David, now she's using Melanie's disappearance. Believe me, Janey can switch her behaviour on and off as simply as a bedside light. She can be extremely devious. I'm up to here with it really. I've had about enough of Janey and her ongoing problems, and you're a fool to be taken in by her latest performance.'

Sonia was nonplussed. Never before had Marian

spoken unkindly of Janey. Sonia was uncomfortably gratified by the bitterness there. She realised she hadn't needed to work so hard on the split between Marian and Janey. It had been wider than she thought long before she tried to drive her own wedge in. There was very little chance Janey would come gossiping to Marian now.

But Sonia suspected that Marian was wrong in her conclusions. Janey wasn't attention-seeking, not this time. It was fear. It had a sourness you could almost smell. And the look she'd seen in her eyes at the village hall last night, before she turned away and tried to hide it, was the same look Sonia had seen on her father's face at *Moorview*.

Sonia, having left her car at home on this fine but chilly morning, was walking home when the reason for her unease came to her. The leaves had finished falling, and the limbs of the trees stood out in fine outline against an incredible blue sky. She was walking along the road in air made rich with pungent smells as farmers spread manure over newly-harvested land. She had to pick her way as she went, where overladen muckspreaders had dumped a complicate crazy paving of clods of muck and straw and she didn't want to get her boots dirty.

The funeral had been held on a morning just like this. A November morning. How cold she had felt, standing there at the graveside with her mother and nobody else except for the vicar who'd had a cold. How chilly and uncomfortable the dark earth hole had looked. How she'd wished she hadn't said so glibly to Paul at breakfast that morning, 'No, don't bother, Paul. After all, you hardly knew him . . . not as he was before he went away. No, you're busy today at the gallery, don't bother to come. Mum'll understand.' There had never been any question of bringing the children back from school to attend. Her eyes had streamed, as they were starting to do now, against the smarting breeze, and her nose had started to run. She'd known it would be red at the tip. And when she'd stamped her feet the noise had echoed up hollowly with the mournful sound of a lone drum in her head.

She'd noticed her mother's hands, red raw without gloves. She'd thought her silly to have forgotten such an essential thing at a time like this.

She'd bent forward to whisper, 'Here, Mum, take my gloves. Your hands are frozen.'

Sonia's mother made no sign of having heard her, but just kept staring into the hole in the ground.

She hadn't spoken until it was over and they were making their way back through the tangle of old gravestones towards the waiting car. Then she'd turned to Sonia and said, 'He wasn't mad, you know.'

'I know he wasn't mad, Mum. That's a horrible word. Dad was just old and tired.'

'No, Sonia.' Her mother had been full of a

flustered urgency, desperately in need of making Sonia understand. Sonia gave all her attention, bending down so that her mother knew she was listening.

'No, Sonia. Dad was frightened. That was all.'

'Frightened? What of?'

'Dad was frightened of . . . oh . . . everything.' Her mother, made older than ever by the cheap chiffon headscarf and the coat with the black astrakhan collar that stank of mothballs, had searched the sky with watery eyes for meaning. Only the rooks had cawed back an answer. It seemed to suffice, however, for on a new wave of energy her mother had explained, 'He was old. He was tired. They said he was confused. But I know different. I know that he was frightened . . . and it was fear that made him the way he was.'

'But you haven't answered me, Mum. Frightened of what?' She tried to catch her mother's arm to steer her towards the car. The old lady seemed to have become rooted to a spot, high on the hilly graveyard, that caught every vicious streamer of wind.

'Frightened of getting old. Frightened of becoming a burden. Frightened of not being able to look after me. Frightened of being an embarrassment to you . . . oh, yes, Sonia, no need to look like that. He knew how important it was for you to rise in the world. And he was proud of you with your antiques and your house and your clever, well-spoken children. But it was all

246

part of what made him so frightened. But I knew, oh yes, I knew. Fear can do that to people, you know. It often happens . . . and they put it down to other things because they don't like to talk about fear. But basically that's what it is . . . it's fear.'

'But you could have told him that everything was all right. You could have reassured him . . . maybe helped him to overcome his fear . . .'

'How could I, Sonia? He was right! All his fears were quite justified.' And appearing content, having worked it out to her own satisfaction, Sonia's mother had left her windy spot and made quickly for the car, and home, and the inevitable cup of tea.

Fear. That was what most of it was all about, anyway. Fear of what strangers might be saying about you. Fear of making a fool of yourself in public. Fear of not meeting up to whatever requirements you had made of yourself, or that others had imposed upon you. Fear of madness. Fear of loss. Fear of death. And for Janey, fear of something else, too. But fear of what?

Sonia might have been able to prevent her father's intense fearfulness . . . by offering him a home . . . by taking over his responsibilities . . . by assuring him he was wanted and loved. Things her mother was too tired and played out to do. Sonia could have . . . if she'd bothered . . . if she'd recognised it for what it was. She should have recognised it — being such a cowardly kind herself. She recognised it in Janey. She seemed to be the only one to recognise it in Janey.

Sonia was not a wicked woman. There is no such thing. She was just totally selfish. As she walked along the road Sonia pondered. As she walked along the road her conscience, which had never troubled her unduly before, made her more and more uncomfortable. She had gone too far. That's what she'd done. If there was a God, if there was anything controlling events up there, was she perhaps being given a second chance? It was easy to believe in a greater being on such a morning . . . it was alight with glory . . . it was the kind of morning they wrote music and poems about . . . it was a morning that got through to even Sonia's soul on shafts of dusty white sunlight as she walked along the road to her house, tiptapped along the road taking care not to step into the dung.

Janey Tandy was in the process of retreating into a private world of her own, as Sonia's father had done. And she, Sonia Hanaford, by her self-centred manipulations and cruel schemings had probably made Janey's fears much, much worse. She had deliberately tried to take her friend, Marian, away from her. Although, from what she'd heard this morning, Marian was already fed up to the teeth with Janey. She had kept distant from Janey herself, afraid, until lately, that Stanley might have been involved in the disappearance of Melanie. And only this week she had gone round to Janey's house and, ignoring the woman's obvious distress, had insisted Janey keep quiet about that unfortunate incident between herself and Stanley.

Thought about like this, it was a sobering situation. She hadn't behaved much like a friend, had she? No one seemed to have been much of a friend to Janey at this time when she needed one most. And the woman was terrified of something, Sonia was sure of that. Somebody had to take notice . . . somebody had to take her in hand. Marian certainly wasn't going to. Perhaps she should talk to David about her? But he was such an appalling mess himself. What good would that do? Well, should she have a word with Jeffrey the vicar? Yes, that might be the best idea.

And on top of that, she would go round to Janey's house again tomorrow and insist that she come out to lunch.

Feeling much better about herself, Sonia opened her mock Georgian front door, took off her coat, and poured herself a Bristol Cream in a lemonade glass.

Cheers! But Sonia . . . life is not as simple as that. And, sadly, you are a good two months too late!

CHAPTER EIGHTEEN

I put the story together from fragments — preserved, crumbled or missing, like dinosaur bones, like ancient urns from pharaohs' tombs, like statues half-dissolved in desert dusts. We put them together again for posterity, using experience and imagination as glue to fill the gaps.

She made one last attempt. One last, wild bid to try and prevent herself from doing what she knew she had to do. It was a brave gesture, if a confused and a pathetic one. But it was a gesture just the same.

Bloody amateur dramatics! Stuart Hubbard-Granger, chief reporter on the *South Sarford Citizen*, cursed his misfortune at being lumbered with the Meadcombe job. He normally picked his diary events carefully so that he could get home early to Jilly and their newly-born infant, Charles. Jilly was scratchy these days, unable to cope with endless hours alone with her child, closeted away from any form of recognisable life in their open-plan new townhouse, where even the trees grew in an orderly fashion. She desperately needed him home. So he worried.

Nobody chose to go to Meadcombe because it was on the road to nowhere, a village between villages with long stretches of farmland in between. And he would be pressured into staying until the end of the evening if he wasn't careful, probably have to sit through the rehearsal trying to look interested, with the name of the play — the reason for his inconvenience — drawn at the end. But he couldn't get out of it. Everybody else was busy and Chris Earl, the editor, wanted the event covered.

'We can pick it up in the morning, Chris.' He had tried to get out of it for Jilly's sake.

Chris had shaken his head, so a pattern of languid cigarette smoke lay like low-lying mist pockets before his face. He was of the old school. It was time he retired. 'Local interest,' he said. 'Important to let them see we care . . .' and on and on he went. 'Never know when something big might happen in these little places . . . good to maintain contacts . . .'

Something big in Meadcombe? The man was off his head. Stuart thought of Jilly alone by the cot this evening, and anxiety gnawed and squeezed at his temples. He realised that he was frowning a lot these days. They didn't tell you the truth about babies . . . nobody did.

So on this dark December evening he left the office at six-thirty and went for a pub supper at the Garden House, a soulless red brick building next to the bookie's up an alley in the new town. He chose a pasty. The Garden House was renowned for the practice of warming and rewarming its pasties. Stuart hadn't heard about that. He only knew that it wasn't worth going home first. There would only be tears when it came to the time for leaving.

It was Christmas time on television — only twenty more shopping days to go. The Christmas jingle, couched in an oval surround of holly and red ribbon, heralded lists of epic films, glittering game shows, and carol services for the young, the sentimental and the ancient. Advertisements showed rosy-faced consumers stepping high. In fur boots and high collars they swung carrier bags full of goodies and laughed their way merrily through the bustling crowds. On the screen there was an atmosphere of desperate jollity which Janey watched slack-jawed.

But she could not get out. Nor could she contact anybody even if she'd felt it safe to do so. Christmas wasn't touching her. She didn't consider Daniel or Justin. It was an event that was happening to everyone else, not the Tandy family.

Whenever she went to try the phone it was with a weary resignation. She didn't even bother to ask David why there was no dialling tone. He would have told her, 'We've been cut off again . . . and if you bothered to concern yourself with the state of the family finances instead of moping around making yourself ill over Melanie you'd know why and not have to ask.'

Money! Money! And off he would go, tumbling down that old road again, a big fat snowball of irrelevancies. It would be a waste of time. Janey knew the reason why the phone didn't work.

Her short trip across the square to try the pay phone had also been a matter of going through the motions. At every step her legs had grown heavier, shaking until she felt they wouldn't hold her, and thunder rolled in her head. She had clung to the metal frame for support, fighting a fug of confusion. She had seen the neatly-cut cord through spiralling eyes, and struggled to remember why she had come.

'They' allowed her to visit the shop without hindrance. She could reach the village hall without being affected by dizziness or nausea, and that was twice the distance of the phone. 'They' were keeping her prisoner. A laboratory rat, she was punished by electrical impulses if she made a wrong move. And everywhere she went they were watching . . . she saw beady Meadcombe eyes wrapped in bland, Meadcombe faces, and she wondered if she were the only one not involved in the vile conspiracy.

By now she was not even certain that Melanie wasn't one of them — or Justin — or Daniel — because the boys were watching her hard, oh yes, all the time.

The police? Which one? How could she be certain? And if she made a mistake what would they do with her daughter?

'What did Sonia want?'

David's question was unexpected, for how had he known Sonia called again this morning? Who had told him and why? 'I don't know what she

253

wanted,' was the truthful answer. 'She just called round for a coffee.' It had always seemed to Janey that the women round here were worse than the men, as if, instead of sticking together and giving support to each other, their weakness and dependency made them small and withered inside, and the only reason they stuck together over anything was to stamp on one of their kind. Having someone to decry seemed to give them strength. At least the men didn't pretend to be anything more than drinking companions. She knew that Sonia only called to find things out so she could go back and report to whoever she'd been sent by.

'Melanie's all right,' was the standard response given by everyone she had ever talked to about her missing child. 'Melanie's all right . . . oh, yes, don't worry, I'm sure Melanie's all right.'

They all knew . . . they all knew where she was . . . and Sonia had repeated the same words in the same reassuring way this morning.

They'd got to talking about babies, which was rare, because Sonia didn't often speak of her children. It seemed it was out of sight out of mind with Sonia. The impeccable twins, Phineus and Flora, were mysteries to most of Meadcombe. Sonia never created a whole picture. All she ever talked about was their successes . . . their grades in music . . . school visits abroad . . . using these as a sort of landmark when others, closer to their children perhaps, used more personal illustrations, like measles or head lice.

Home for the holidays and they didn't mix with the local children. They seemed contained unto themselves, contented with their own company. They were not offish, or snobbish. It wasn't quite like that. They sailed through the village on identical bicycles sporting smart, black saddlebags, open and friendly, likeable, too. But they kept themselves to themselves.

'I'm looking forward to the holidays.' Sonia had even seemed a little embarrassed at her uncharacteristic confession. In fact she was merely over-eager to make amends. 'I have really missed them both this term. Perhaps it's because they've reached a good age . . . eleven is a good age, isn't it? They become more like reasonable people . . . you know . . . you can even have a sensible conversation, and they have ideas of their own all of a sudden. Yes, I miss them.'

But at least you know where they are, Janey wanted to scream. Can you imagine how I feel? But of course she couldn't say it because Sonia was just waiting for that sort of outburst. Perhaps that's why she raised the subject of children in the first place.

Sonia had waffled on while Janey had stood at the sink and scraped the carrots, knowing the importance of these little actions to her slipping sanity. 'I wanted them to be confirmed this year. But they weren't interested . . . and Paul was against it.'

'Oh?'

'I know I'm not a churchgoer, but one likes

these things to be done properly. One never knows when it might come in handy.'

Janey couldn't think of any circumstances when confirmation might come in handy unless you believed in it.

'Of course I always felt a little miffed that I couldn't be at the twins' christening. I don't like missing any of their big days . . .'

The knife Janey was holding slipped and nicked her finger. She drew in a quick breath and held the cut under the tap, feeling nothing. 'Why weren't you at the christening?'

'I was ill,' said Sonia vaguely, already thinking of something else. 'I think I had flu or a bug . . .'

Janey's three children had been christened without her being there, either. She stopped scraping and thought while she watched the water dilute her pinky blood and take it, almost before it had time to appear, off down the plughole.

Melanie had been christened at three months old. Janey had come down with a bad bout of mumps which had been rampaging through the village at the time. Everyone had said how good it was that Melanie hadn't been a boy because she might have caught it and it might have affected her badly. The arrangements for the ceremony had already been made. They couldn't put it off. So she had stayed in bed and not much minded.

The day before Daniel had been due to be christened, Melanie's temperature had risen to a hundred and six. All night Janey had been up trying to control it with Disprin and cold flannels.

It had dropped by morning, but David had insisted she stay at home with her. 'You don't need to come to the christening,' he'd said. 'Melanie needs you far more than Daniel does today.' So she had acquiesced, and, feeling very tired, had not much minded.

A year later, when Justin's christening had come along, she was the sort of person who didn't go to christenings, so when, at the last moment, she'd found herself with a violent sick headache, she hadn't made much effort to fight it. 'I'll stay here,' she told David.

'If you're sure.'

'I'm sure.' She had done up the pearly buttons of the christening robe, closed her eyes against a dull red pain, and the room had stopped its turning. Again, she hadn't much minded.

But now she minded. Now she minded a great deal. Now she thought of sacrifice, of innocent children being offered to the Devil.

But Sonia had moved on to the big Christmas Eve event. 'I have agreed to buy the cocoa,' she said, watching as Janey delved in a biscuit tin where she kept her bandaid. 'Well, we can afford it and it seems that funds can't run to a large tin and it would be a shame not to do it properly. They want to boil the water in a nearby house and roll the urn out into the square on its trolley when it's ready. Apparently it takes over an hour to boil.'

'They can plug it in here,' said Janey carefully, wrapping her white puckered skin in plaster.

257

'They can roll it in over the step and plug it in to the kettle point, look, it's very handy.'

Sonia was pleased to have Janey's cooperation. She was desperate, now, to retrieve something out of what she saw as her shockingly bad behaviour. Janey wouldn't tell anyone about Stanley. Janey probably didn't even remember. Janey was a mess . . . a real mess. And Sonia felt partly responsible. 'I'll bring the cocoa here then. We can mix it in at the last minute . . . just before midnight. People will be glad of it . . . they'll be frozen stiff by then.'

'Yes,' Janey mused. 'Yes, I suppose they will.'

Tonight was going to be a real event. Stuart Hubbard-Granger was here and the name of the play would be chosen.

Some people took it very seriously. Alan Faraday had been through his giant book of quotations and his compendium of poetry from beginning to end, to find a witty title. From his resulting maze of confusion the domed-headed bank manager, who was playing a King's man and dressed in an uncomfortable assortment of old armour, had surfaced with, *Of Oafs and Yokels*, and a second title which he suspected might be a better one but which he was not allowed to put in the hat — *The Chimney of Time*.

'What if the young man from the *Citizen* picks out something hopeless?' Mrs Blogg was concerned. 'I've always said it should have been done by a panel of judges. I mean, some of these people here haven't a clue about titles.'

Mrs Henley frowned at her, and tapped her leather briefcase reprovingly with the tips of her glasses. 'The truth of it is, Nancy, that it doesn't really matter what the play is called. But it gives everyone a feeling of being an equal part of the decision-making process.'

Mrs Blogg had always disliked Mrs Henley's rather laid-back political attitudes. At least she had managed to convince the writer to stop the village children from taking part. The results of that would have been too silly. She feared the results would be a bit silly anyway.

'This is our first proper dress rehearsal,' Grant was telling the reporter. 'It is the night everything is destined to go terribly wrong, I'm afraid. Patience will have to be our watchword.'

Stuart didn't think Grant looked patient at all. A tic had developed in one blue eye, and the lock of hair that was generally smoothed back, fell forward and bobbed about anxiously over his broad forehead. Stuart was concerned about Jilly.

'It wouldn't be possible, would it, to have the draw first, and do the rehearsal afterwards?' He looked at his watch. 'I am a bit pressed this evening.'

Grant looked more flustered. 'Well, we hadn't planned . . .'

'I wouldn't ask, but something has come up at home.' Stuart looked at his watch again, and then round the hall. It was a mess of confusion. People half in and half out of their costumes . . .

Mrs Brierly scurrying round adding the last touches to her make-up jobs . . . wigs askew on heads and half-empty coffee mugs in precarious places about to be kicked over. It would be a while before they could even get started. 'I'd be most grateful.'

It was hard for Grant to understand how anyone could bear to miss a performance of his play . . . even a dress rehearsal. But he saw that Stuart was serious, and clapped his hands for order. The pieces of paper were already in the hat. People had dropped in their choices as they came through the door. There was really no reason why the schedule shouldn't be changed.

'Right!' called Grant, over the hullabaloo. 'We're having the name draw now instead of later. Could you all be quiet please while I ask Stuart Hubbard-Granger from the *South Sarford Citizen* to take the stage.'

Those on the floor of the hall nearest the stage moved back to get a better view. Stuart fought with the curtains as he made his way along the front of the elevated platform. Grant handed him the hat from below. Stuart looked down at the waiting faces and gave his little boy grin.

'I am honoured,' he started, 'to be the one to pick the name of this most traditional village event . . . the annual Christmas play. I understand all the members of the cast have been invited to choose a title,' he delved into the grey top hat, 'and let's hope we come up with something everybody approves of!' Let's hope this is over quickly so that I can get home!

He juggled with top hat and paper before handing the former down to Grant who waited below with aching neck. Stuart Hubbard-Granger carefully unfolded the paper, trying to draw the moment out, for this is what he was here for. I couldn't live in a village, he thought to himself, as he held the result up to the light. I couldn't live in a close community like this. It would drive me mad in a week. The atmosphere in here was stifling, or was it something he'd eaten?

He frowned as he read the hard black print. He frowned and he looked down at the sea of faces. He cleared his throat and straightened his tie, and read it a second and third time. He gave a small laugh as he handed the paper down to Grant. 'I can't read that out!' he said in a low voice.

'Pick another,' said Grant uneasily. 'Someone is obviously playing a joke.'

The hat was handed up again, balanced on the flat of Grant's hand. Again Stuart picked a paper, having first poked the little bits about firmly with his finger. 'Right,' he smiled down at everyone. 'Here we go again.'

But it was the same message. For the first time his audience was silent. Something had gone wrong so the ceremony was worth watching.

'It's exactly the same.' Stuart, embarrassed, had to get on his knees at the front of the stage to communicate confidentially with Grant. 'They're all the same . . . look.' He opened another one, quite angrily, to prove it.

'Pretend . . .' said Grant quickly. 'Pull one out and use your commonsense. Any old title will do . . .'

'I can't think of a title! I don't even know what the bloody play's about!'

'*The Plague Stone* will do. Go on! Get it over with for Christ's sake!'

Stuart straightened up once again, forcing a smile. He picked out yet another small, tightly-wrapped piece of paper, and smoothed it before declaring clearly and slowly. '*The Plague Stone,*' he said. 'I hearby christen this play, *The Plague Stone.*'

There was a brief, bored flutter of applause. And the cast went back to their preparations. 'What a waste of time,' said Jeffrey fatly, red from previous exertion. 'We could have called it that from the start. You tend to forget what limited imaginations some people have . . .'

'You've got a raving lunatic in your midst,' said Stuart, relieved as he inched his fingers into tight leather gloves, ready for leaving, safely off the stage and out of the limelight.

'Someone tampered with the hat,' said Mrs Henley crossly. 'The possibility of that happening had never occurred to me.'

'It must have been children,' said Mrs Blogg.

'It doesn't look like a child's writing to me,' said the reporter.

'Children, or a practical joker.'

'Not a very funny joke though, is it?' said

262

Stuart, looking mildly round him.

'I'm sure it's the work of children,' Grant assured him as he escorted Stuart from the hall. 'Nothing to worry about. These things happen in a village . . .'

'Do they?' Stuart felt he was being hurried away, and he wasn't sorry. The sooner he got home, the better. He was uneasy. He had been uneasy all evening and now this . . .

'I hope someone from the *Citizen* will be able to cover the event itself,' Grant told Stuart as he ducked down into his driving seat. 'You normally send someone.'

'Christmas Eve is a difficult night, but of course we'll see what we can do . . .'

'And a photographer?'

Stuart started his engine, peculiarly delighted to hear it fire. 'If we can. I can't promise anything . . .' Exhaust smoke sat on the cold night like rounded, stubborn rain clouds.

'Naturally you won't write anything about this evening's unfortunate . . .'

'Of course I won't. It's hardly the sort of news the *Citizen* likes to cover.'

'No. Well.'

Feeling faintly nauseous, Stuart drove away, glad to be off. As he looked back at the village hall through his driving mirror, the lights from the windows put an eerie green effervescence into the chilly darkness and he shivered and turned on his heater.

Worried though he was about his wife, and

driving fast in order to get home, he could not get the messages out of his mind. They had been aimed at him. There was an urgency about them that certainly spoke of madness. Try as he might he could not get the picture of those words, written with such force and deliberation, out from before his eyes. They danced on the windscreen so that, foolishly, he wanted to turn on his wipers to erase them.

'THEY HAVE TAKEN MY CHILD FOR INITIATION TO THE SECT. LOOK AT THEIR EYES AND SEE THE EVIL THERE. THEY OFFER THEIR BABIES TO THE DEVIL. HELP ME PLEASE, AND GET AWAY FROM THIS SATANIC PLACE.' And Stuart knew that every single piece of paper said the same thing.

Extraordinarily, no one had thought it sinister. Stuart Hubbard-Granger wiped sweat from his forehead and realised that he had detected not an inch of concern on anybody's face. If he lived in Meadcombe he would be worried sick that one of his neighbours was going about writing things like that . . . because one of their number was clearly stark staring mad . . . unless . . . unless . . .

And he was so deep in his thoughts he didn't see the bend before he was on it. The tree was far too strong to budge . . . so it was the car that gave . . .

CHAPTER NINETEEN

Ah! To commit an act so heinous that the wind holds its breath and the waves are repulsed by the shore and roll their heads backwards in abhorrence. Infamy!

A civil act, not war. A crime against humanity by one single human being. To mark the pages of outrage so that for generations to come one name can cause a shudder.

Janey Tandy trembled on the brink of notoriety. She knew what she was going to do long before she did it. And how. And when. And why. She had to act, not just for Melanie's sake. They were killing people . . . that poor young man with a wife and baby at home . . . brain damage . . . and all because of her note.

'Melanie, God damn you!' Out between bared teeth came the high-pitched scream, the words tasting like old cobwebs in her mouth. 'Melanie, God damn you, why didn't you die?'

But Janey Tandy was a sensitive woman, oversensitive, some might say. Notoriety would kill her! She was the sort of woman who was embarrassed to see her name in the paper in lists of prize winners at the Sarford flower show. She was the sort of woman who, muttering a thank you through an open car window, slumped in pain if her gesture was not acknowledged, who withdrew her finger from her nose while driving in case strangers might see and despise her. Insensitive shopkeepers could ruin Janey Tandy's day with a sharp word or the abandonment of a platitude.

But that was the old Janey Tandy. The woman who sat on the floor of her daughter's room that December day was quite different. She was at the point where there were no consequences. They simply didn't exist. And that, for sure, is madness.

But what about the boys? She was still their mother. They still needed her, particularly in view of their totally incompetent, inept father, so wrapped in himself he hardly knew of their existence. It was too late for the boys. Unfair, because they have done nothing wrong. They had not asked for such gross withdrawal of mother love. Unfair! Unfair! But then life's unfair. Janey was afraid to love the boys lest they were taken, too. And David? Well, she blamed David for Melanie's disappearance, but could not tell him so. There's the rub . . .

When she thought what they might be doing to Melanie . . . even at this very moment! Jesus Christ . . . and I so wanted there always to be lambs in the fields for my children!

By now Janey saw it like this . . . On the night of the nineteenth of September, David Tandy had deliberately driven his daughter from the house. Knowing Melanie like Janey knew her, knowing her like David knew her, it was obvious she would fling herself out of the door if driven in a corner like that.

He had forced her out . . . for a purpose, and Janey, like a weak-minded fool, had helped him.

Someone had been waiting in the square, lurking, skulking, hiding out there in the darkness.

Janey couldn't bear to be around her husband. He was evil. They were all evil . . . but after her warning note to the *Citizen* reporter which had caused such calamitous results, there was nothing more she could do, no one else she could tell. She saw no one, and could go nowhere. She felt sick and ill and tired all the time. It was as if 'they' were draining her, daily of her energy, sucking it from her like blood from a sacrifice. She had no spirit. She was exhausted. She peered out at life through red-rimmed eyes. She wanted Melanie back. She grew terribly afraid.

Through the gloom of her exhaustion, however, one bright light stayed shining . . . revenge. It took everything she had, but she managed to concentrate on this one piercing spark of hope that she stoked and poked until it roared from a dull red ember into a white-hot, searing flame. 'They' would not get away with it. Whatever happened Janey would make sure of that.

For if David had driven his daughter out that night, one of two things was possible. Either he had offered the baby to the Devil at the time of her christening, and her time for confirmation had come. Confirmation, initiation . . . The other possibility was that Melanie, out and about in the dark like she was, knew something she shouldn't know, and had to be silenced.

Janey's mind, in constant turmoil now, turned again to the pictures.

That her daughter had been talking to Stanley did not surprise Janey. That he was involved up to the hilt was a foregone conclusion. The pictures said so . . . and she believed everything the pictures said. Well, it wasn't for long. She would soon put a stop to their satanic games . . .

She looked nervously out of her window and only saw the Plague Stone looming, stern and forbidding, lording it over the mortals who scuttled by. She saw Sonia strutting across the square in the direction of the Rectory. Sonia wasn't in Melanie's pictures. But that didn't mean she was not one of them. She was a newcomer to Meadcombe, like herself, and Janey realised that only children born in the village were involved with the coven. Sonia was working for them from the outside. You could see it in her face . . . and why else would she fraternise with such as Stanley?

To stop the witches taking your child you had to scream its name . . . out there . . . in front of them all, with your back touching the Stone. Well, she would do that, but at the right time. Janey Tandy had her plans, and she was going to stick to them now and carry them out to the

268

end. She had nothing else left.

Sonia was on her way to see the vicar for poor Janey's sake.

On the road to the Rectory, Sonia pictured Marian watching the square from Constance's room in the early hours of the morning while behind her, in the same room, the old woman was dying . . . or already dead?

Marian said she'd seen Melanie talking to Stanley. But she'd only admitted that after Stanley had said he'd seen her. Up until then she'd kept the fact mysteriously quiet. Why hadn't Marian spoken about that at once as soon as she knew the child was missing? Why the secrecy? Could it possibly be that Marian had something to do with her mother-in-law's death? Surely not! Not Marian!

No. It couldn't be that.

Sonia strode out purposefully. Sometimes she took her car to the village, sometimes not. It all depended on the weather. Today it was cold but sunny, and clouds that hinted rain were broken, high overhead.

There was much going on at the moment that Sonia didn't know about. She didn't like it. She needed to know what was happening within her immediate environment so that she could manipulate. Marian was getting colder and colder, Janey was going madder and madder . . . and nobody, as far as Sonia could see, was taking any damn notice!

The poor soul had nearly passed out at the rehearsal when Marian had dressed as a witch and gone round the hall spitting venom. Sonia had watched her from across the room . . . Janey had been forced to hold herself up on the heater, had burned her hand, and after that she had run out, to the toilet probably, to be sick. Before Sonia's eyes Janey had changed colours violently, until she'd ended up a sickly sort of beige . . . Marian had certainly looked convincing as a witch, but not as frightening as that!

And that business with the choosing of a name for the play. Something funny had gone on there, but when she asked Marian, Marian had virtually told her to mind her own business and turned back to her discussions with Jeffrey and Mrs Henley. Sonia, considering herself to be a cornerstone of village life and certainly of the drama group, didn't like to be excluded in this way . . . not at all.

And that dreadful accident on the road when that poor young man from the *Citizen* had been concussed and was still, as far as she knew, in intensive care with damage to his head . . .

Without being aware of it, Sonia had stopped to sit down on a roadside seat dedicated to the people of Meadcombe by someone called Ron Blake. She was feeling sick and shaky. Everything seemed to tie in with the disappearance of Melanie . . . it was on that night that she had met Stanley . . . on the night Constance had died . . . and only a short time later Janey had started behaving in this unnerving manner. Thoughts of Devil worship would never have entered Sonia's head . . . she was too straightforward for that. She scorned anything even vaguely supernatural — straight religion was too strong for Sonia. No . . . that didn't enter her mind . . . but scheming and scandal did, and something was going on.

Oh, Ron Blake, whoever you are, what is it? Sonia couldn't bear to do nothing, which is why she had made this appointment with the vicar.

'I'll pop round to see her — no, don't worry. I won't say you called. I'll ask her for help with the church flowers. I'll suggest she attends my wife's coffee morning. She won't know you've been to see me, or what you've said. Trust me.'

Sonia kept her coat on. She was always uneasy in the environs of the church. Nowhere round here was ever quite warm enough. Even on a hot day the sun, high behind the spire, was blocked from the porch which was as far as Sonia ever normally got . . . to peer at weddings or read notices.

'I don't want you to think I'm interfering . . .' She was looking particularly fresh this morning in a cherry red Jaeger coat with matching boots and gloves. Her cheeks burned from the cold, her wide eyes bright and interested.

'No, I certainly don't think that. It was good of you to come and see me. That's what I'm here for, to help in times of trouble.'

'Or that I'm over-reacting . . .'

The vicar, drab in his hand-knitted sleeveless jersey before this coutured lady, clasped his pudgy hands and leaned them on the desk before him. 'I think, if anything, you've under-reacted, Mrs Hanaford. Mrs Tandy is clearly deeply disturbed.'

'It makes it all the more difficult because of David. He's not the most dependable of men.'

The vicar was not prepared to discuss a member of his flock with one who so blatantly was not. The Tandys did, occasionally, attend church, for the sake of the children. The Hanafords did not. And in Meadcombe it was a well-known fact that the villagers liked to help each other. This they strived to do before calling for outside help. Jeffrey didn't recognise it, but deep inside he resented interference from outsiders. He should have realised Janey's need. He should have gone round earlier, under the circumstances. But everyone knew Melanie. Everyone knew that the naughty girl would, eventually, come back.

He now knew who had sabotaged the draw for the name of the play. He was, understandably, worried. And now he thought about it, he had not seen Janey out and about as much recently. Although she rarely missed a rehearsal . . .

'Marian was always such a pillar of strength to her,' Sonia was saying. 'But now she's fed up. She's withdrawn her friendship, and I think that has made the situation far worse.'

Jeffrey nodded his fat head and smiled benignly. 'These things happen in village communities,' he said, talking to her like a presenter from *Play*

School. 'We all have our ups and downs, our ins and outs, and Mrs Law has been having her own problems lately.' He didn't add what else he knew . . . that dear Mrs Tandy could be a pain in the arse if given her head . . . that it was sometimes necessary, for one's own sanity, to close the door, with caution, and forget about charity. He sighed.

Sonia didn't like Jeffrey, and Jeffrey knew it. She considered him weak and waffly . . . an attitude she despised in men, even vicars. She had not heard him preach from his pulpit, had missed his transformations there, when, every Sunday he shed his lambskin and emerged as a lion. She only saw him dithering about in the drama group, a situation and an activity with which he was not easy. His skin was smooth like a baby's. His cheeks reminded her of a freshly-lotioned baby's bottom, his little mouth suggestive of a different orifice, and she disliked him.

But her duty was done. She had, in this small way, absolved herself of her scheming behaviour. What happened now was no longer her fault. She had been to Confession although she had not confessed. She had purged her soul.

Her step was lighter as she left the Rectory where leaves lingered longer and made carpets down the path. The little iron gate was a church gate. The smell of the garden was a church smell, old, decayed, prayer-booky. Rooks rose and cackled when she clanked the iron latch. She wouldn't like to live here . . . so close to the graveyard. But Sonia was not a superstitious person.

Janey Tandy watched her progress through curtains tied back with red bows. One of Melanie's little touches. She always liked her room to look nice. It was not cold and prickly like its owner. It was soft and girly, made so by these little additions. Now old coffee rings of Janey's stained the neat surfaces. Papers littered the bed and the floor. Books were scattered, disorganised, and a wine glass sprouted white mould from a liquid, purple surface.

Next door's cat was on the prowl again. It lived there, between her house and Marian's, with the old couple who had moved in comparatively recently, having first used the house as a holiday cottage before retiring and moving permanently in. They hadn't brought the cat with them. It had adopted them and they had accepted it. No one knew where it had come from. No one bothered to ask. Prior to this, the animal had tried to attach itself to the Tandy household. Janey had kicked it out, over Melanie's loud protestations. 'Why can't we have a pet like everyone else has? Why can't we be normal for a change? There's nothing wrong with having a cat. They're not demanding! They don't need taking for walks! Why can't we keep it? Why?'

Janey had responded automatically, 'Your father wouldn't like it. You know he doesn't approve of household pets.'

Melanie had flung herself upstairs to sulk. And the couple next door had taken it in.

Janey watched the creature avidly as it approached Sonia, its back arched, its tail high, its head waving, snake-like as it reached the woman in red. It caught her as she turned her back, trying to fix the vicar's gate catch. It nearly tripped her, circling her legs.

Sonia looked round in a way that suggested she felt she was being watched. Convinced that she was, she didn't kick the cat away, but bent and stroked it so that it purred and circled again, hoping for some titbit. But Sonia didn't have time for this sort of nonsense. She straightened up, stared at the windows in the square, and, gently dislodging the cat, strode across to the shop where she was to order her weekly groceries for later delivery, and you can't get that sort of service in many places these days.

She would play her part. Would continue to humour Janey and encourage her to help with the cocoa on Christmas Eve. What the woman needed was to be kept busy. Everyone knows that idle minds make mischief. Well, Sonia would do her damnedest to make sure Janey didn't remain idle. She could do no more than that, could she?

The vicar made his move that very afternoon, stung into action by what he perceived as veiled criticism from Sonia.

Sensibly and forcefully he persuaded the con-

fused Mrs Tandy to accompany him to the Bloggs'
tea party, proceeds in aid of the pew replacement
fund.

This, she knew, was Sonia's doing. Janey didn't
believe for a minute that she would get to the
tea party. She sat, poker-faced, in Jeffrey's car,
waiting for it to turn off the road into some dark
dell, waiting for him to tell her what was going
on. Neither of these things happened. He chugged
along, chatting about this and that, watching her,
she realised, through the off-side wing mirror.
She smiled a little wanly. She knew what this
man looked like with nothing on. Melanie had
shown her.

But she was prepared to go with him in case
he took her to Melanie. She offered no resistance
to his suggestion for the outing, but meekly went
upstairs to fetch her coat and throw water on
her crumpled face as though under orders. When
she came down she looked no better, and Jeffrey
realised there was something badly wrong.

He had already spoken with Nancy Blogg on
the telephone, so the hostess was warned before
their arrival.

Mrs Blogg had always reckoned, and declared
quite openly, that she lived on the edge of insanity
herself. But in this she was wrong. Her rather
safe eccentricity, her fervent likes and dislikes,
were very different to Janey's state of mind. She
smoked like a train and drank like a fish, but
she functioned very efficiently, she adored her
husband and children, and was one of the sanest

people in Meadcombe. Though, if anyone had told her so, she would have felt insulted. So her warmth, her good intentions, which she wrapped round poor Janey that afternoon, were frankly to no avail. She was not a kindred spirit. But it was kind of her to bother.

They were all there waiting for her, as Janey had known they would be . . . all smiling . . . sitting round the room nodding like dachshunds in the back windows of cars . . . so she nodded back and sat where Nancy Blogg showed her she should, next to the hostess, in front of the wallpaper tables covered with the sale of work. But no Melanie. Not even a mention of Melanie.

Janey was not an easy guest. Her attention seemed to slip, not sometimes, all the time, and her eyes darted about as if she was afraid of missing something. What with her unkempt wiry hair and her haggard, pinched features, Nancy Blogg decided the woman must be ill, and promised herself to see about it, soon.

Janey slipped away to visit the 'john' as Nancy Blogg still called it. She had no intention of going there, but marched through the back door and out into the farm office, a functional little room made warm with a two-bar electric fire in one of the old-fashioned shippens which had not yet been converted.

The office was not locked. Janey hadn't expected that it would be. She had been here before, most of the villagers had, to buy eggs or ask for favours from the farmer . . . the loan of a link box, the cutting of a hedge. In an old bath-room cupboard on the wall above the table, a cupboard covered in faded information about sheep scab, warble fly and lugworm, she found what she wanted. She brought out the small, brown bottle with warnings on the label and dropped it into her handbag before returning to the tea party in the drawing room. But first she'd stopped in the 'john' to get it out and marvel — that one small bottle could kill a hundred people. Phostrin . . . agricultural pesticide . . . it had all been so easy . . . as she'd known it would be.

But this was only a back-up to her plan, oc-curring to her just a moment ago. She had the paste already . . . mashed up under Melanie's bed in a kilner jar which once held pickled onions, with a firm screw top . . . waiting for Christmas Eve. *Hubble, bubble toil and trouble* . . . Amargil, Thorazine, Largactil, Megaphen, Lithium and the contents of many, many more little bottles, some with their labels erased or torn off over the num-ber of years they have been hoarded and stored by David Tandy, in a box by his bedside table.

Janey had filled them all with Smarties and re-placed them in careful order. He only liked to *have* them. He never, ever looked *inside*. Well, why would he?

CHAPTER TWENTY

Janey used a wooden spoon to stir the whitish-grey paste in with the Cash and Carry cocoa powder. The Phostrin liquid turned it a good, healthy brown again.

'The boys deserve a Christmas,' David felt compelled to say, at last, though by doing so he recognised he lost some credibility. He was not supposed to notice Christmas, let alone its coming.

'You have done nothing, made no preparations, no plans.' He must have gone searching in Janey's stand-up larder, looked under the bed where she normally hid the presents prior to wrapping.

Poor David. A victim of his neurosis, he could observe but was impotent to act. He was too old, too miserable to suddenly have to take up such challenges. He sadly pondered why his wife had abandoned him. And yesterday he had had to iron a shirt . . . the day before had saved a casserole from burning. And where was Janey while all this was going on? Sitting, living, sleeping by herself in Melanie's room, behaving just like a sulky teenager herself.

No lightweight, the Kays catalogue landed on David's knee and nearly winded him. 'There's the catalogue! Order! Or maybe there's no money for a Christmas this year.'

'I don't know what the boys want.'

'Ask them!' Janey knew it didn't matter anyway.

In a fair world, by now David ought to have been well on the way to achieving the breakdown he'd never had. And although nervous breakdowns are not to be recommended, in some ways the experience would have been kinder. He would not have to cope with the chaos in his house, the rampagings of his wife and the responsibility of his children. But it was not to be. When he held out his hands they were steady as rocks. When he pulled down his eyes before the bathroom mirror while shaving, searching hopefully for pink and stringy signs of strain, they looked back at him steadily as if they had never been so true.

'And then there's your mother. I can't choose for her.'

'Well, leave her then.'

'We can't. She always gives us something.' Yes, sweaters in dull, unimaginative colours that looked as if they had been knitted with a curse worked into every stitch. Melanie was the only one who'd ever seemed to like them. This role reversal with his wife undermined him. They were sitting there, playing each other's parts. It didn't feel right at all. 'Are we going to ask her round for Christmas Day?' He was relieved that his own parents were dead so he didn't have to juggle with them, as well. He didn't like Janey's mother. Well, she was a hard woman to like. She had the brutalised face of one who had spent a lifetime drinking too much, smoking too much, resenting too much. She was bored and bitter. Hardly the sort of company associated with a joyous Christmas Day. But she was Janey's mother, and shouldn't be left wandering, lonely, between the perspex doors of her miserable new town home at Christmas time. And he couldn't stand the thought of spending Christmas alone with Janey in this frame of mind.

She left him, and he ordered from the catalogue, obediently, having to think hard and long about the likes and dislikes of his remaining children. He was a maths teacher, so he had no trouble at all with the adding up of the total and the working out of the postage and packing. And where did Janey keep the decoration box? And where should he go for the tree?

The children, bless them, closed in around Marian Law in the run-up to Christmas.

'We will do everything,' said Sally, her large, unusual face rucked with reassurance while Lloyd stood beside her nodding. 'We don't want you to worry about a thing. We're going to make it nice, and we don't mind if you don't enjoy it, do we, Lloyd?'

Lloyd, too tall for the small room really, nodded again and cleared his throat. A true son of his father, with large, flat working hands, he found these confrontations hard, preferring to speak through action, a hundred little kindnesses that he wasn't sure his mother even noticed. The wood was always chopped and neatly stacked, the garden, though not beautiful, was clear of leaves, the car was serviced regularly and its tyres and oil checked . . . all jobs his father used to do, he knew, jobs he suspected his mother could not cope with.

Marian found it hard to respond to their festive efforts. She was numb. She just couldn't imagine Christmas without Roger. Did they, were they really expecting her to take part in this farce now he'd gone? Yes, they were, and amazingly, they were doing it for her sake! How could she tell them she'd rather be left alone to weep upstairs by herself . . . to rake through her memories, torturous though they were. But that awful self-indulgence was not allowed at Christmas. How could it be? It would be like allowing a madwoman to deliberately tear out her hair or pluck out her eyes. But really, that is what Marian would have liked to have done. All alone, with no one watching.

'I might be a bit of a damp squib,' was merely all she said.

'We know! We understand!' Sally rushed in, comforting. But did they? She fervently hoped they did not. For if they did how could they continue, in all reasonableness, with their own little love affairs that would sprout over the years into the massive, oaken, powerful yet gentle love her own had been, only to have someone come with a chainsaw and cut off its beautiful head. Oh! Roger!

At least she wouldn't have Constance to cope with. That should have brought relief. But strangely it didn't. Constance had been a powerful force, in her own way, during her short stay at *Dunoon*. A kind of pivot around which they could all revolve, however reluctantly. Now there didn't seem to be a pivot . . . not for Marian, anyway.

And she missed Janey, even with her trail of trials and tribulations. For they, too, had been a diversion . . . my God . . . she had been feeding off other people's misery, shamelessly, like a leech sucking infected blood from its victim. Better she leave their friendship dead, better than sucking from Janey. She had Sonia. But Sonia was a treacherous friend with many faces. And whenever she left, Marian felt she'd been forced into being unpleasantly conspiratorial. No, she could do without Sonia. There was nothing satisfactory about Sonia.

No. She joined Lloyd and Sally, and Harry Blogg and Donna, twisting the streamers and sticking bits of holly into the dusty little spaces between the pictures and the wall. No. She sipped her sherry and nodded acquiescence as Lloyd held up the Jim Reeves Christmas LP. 'Yes, put it on. We always do when we decorate.'

Numb. Numb. If she tried very hard she could put herself into neutral and feel nothing. After all, no one was causing her pain. She wasn't being stretched on some medieval rack. It was she who allowed the thoughts to come in, determined the coming and the going thereof. But there were so many ignition keys . . . wherever she looked great bunches of shiny, traitorous ignition keys, waiting to start up the engine and send her roaring, top gear, into purgatory again.

Sonia and Stanley. Whatever it had been, it was over. And now they avoided each other in shame and embarrassment, unable to understand what had set them off in the first place.

Mortified, Sonia ceased to be so critical of Paul's appalling father, and of his mother, too. This helped the atmosphere at the Manor, and the twins were home, and everything was getting back to normal again. Stanley and Beryl had even been invited to come and watch the Christmas Eve play.

Peculiarly childlike and keen to make amends, Sonia bustled around Janey, while paying her visits to Marian, taking news from one to the other, though less vindictively.

Sonia loved Christmas . . . the freezer was full of goodies. And then there was the play . . . and she the star . . . and Paul had bought her, she knew because she had looked, an enormous antique doll's house, something she had craved for ages and yet not felt able to buy, that she would take years to fill. She might even let Flora help her make the little curtains. It was hidden in the garage under a blanket . . .

Their evenings were taken up with dinner parties, supper parties, theatre visits. She loved to dress up in furs and jewels, and Paul, of course, always looked his best in a dinner jacket. But no matter how she tried, no matter how long she perused the Clinique counter, she could not get that hard look off her face. No matter.

The Manor leant itself marvellously well to Christmas. The huge tree sparkled in the hall, the log fires, unnecessary because of the central heating but essential all the same, burnt merrily in their antique grates, the sound of children's voices playing nicely came from upstairs. Oscar wore tinsel in his collar. And really, for Sonia, all was well with the world. She felt she was further away from Sonia Doris Burridge than she'd ever managed to get before . . . a real lady of the Manor . . .

Christmas Eve, and in spite of Grant's forebodings, the play got off to a good start.

It had rained all day — a grey, cold sleety sort of rain that chilled even if watched through a window. But by evening the sky, though overcast, had stopped dripping, and the forecast said it would keep dry. But tomorrow, Christmas Day, it would rain again. How depressing! And David had chosen sledges for Justin and Daniel's main presents. Typical, he thought to himself . . . and it was possible to wonder if David hadn't chosen sledges, perhaps it might have snowed.

The WVS urn had been wheeled, early on, into Janey's kitchen, and there it groaned and moaned and boiled and bubbled, taking, David thought woefully, more electricity than was necessary for efficient performance.

Sonia was gratified to see that her ministrations had been effective, for Janey had got herself together enough to mix the cocoa powder and share it out between the five huge enamel jugs into which the boiling water would be poured when it was time. She had laid out the biscuits on paper plates, too, and in every way was behaving as quite the little hostess.

Out of a village of four hundred souls, surely there were well over two hundred gathered in the square this evening, watching.

'They won't all want cocoa,' Mrs Henley had pointed out when they were discussing the amount to be used.

'Why not?' Janey had asked.

'Well, they won't all like it.'

'Well, we could manage coffee and tea . . .'

'We won't have time to mess about,' said Mrs Henley sharply, for by this time she was becoming nervous, fiddling with her spectacles chain. 'We'll only have five minutes or so before we're due in the church. The service has to start at midnight.' She poked about with a spoon in the paste, in danger of marking her rather good sheepskin coat.

'A bit lumpy?'

'It's always like that,' said Sonia, down her nose. 'It's cheap cocoa . . . not the proper kind.'

'From witches and wizards, and long-tailed buzzards, and creeping things that run along hedge

bottoms, good Lord deliver us!' Janey's voice was reedy in the harsh, night air. She must be cold in that threadbare skin. She had a headache, and her scalp was itching. She can't be too bad if she can act like that, thought Sonia, as Janey remembered her lines and came in at the right time and put the timeless tone that Grant wanted into her voice.

The villagers were supposed to line the square, but, of course, they hadn't. They were huddled up at one end, the end nearest the houses, as if by keeping their backs to something familiar they were somehow less exposed to ridicule. But they were only the watchers . . . not the actors . . . so they shouldn't have been afraid of ridicule.

'I never told anyone this before, but I always yearned to kill my father.'

The costumes, after all the trauma associated with their choosing, were fine. The real problem was the sound system. It was hard for the audience to hear the words clearly . . . but it didn't really matter, it was mostly action, and atmosphere, and there was plenty of that.

No one played the Stone. It played itself. John, on lighting, had imaginatively placed a blue bulb behind it, so that what it gave out was an aura rather than an actual presence. The effect was spine-tingling.

It was quite a spectacle. The actors came on and off the set by way of lighting. Spotlights set up on the flat roof of the village shop depicted a speaker or a group of speakers while blanking out the rest. Perversely, something about the way the lights had been positioned illuminated, quite grotesquely, the unfortunate word *SPAR*, so that everybody thought, until the play was over, that this was something to do with the story-line, and kept glancing up at it.

The Plague Stone. It was the sort of play which made it difficult to know when to clap. On top of that, with gloved hands, it was hard to make the sort of noise that counted, so the actors played to sporadic, fragmented applause, which was, at times, a touch disconcerting. But they rose to the occasion, and Grant could relax. Even the children behaved themselves.

Secretly Mrs Henley congratulated herself on having had the foresight to include a brief synopsis of the story in the front of the programme. The audience couldn't hear the words, but at least they had some idea of what was supposed to be going on. She felt a weight lift from her shoulders as the play moved on. Another year . . . another play nearly over . . . she wished they would choose something out of a book, an acknowledged, recognised play. She knew the subject was discussed annually, but the village invariably voted for one of hers. While she'd found this vote of confidence flattering at first, now it was merely irritating. Well, she couldn't really enjoy the process, could she, with her reputation riding on it? And she would have liked to take part as an ordinary member of the cast. But she couldn't say anything. She didn't want to let them down.

How nice it was, thought Nancy Blogg, to see Marian's children rally round her as they did. They were there in the audience, trying to take the place of Roger, supported by Donna and her own son, Harry . . . and they talk about youth of today . . . A shiver of pride mixed with compassion moved through her, bringing brief tears to her eyes. Marian made a marvellous witch. Mrs Brierly had lived up to her reputation tonight.

A clever revolving action with lights under scarlet paper made it seem that the bonfire was alight. Sonia, tied to the stake, was in her element — screaming and moaning and disgracefully overacting as John, on lights, sent a smoky gauze around her. A grander finale could not have been wished for. The frozen villagers stamped and cheered, sensing that this was the end. There was much flinging of scarves and pulling down of bobble hats. The smaller children were led away. The anti-Christians crept away, not wanting to attend the service. Gratefully, David, watching from the house with one eye on the meter, unplugged the urn and wheeled it on its trolley out into the square.

She watched as they queued, automatically circling their paper cups with cold hands as they gratefully received their cocoa . . .

'Mm . . . this is nice . . .'

'Just right . . .'

'Keep the cold out . . .'

'Wasn't it good?'

'Best yet . . .'

'Isn't it cold?'

'Isn't it dark?'

'Please throw your empty cups into the bin provided.'

She watched as the empty bin, splayed at the top like a wired imitation of a lily flower, turned white from the bottom with discarded cartons that threatened to spill over. She watched as the Devil's children chatted and waited, watching for the church lights to go on. She watched as the light from the stained glass windows patterned the gravel they stood on, patterns that looked like snowflakes on the ground. The square turned into a Christmas card.

Her head ached and her legs itched and she walked directly to the Plague Stone. She stepped up so that her body was pressed against it. Miraculously, the itching stopped, her head cleared, and she was alert and calm as she hadn't been since Melanie disappeared.

Only a few people watched her. It took time to manoeuvre into the correct position . . . the position she knew she had to adopt. She stood like a martyr with her back to the Stone, her arms behind her and wrapped round it so that she felt every nub and crevice, cold against her skin. It seemed to fit her . . . never had Janey felt more right and comfortable. And then she began to moan.

What was this? Was the play not over? Was this some clever act tacked on the end to take them unawares? They stamped their feet and turned to watch, warmed and comforted by the cocoa.

'Oh God, oh God,' moaned Janey, her voice rising from something slight that stirred the breeze, into a piercing scream that rode it.

'Oh God, oh God, oh God. In the name of God, in the name of all that is Holy, give me back my daughter!' And then she screamed her name, *'Melanie! Melanie!'* while throwing her head violently from side to side.

No one liked to approach her, this savage woman in the hairy skin. The truth was slow to dawn. No, this was nothing to do with the play. This was the wretched Janey Tandy who had clearly lost her mind. What should we do? Who is responsible? And on Christmas Eve . . . how sad.

It was only because everybody was looking at him that David Tandy acted. He acted by edging his way across the square towards his shrieking wife. With his arms pathetically out before him, a blind man, he tried to touch her.

'Get thee behind me, Satan,' she spat, and there was no recognition in her eyes. He stepped back, burnt, embarrassed. Jeffrey, a paunchy Gabriel, stood at the church door, having opened it wide to accommodate his flock. He whispered to his wife.

'I think we should call an ambulance.'

His wife, as always, scurried away to obey.

But nobody else moved. They stood, as they

had done before, enthralled by the performance. The Plague Stone, all in blue, stood out with a menacing incandescence . . . almost protecting its petitioner . . . daring anyone to come near. Nobody wanted to . . . John didn't know whether to turn off the lights.

Daniel and Justin, both in the choir, were mercifully spared the ordeal of their mother's behaviour . . . and the cocoa. They stood in the stalls in the candlelit church and wondered, with the others, why the congregation weren't filing in. David, on the other hand, was spared nothing.

'Melanie! Melanie!' Janey called. Nothing, it seemed, was going to silence her. Sonia approached, but backed away. Marian watched with tears in her eyes as she squeezed Sally's hand, knowing she could not go near, knowing much more than that.

Such was the power of the Plague Stone that it was at that very moment that Melanie Tandy decided to come home.

She had wreaked an awful punishment, but a just one . . . it was done. She felt weak and empty. It had taken all her powers.

Now she wanted her own little room again, and to take up her life, different now though it would be. Meadcombe, she knew, would never be the same. And that was good.

Isobelle looked at the child . . . child? It was not an appropriate word. The dark one. Never had she taught such a responsive pupil. Her tutelary days were over. There was nothing more she could teach her. Night and day, night and day they'd worked at the altar of night magic, where, within the gammadion, grotesque cartoon drawings hung to the cloth, until, at times, she'd felt her own powers failing, milked by the granddaughter she had always known had a greater magic than her own and would one day come . . . the art often skipped a generation . . .

Melanie was going home. Vengeance was hers. Let it be.

The celebrants solemnly crossed the room and lit the black candles.

They slumped in the pews, they slumped in the aisles. And Jeffrey dried up in the pulpit.

One hundred souls . . . murdered in cold blood . . . by the woman they took away on that infamous Christmas Eve.

They found them in the early hours of Christmas morning. But it was Boxing Day before Meadcombe hit the headlines. Not one member of the drama group survived. Nor did David Tandy. Or Paul. Or Stanley. Or Lloyd. Or Donna. Or . . .

I am not a superstitious man. And although I work with relics of dead times, the relics themselves are not dead. They carry power. They vibrate with energy. Some of them, not all, but some of them wear evil like a shadow.

And so when I first saw Melanie Tandy I knew

immediately what had happened here. And it was something you couldn't write about in official reports. At first I thought that it had nothing to do with the Plague Stone. I thought that she and her grandmother had worked the evil alone. But I supervised the removal of the megalith. They wrapped steel hawsers round its frame. They dug it deep from the ground with heavy, earth-moving machinery. They came with cranes to lift it. They took it to a heath where it could be approached by public footpath. They put up a plaque. It dominated its new domain, made small its vast surroundings.

But I had to return to Meadcombe to see the finished work. I stood by the freshly-laid paving . . . stained already with rust, and seeping corrosive. They had planted an oak in its place — a tiny, leafless thing with a label on its stem. Yes, it would have looked lovely, a hundred, two hundred years from now, but I knew it would never survive.

Because although the Plague Stone had gone — certainly the embodiment of it was no longer there — the substance, the essence of the thing, that sulphurous stench had been left behind.

Night — and the village of Meadcombe is buried by the mauve candlewick of the surrounding hills. White, it peeps from its covers like a slumbering unicorn curved round a church spire horn. White-washed walls, gloss gates, and, by day, Persil-white washing flapping on its garden lines.

The Plague Stone has always looked uncomfortable slumped in the centre of the square like that. In such a very ordinary village.

The employees of G.K. HALL hope you have enjoyed this Large Print book. All our Large Print titles are designed for easy reading, and all our books are made to last. Other G.K. Hall Large Print books are available at your library, through selected bookstores, or directly from us. For more information about current and upcoming titles, please call or mail your name and address to:

G.K. HALL
PO Box 159
Thorndike, Maine 04986
800/223-6121
207/948-2962